"This wa
shouted.
And I
no lynch mob!"

He drew his pistol and waved it around, threatening everyone in the room. "I ain't goin' to jail!" he hollered. "You all go to hell!"

Hawke, who had watched the scene quickly deteriorate, pointed his finger at the cowboy. "Shorty! Put your gun down before you make things any worse!" he ordered.

"Ain't no damn piano player goin' to tell me what to do!" Shorty shouted. He swung his gun toward Hawke and fired, his bullet frying the air no more than an inch from Hawke's ear. Hawke drew his gun so quickly that, to the witnesses in the room, it seemed as if it had appeared in his hand by magic.

Hawke returned fire, and his bullet hit the cowboy high in the chest. With a gasp of surprise, Shorty fell forward, tumbling down the stairs, winding up on the floor alongside the dead prostitute. He raised himself up on his elbows.

"Kilt by a piano player," he said. "Who would've thought?"

Shorty fell forward, and lay quietly.

Books by Robert Vaughan

HAWKE

THE LAW OF A FAST GUN
VENDETTA TRAIL
SHOWDOWN AT DEAD END CANYON
RIDE WITH THE DEVIL

ROBERT VAUGHAN

HAWKE

THE LAW OF A
FAST GUN

HarperTorch
An Imprint of HarperCollinsPublishers

This is a work of fiction. Names, characters, places, and incidents are products of the author's imagination or are used fictitiously and are not to be construed as real. Any resemblance to actual events, locales, organizations, or persons, living or dead, is entirely coincidental.

❧

HARPERTORCH
An Imprint of HarperCollins*Publishers*
10 East 53rd Street
New York, New York 10022-5299

Copyright © 2006 by Robert Vaughan
ISBN-13: 978-0-06-088846-6
ISBN-10: 0-06-088846-6

First HarperTorch paperback printing: November 2006

HarperCollins®, HarperTorch™, and ❧™ are trademarks of Harper-Collins Publishers Inc.

Printed in the United States of America

Visit HarperTorch on the World Wide Web at www.harpercollins.com

10 9 8 7 6 5 4 3 2 1

This book is dedicated to Captain Frank S. Virden, USN (Ret). We owe our freedoms to such men.

HAWKE

THE LAW OF A
FAST GUN

Chapter 1

St. Louis Globe
April 10, 1864

TERRIBLE RAID IN SIKESTON, MISSOURI
CONFEDERATE IRREGULARS KILL WOMEN
AND CHILDREN

Special to the Globe—Intelligence received by
this newspaper says that thirty-seven people
were killed when Rebel raiders invaded the town
of Sikeston, Missouri. It is said that the leader of
the Rebels singled out all males between the age
of sixteen and sixty, led them to the center of
town and shot them before the eyes of their
wives and children.

It is not certain who led the raid, though
initial reports stated that that the leader was

none other than William Quantrill. However, subsequent information suggests that it was more likely either "Bloody Quint" Wilson or Jesse "the Executioner" Cole.

The attack, it is said, took place just at sunrise, catching many of Sikeston's citizens during their morning ablutions. There appeared to be no military purpose to the raid, which resulted only in wanton killing and the looting and burning of homes.

"Are you sure the train will stop here, Major?" Kincaid asked.

"The train has to have water, doesn't it, Sergeant?" Jesse Cole replied.

"I reckon so," Kincaid answered.

Jesse pointed to the water tower that stood alongside the railroad tracks.

"Well, there's the water. That means the train will stop."

Jesse climbed up the rock-covered berm and stood on the track, looking back toward the east. "I sure wish it was a little darker, though."

The full moon made it almost as light as day, making the twin ribbons of steel gleam softly.

"Hey, Jesse, do you really think there is Yankee gold on that train?" Gus asked.

"It's Major Cole, not Jesse," Kincaid said, correcting him.

"I didn't mean no disrespect or nothin'," Gus said. "But technically, he ain't no major. The Confederate Congress ain't never give him a commission."

"No, but West Point did, and that's good enough for me," Kincaid said.

"West Point is a Yankee school," Gus said.

"Robert E. Lee went to West Point," Kincaid said.

"Yeah, I guess you're right," Gus agreed.

"So, what about it, Major? Do you really think there is Yankee gold on the train?"

"According to the letter that was on that courier we killed the other day, there is," Jesse said.

"What are we going to do with it? I mean, with the Yankees all around us, there's no way we can give it to the Confederate cause."

"We're Confederates, aren't we?" Jesse replied. "We'll just give it to ourselves."

"Yeah!" Kincaid said. "Yeah, now I like that idea. I like that a lot!"

"The only thing is, if there is Yankee gold on that train, then there's bound to be Yankee soldiers as well," Gus said.

"What if there is?" Jesse replied. "We've killed Yankees before, haven't we?"

Gus laughed. "Yeah, we have at that. Fact is, I reckon Cole's Raiders have killed more Yankees than just about anybody. More'n Quantrill or Anderson, or Quint Wilson."

From behind, they heard the sound of someone urinating.

"Damn, Van, that's the third or fourth time you've taken a piss since we got here," Kincaid said. "What's the matter? Have you got a leak in you, somewhere?"

"I can't help it," Van said as he finished his business and buttoned his pants. "I'm nervous, and whenever I get nervous, I pee."

"Yeah, well, there's nothin' to be nervous about, is there, Major? I mean there are ten of us and there isn't likely to be any more'n a hundred or so of the Yankee soldiers. I'd say the odds were about even." Kincaid laughed at his own observation.

"Kincaid—"

"It's Sergeant Kincaid," Kincaid corrected.

"All right, Sergeant Kincaid. You're as full of shit as a Christmas goose," Gus said, and the others laughed as well.

"How many soldiers do you think they'll have, Jesse . . . uh, I mean, Major."

"Probably no more than three or four to guard the gold," Jesse answered.

In the distance the men heard the long, lonesome wail of a train whistle.

"There it is," Jesse said. "Sergeant, get the men in position, and stay out of sight until I give the word."

"Yes, sir," Kincaid answered.

"I don't see it yet," Van said.

"You will. Just keep looking that way," Jesse said.

They heard the whistle a couple more times before they saw it. And even then they didn't see the train, but they did see the head lamp, a gas flame behind a glass, set in front of a mirrored reflector. The reflector gathered all the light from the gas flame, intensified it, and then projected it forward in a long beam that stabbed ahead, picking up insects to gleam in the light.

The train whistled again, and this time they could hear the puffing of the steam engine as it labored hard to pull the train through the night.

"Remember, nobody makes a move until I give the order," Jesse said. "We don't want to take a chance on being seen."

Jesse walked up onto the track and stayed there until all his men were in position. He looked to see if any of them could be seen from the approaching train, then, satisfied that they could not, he ran back down to join them. He watched the train approach, listening to the puffs of steam as it escaped from the pistons. He could see bright sparks embedded in the heavy black smoke that poured from the flared smokestack. More sparks were falling from the fire box, leaving a carpet of orange-glowing embers laying between the rails and trailing out behind the train, glimmering for a moment or two in the darkness before finally going dark themselves.

The train began squeaking and clanging as the engineer

applied the brakes. It grew slower, and slower still, until finally it approached the water tower. The engineer brought his train to a stop in exactly the right place. By now the fireman was already standing on the tender, reaching for the line that hung down from the curved mouth of the long water spout.

For a long moment the area was very quiet, the solitude interrupted only by the sigh of escaping steam and the snapping and popping of bearings and fittings as they cooled. The fireman grabbed the water spout, swung the spigot down and guided it to the open mouth of the tender. He pulled on the valve rope and the water started thundering into the cavernous tank.

The door to the express car slid open and the express messenger stood in the door a moment, backlit by the kerosene lanterns that burned inside. He jumped down and walked forward to call up to the engineer.

"Hey, Ben! How long are we going to be here?" the express messenger asked.

"No more'n fifteen minutes," the engineer answered. "Why?"

"It's stuffy in there. I thought I might get out and take a walk around."

"Be my guest," the engineer replied. "But if you aren't back by the time this water tank is filled, I'm pullin' out without you."

"I'll be back in plenty of time," the express man responded.

The express man walked up the track a few feet, then stopped and looked directly toward Jesse and his men, all of whom were waiting just under the berm. His eyes grew wide in fear when he realized what he was seeing.

He turned to run back to the train, but before he got more than a couple of steps, Jesse threw his knife. The knife buried itself in the express man's back, and he fell, then rolled back down the berm, winding up in a ditch alongside the track.

"You men," Jesse said. "Spread out and cover us. Sergeant

Kincaid, you take charge of security. Van, Gus, you two come with me."

The three men ran alongside the track, bent over behind the berm so as not to be noticed by the engineer or fireman, until they reached the express car and climbed in through the open door.

There were two soldiers in the car. One was asleep, the other was smoking a pipe and looking at a newspaper by the light of a lantern. The soldiers' rifles were in the corner.

"What the hell?" the soldier reading the newspaper said in shock and alarm when he saw Jesse and the other two climb into the car. He started for his rifle, but it was too far away. Jesse shot him, and as the other guard woke up in surprise, Gus shot him.

Sitting in the floor of the car was a strongbox, held closed by a clasp and padlock. It took two shots to blow the lock off. Jesse jerked open the lid, then smiled at seeing several stacks of money.

"There it is, boys," he said.

"It's paper!" Gus said. He spat in disgust. "We did all this for paper money? I thought we was doin' this for Yankee gold."

"It's Yankee greenbacks," Jesse said. "That's as good as gold, and a lot easier to carry." He began stuffing bound packets of bills into his pockets and shirt. "Start grabbing," he told the other two men.

But before either of them had even reached for the money, they heard shots outside.

"Gus, take a look and see what's going on," Jesse ordered.

"Son of a bitch!" Gus shouted, peering out the open door. "It's Yankee soldiers. Dozens of 'em! I thought you said there'd be no more'n three or four!"

"This must be a troop transport train," Jesse said. He came to the door to look out. As Gus had indicated, there were dozens of soldiers already out of the passenger cars, and dozens more were following them out. All were armed.

"We've got to get out of here!" Jesse shouted. "Jump!"

Jesse, Van, and Gus jumped down from the express car, then ran back to join Kincaid and the others, who were already engaging the soldiers in gunfire. Van didn't make it back.

The soldiers were infantrymen, carrying rifles that were accurate and hard-hitting weapons, but had to be reloaded after each shot.

Jesse's men were all armed with at least two pistols each, which meant they could fire six rounds to every one round fired by the soldiers. That gave them enough of an advantage to be able to hold their own, despite the imbalance in numbers. They began cutting the soldiers down, shooting them until bodies were piling upon bodies. However, the sheer number of soldiers arrayed against them was having an effect as well, and all around him Jesse could see his own men going down.

The train started moving, and realizing that it was pulling away, the soldiers now hurried back to jump in. They paid no attention to the bodies they were leaving behind.

In frustration, Jesse fired at the train, but it gathered speed quickly and within moments was disappearing down the track. He remained standing on the track, pistol in hand, his arm hanging by his side. Only then did he look around. He saw nothing but bodies; bodies of slain Union soldiers as well as his own men.

"Kincaid?" he called. "Gus? Teague, Chandler, Van? Is anyone left alive?"

"I think it's just you and me, Major," Kincaid answered.

"God have mercy, this was a slaughterhouse," Jesse said.

"There's no God here, Jesse. This is hell," a strained voice said.

Jesse whirled toward the voice, his pistol at the ready, and saw a wounded man in the uniform of a captain in the Union Army.

"I'm no danger to you," the captain said easily.

"Bert?" Jesse said, lowering his pistol. "Bert Rowe, is that you?"

"Captain Bert Rowe, at your service, sir," the Yankee said. "It looks as if you, your sergeant, and I, are the only ones left alive."

"How badly are you wounded?"

"Perhaps more in dignity and spirit than in fact," Bert said. "I expect I will survive. How about you? Were you wounded?"

"No," Jesse replied.

"Good."

"You'd better throw your pistol over here, Bert," Jesse said.

"Come on, Jesse. Do you really think I would shoot you? My old roommate?"

"We aren't West Point roommates anymore, Bert," Jesse said.

"It's empty," Bert said, pointing it straight up and pulling the trigger. The hammer fell on an empty chamber.

"Throw it over here," Jesse insisted.

"All right," Bert agreed, tossing his pistol.

Jesse picked it up and looked at the cylinder. There was a round in one of the chambers.

"Bert, Bert, Bert," Jesse said, clucking and shaking his head. "You were holding back on me, weren't you? I'm ashamed of you."

"It was my duty as a soldier," Bert said. "You do know what it is to be a soldier, don't you? You stood on the plains at West Point with me and the rest of our class, taking an oath to serve your country. Tell me, Jesse, did the words duty, honor, country, mean nothing to you?"

"The words mean everything to me," Jesse said. "But sometimes a man's honor requires that he serve a greater duty."

"Jesse, is it true what they say about you? Did you really kill all those women and children when you raided Spring Hill?"

"You talk too much," Jesse said.

"We were coming to get you, you know. That's why there were so many soldiers on the train. The army's determined to get you, Quantrill, Anderson, Wilson, and all the other irregulars. That means that even after the war is over and all the other Rebs go home, we'll still be looking for you."

"Major, we've got to get out of here," Kincaid called to him.

"He's right, Bert," Jesse said. "I've got to go."

"Yes, you'd better. Oh, you wouldn't have a blanket, would you? I don't know how long it'll be before the train comes back."

"Yeah, hold on, I'll get it."

Jesse walked over to where the horses were tethered and reached for a blanket.

"Major, we can't leave him alive," Kincaid said quietly.

"What do you mean we can't leave him alive? Bert and I are old friends. We were roommates through four years of West Point."

"Like you said, Major, you ain't roommates anymore. If they come back and find him dead, and all of our men dead, they'll think everyone was killed. If he's still alive, he'll tell them we survived, and probably even tell them which way we went. Hell, he was going to kill you, remember? What did he say? It was a soldier's duty?"

Jesse stood there a moment, as if trying to make up his mind.

"We don't have much time, Major," Kincaid said. "You know damn well that whoever is in charge of the soldiers on the train will get to the engineer and order him back. We don't have much time to hang around. We need to get out of here. And we don't need anyone left."

"Jesse, how are you coming with that blanket?" Bert called.

Jesse pulled his pistol and cocked it. "You're right," he said as he started back.

Bert saw him coming, and saw Jesse raise his pistol.

"If you're going to shoot me, Jesse, get it done," he said. There was no panic in his voice. "You see where my pistol is. There's nothing I can do to stop you."

Jesse pulled the hammer back and aimed it. Then, sighing, he lowered the gun.

"Do it, Jesse, it's your duty. You know that if our roles were reversed, I would shoot you."

"Don't tempt me, Bert," Jesse said. He walked back to the horses, grabbed a blanket from one of them, then returned to where the Yankee captain was lying.

"Here's the blanket," he added, tossing it toward him.

"God go with you, Jesse," Bert said.

"God?" Jesse shook his head. "No, you were right the first time, Bert. There is no God for the likes of us."

Jesse walked around to examine the carnage. There were seventeen dead Yankee soldiers, as well as eight of the men who had come with him. That was nearly one-fourth of his entire outfit.

Jesse heard the train whistle and knew the train was coming back.

"You'd better get out of here," Bert said.

Jesse hesitated.

"Go on," Bert said. "I'll tell them that everyone was killed."

"Careful, Bert, that's very close to a violation of duty, isn't it?"

"Yes, well maybe some of my old roommate's bad habits have rubbed off on me," Bert answered.

The train whistle was much louder now, and the puffing of the steam engine could be heard quite near.

Jesse went back to the horses, where he scattered all of them but the ones he and Kincaid were riding.

"You couldn't do it, could you?" Kincaid asked.

"Let's get out of here," Jesse said without answering him directly.

As they rode away, they could hear the train braking behind him.

One year later

The victorious Union Army was encamped in a five-acre field just outside Independence, Missouri. The field was dotted with white tents and red, white, and blue flags. To the south of the field, in an enclosed area, nearly one thousand men, former soldiers of the Confederacy, were being detained until their repatriation.

"Hey, Yank! When you goin' to let us go home?" one of the detainees shouted. "You done said yourself that the war was over."

"When we get all of you Rebel trash to sign the oath of loyalty," the Union sergeant answered. "But if it was up to me, I'd just keep ever'one of you right there in that pen for the rest of your lives."

"Yeah, well if it was up to me, we'da never surrendered," the prisoner called back.

"Sergeant," someone called. "Send the next twenty men over here."

"Yes, sir," the sergeant answered. He counted out twenty. "You men," he said, pointing to a couple of tables, behind which sat Union officers. The tables were flanked by armed guards. "Go over there and take your oath."

"Then what?" one of the men asked.

"Then you're free to go home. Or wherever you want to go," the sergeant said. "Just so long as you don't bear arms against the U.S. government ever again."

For the rest of the morning groups of twenty were marched over to the tables where the oath was admitted. The group Jesse was in was taken over at about noon.

"You fellas get in line there, and listen up to what the captain has to say," a sergeant ordered.

"Men, the generosity of the United States government knows no bounds," the captain began. "Even though you have taken up arms against us, we are a forgiving people. In a couple of minutes I'm going to ask you to take an oath of loyalty to the U.S. government. Once you take that oath, you are free to go."

"Will I be a'gettin' my rifle back?" one of the men asked.

"No. Officers may keep their sidearms. All other weapons are confiscated."

"But, we'll be a'needin' them weapons for huntin' and sech," the man said.

"You should have thought of that before you took up arms against your country," the captain said. "All right, now, step up to the table, one at a time."

Jesse was third in line, and close enough to the table to hear what was going on.

"What is your name?" the captain asked the first man.

"Sergeant Ken Waters."

"You aren't a sergeant anymore, Mr. Waters. The Confederate Army no longer exists. Who were you with?"

"I was a Confederate," Waters replied.

"You were all Confederate trash. I mean who was your commander?"

"First one and then another," Kincaid said. "I don't know how you Yankees did it, but we moved around a lot."

"Did you ever ride with William Quantrill, Bill Anderson, Quint Wilson, Jesse Cole, or any other irregular unit?"

"What if I did?"

"I'll ask the questions, Mr. Waters."

"No, I never rode with any of them."

"Very well, hold up your right hand and repeat after me. I, state your name."

"I, Ken Waters."

"Swear that I will never take up arms against the United States government again, and that I will bear true faith and allegiance to same, so help me God."

Waters repeated the oath.

"You're free to go, Mr. Waters."

"What about lunch?" Waters asked. "You fellas haven't fed us any lunch yet."

"You are a free man, Mr. Waters," the captain said. "You are no longer our responsibility."

"But I don't have any money or anything. I don't even have any cornmeal."

"Next," the captain said, ignoring Waters's complaint.

Just before Jesse stepped up to the table, the captain who was doing the interviews was replaced by another officer.

"Who's next?" the new officer called.

Jesse took a deep breath. The new officer was Bert Rowe, now a major.

When Jesse stood in front of the table, Bert looked startled. There was a long, silent moment while the two men stared at each other. Jesse braced himself for the inevitable.

"What is your name?" Bert asked.

Was Bert saying that he wasn't going to betray him? Or was he just testing him?

Jesse took a chance.

"My name is Tobin. Don Tobin."

"Mr. Tobin, have you ever ridden with Quantrill, Anderson, Wilson, or," Bert paused for a long moment before he said the last name, "Cole?"

"I've never ridden with any of them," Jesse replied.

"Are you willing to take the oath?"

"I am."

"And abide by it?"

"Major, to me, abiding by an oath is a sacred thing," Jesse said.

"Is that a fact? You mean like, an oath to duty, honor, country?"

"Yes," Jesse said. He stared pointedly at Major Rowe. "Just like that."

"I'm glad," Bert said. "I'm glad that this war is over and the animosity and all its horrors are being put behind us."

Bert administered the oath, then he and Jesse shook hands.

Jesse started to walk away, but Bert called toward him. "Mr. . . . Tobin . . . is it?"

Jesse stopped. Had Bert just been playing with him?

"I wouldn't spend much time in Missouri, if I were you."

"Thanks," Jesse called back over his shoulder.

Jesse left the camp, walking toward Independence. He had no horse, and on his person he had no money and no weapon. But the war was over, and he was a free man. And he knew where twenty thousand dollars of Yankee greenbacks were buried.

One hour after Jesse left the camp, a lieutenant and a sergeant came over to Bert's table.

"Major Rowe, be on the lookout for a man calling himself Don Tobin," the lieutenant said.

"Don Tobin?"

"Yes, sir. We just got word that the man calling himself Don Tobin is really Jesse Cole."

"And he's here, in our camp," the sergeant added.

"I wish you had come by earlier," Bert said.

"Why?"

"I've already paroled a man named Don Tobin."

"Damn!" the lieutenant said, hitting his fist in his hand. "Do you have any idea where he went?"

Bert shook his head no. "You know how this works, Lieutenant. Once these men are paroled, they are on their own."

"Yes, sir, I reckon so," the lieutenant said. "But we now have authorization to hang him on the spot just as soon as we find him. And after all the killin' he done, well, that's one fella I'd pure dee like to see strung up."

Chapter 2

Ten Years Later

EVEN AS THE FINAL CHORDS OF THE PIANO CON-
certo were still reverberating through the Munich Opera
House, the crowd erupted in thunderous applause.

"Bravo! Bravo! *Wunderbar! Prächtig!*" the crowd shouted
in appreciation.

Standing, Mason Hawke turned to face the accolades and
adoration of his audience, bowing in respect as the applause
continued.

Someone in the audience began to whistle, and the whistling
grew louder and louder until it became the whistle of an incoming cannon ball.

"Get down! Yankee artillery!"

It was then that Hawke realized that he was no longer on a
concert stage in Europe wearing the formal attire of a pianist;

he was on a Civil War battlefield wearing the soiled gray of a Confederate uniform.

Hawke dived behind a nearby rock as the incoming shell exploded above, sending shards of red-hot shrapnel singing through the nearby tree limbs. He could hear the cannonading of Confederate Napoleon 32-pounders as they returned fire.

Thump thump thump.

His stomach shook with each blast.

Thump thump thump.

The acrid smoke of the black powder charges drifted across the field as the cannonading continued.

Thump thump thump.

"Hit 'er again, George! You've just about got her!" someone shouted.

Thump.

Hawke opened his eyes and looked around his room. The shade was pulled, but a small hole in it projected onto the wall a detailed image, not a shadow but a photographic image, of the cottonwood tree that grew just outside the saloon.

"Again!" the man called.

Thump.

"That got 'er. We can get the wheel off now."

Hawke sat up in his bed and swung his legs over to one side. He sat there a moment, gradually getting reacquainted with the world to which he had said good-bye the night before.

He thought of his dream, or rather, the two dreams that seemed to merge into one. Both dreams recalled incidents from his past. He had, indeed, been a concert pianist. "The best young talent to come from America in many a season," was the way the *London Times* put it in the article that told of Hawke being knighted by Queen Victoria for his contribution to the world of music.

Hawke had enjoyed a grand tour of the Continent, playing before the crowned heads of Europe and winning over audiences everywhere he appeared. Therefore his dream of an applauding audience was not without justification.

But the other dream, which had encroached on the first, was equally valid. Hawke had also endured the cannonading of Yankee guns, after he'd abandoned his musical career to answer what he considered to be a higher calling—the calling of honor. Hawke left Europe before his tour was completed, and returned home to join his father's regiment and fight for the South.

It had been his intention to resume his musical career after the war. But as it turned out, that wasn't possible. Many of the men who were not killed were maimed and scarred by the war. And some of the worst scars were not visible.

Hawke was one of those men. For every relative and friend he saw die, and for every enemy soldier he killed, he had lost a small part of himself. Sometimes he found himself envious of his father and brother, both of whom were killed in the war. It would have been better, he believed, to have died with his dreams intact, than to wander through the rest of his days . . . a life without purpose, and a man without a soul.

Padding barefoot across the plank floor, Hawke picked up the porcelain pitcher and poured water into a basin. He washed his face and hands, then worked up a rich lather and shaved.

It was already mid-morning, but the heavy green shade that covered the window kept out most of the light. Not until he was dressed did he open the shade to let the morning sunshine steam in. He stood at the window for a moment, looking out at the street below.

The banging that had intruded into his dream, indeed had shaped it, came from the freight office across the street. There, an empty wagon sat on blocks with one of the wheels removed. Another freight wagon was just pulling away, while a third was being loaded.

Braggadocio, Nebraska, was an industrious town, full of commerce and activity. By painted signs and symbols, the various mercantile establishments made themselves known to the citizens of the town, as well as to the farmers and ranchers who came in to buy their supplies. Next to the freight office, the druggist was sweeping the front porch of the apothecary, his business advertised not by words, but by a large cutout of a mortar and pestle. Next to that, a striped pole advertised the barbershop, and next to that a big tooth led patients to the dentist.

From his position at the window, Hawke could not see the big, painted, golden mug of beer just below him that indicated the saloon. The porch overhang blocked his view. This building, where the Hog Lot Saloon was located, was not only Hawke's living quarters, it was also his place of employment.

After sunset Braggadocio became a totally different town. As industrious as it was by day, it was anything but that at night. Then, for those who availed themselves of the opportunity, Braggadocio was a place of pleasure. And as a piano player in the Hog Lot, Hawke contributed to that pleasure.

"Hmmm. Good morning."

Hawke turned back toward Cindy Carey, one of the other people who contributed to the pleasures to be found in Braggadocio. Cindy was a twenty-two-year-old woman whose copper hair and smooth skin made her one of the most popular of the bar girls who plied her trade at the Hog Lot. Sitting up in bed, she yawned and stretched, and when she did, the sheet slid down, exposing both her breasts. The dissipation of her profession not yet having left its mark, Cindy's small but well-formed breasts were firm and smooth.

"Good morning," Hawke replied. "I trust you slept well?"

"I slept like a log," Cindy said. She smiled. "And I won the bet."

"What bet is that?"

"That you could do more than just play the piano," she said.

"Damn," Hawke teased. "And here I thought you loved me for myself. Now I find out you were just trying to win a bet."

Cindy's smile disappeared. "Hawke, no, it was more than

that," she said. "It was a lot more than that. I just meant that—"

Hawke laughed. "I was teasing you, Cindy," he said. "You're a sweet girl and I enjoy being with you."

Cindy laughed.

"What is it?"

"I don't think I've been called sweet since I was seven years old. I'm a whore, remember?"

"Is there any law that says a soiled dove can't also be a sweet person? *What* you are isn't *who* you are."

"Yes," Cindy said, smiling again. "Yes, I guess that's right, isn't it?"

"You coming down to breakfast?"

"I'll be down soon as I've dressed."

Leaving Cindy still in his bed, Hawke went downstairs into the main part of the saloon. The one connection he maintained with his concert-tour past was in his mode of dress. Whereas the average citizen of the town, as well as habitués of the saloon, dressed in denim and plaid shirts, Hawke wore a suit with a silken vest, often complimented with a cravat. So finely turned out was he that most didn't even notice the Navy Colt .32 that he wore in a holster rig, low on his right side.

John Harder, the man who employed Hawke, didn't own the only saloon in town. There was one other, called Foley's. But the Hog Lot was easily the most popular, and it was the only one that could afford a piano and a pianist. The old upright piano had seen a lot of wear, but with bits of wire here and a few wooden wedges there, Hawke managed to keep it reasonably tuned.

He took a seat at a table halfway between the piano and the potbellied wooden stove that sat in a sand box. The stove, cold now in the summer months, retained the aroma of charred wood from its winter use.

Betty Lou Tinsdale was sitting at the next table, drinking coffee. She had lost her husband during the late war, and turned to prostitution as her only means of support. When she was too old to be "on the line," she became a cook, in the employ of John Harder.

As soon as Hawke sat down, Betty Lou called over to him. "Will Cindy be joining you for breakfast?"

"What?"

"Cindy," Betty Lou said. "Is she joining you, or is she sleeping in?"

"What makes you think—" Hawke started, but Betty Lou interrupted him with a whooping laugh.

"Hawke, you aren't going to try and tell me that Cindy Carey didn't spend the night with you, are you?"

"You know about that?"

"Of course I know about it. Honey, do you think for one moment that she didn't let everyone know who her special beau was last night?"

"I, uh, didn't know it was such common knowledge."

"Common knowledge? Hah! I wouldn't be surprised if Vernon Clemmons didn't wind up doing a story about it in the *Journal*. By the way, I made some gravy this morning. I thought it might go good with biscuits."

"Betty Lou, anything is good with your biscuits," Hawke replied.

"You do have a silver tongue, Mason Hawke," Betty Lou said as she started toward the kitchen.

John Harder came out of his office and sat down at Hawke's table. "Betty Lou," he called. "How about some coffee?"

"Coming right up, hon," Betty Lou called back over her shoulder.

"How'd you and Cindy get along last night?" Harder asked.

"Fine, just fine," Hawke replied, his voice showing his irritation.

"Well, if you were going to do it, last night was the night for it. The Bar-J will be in town today. I expect Cindy and all the other girls are going to be very busy for the next couple of weeks."

"The Bar-J?"

"It's a ranch up in Cherry County, owned by a man named Clint Jessup. He's bringing his cows down to the railhead here, to ship back East. And that's a big herd, which means there will probably be from twenty-five to thirty riders."

"That many thirsty cowboys should be good for your business."

"Yeah, I suppose. . . ." Harder said, almost wistfully.

"Well, won't it be?"

"I'm sure it will be. But there's been trouble every year. You see, the cowboys have been out rounding up the cows, then pushing the herd down. That means they've been away from civilization for about six weeks by the time they get to Braggadocio. They've got a lot of pent-up energy, and sometimes they can get a little out of hand. So much so that there have been a few in town who have suggested that we close down the cattle pens so they have to go somewhere else to ship their cows."

"Is that likely to happen?" Hawke asked.

"No, not really, I don't think. Of course, there are always a few that make trouble. But mostly they just drink and get a little sentimental." Harder chuckled. "If it's true that music hath charms to soothe the savage beast, then I'll be counting on you to play the kind of music that will keep them calm."

"It would be easier for me to play that kind of music if you had a piano worth playing," Hawke said, pointing to the cigar-scarred and beer-stained upright. "With business picking up, maybe you could buy a new one."

"A new one costs too much."

"What I don't understand is why you will hire a pianist, but you won't buy a decent piano."

"It's damned if I do and damned if I don't," Harder said. "If I hire you, I can't afford a piano. If I buy a new piano, I can't afford you. If you want a good piano to play, you can always go down to the church. I haven't spent that much time in the church, but Bob Gary tells me they have a very fine piano."

"Bob Gary is a churchgoer?"

Harder chuckled. "Yeah, a bartender a churchgoer. Who would've thought it? But he's a regular. Anyway, he tells me they have a fine piano, so I reckon you could always play that one if you'd like."

"Thanks, but no thanks," Hawke said. "I'll do the best I can with what I've got."

"I thought you might," Harder said. Then, looking toward the front of the saloon, he added, "Well, speak of the devil."

Harder was talking about Bob Gary, who had just come in. Although the bar wouldn't have any drinking business until noon, Gary came in early every day in order to wash the glasses and take inventory of his stock.

"'Morning, Bob," Hawke called.

"'Morning, Hawke," Bob replied.

Betty Lou came in from the kitchen then, carrying Hawke's breakfast, plus a coffeepot and three cups.

"I seen you comin' in and figured you'd be wantin' some coffee too," she said to Bob.

"Thanks, Betty Lou," Bob said. Then he looked at Hawke. "So?" he asked as he lifted his cup.

"So?" Hawke replied, looking confused. "So what?"

"How was it last night?"

"That's what I want to know too," Betty Lou said. "I asked him, but he didn't seem to want to talk about it."

"What the hell?" Hawke said in exasperation. "Did I leave my damn door open last night?"

Harder, Bob, and Betty Lou laughed.

"What's so funny?" Cindy asked, coming down the stairs in the midst of all the laughter.

"Oh, just a joke Hawke made," Harder said.

"You want some breakfast, honey?" Betty Lou asked.

"Just some coffee," Cindy said. "But I'll take one of

Hawke's biscuits," she added, reaching across the table for it as she sat down.

"Well, we need to get back to work," Harder said. "It'll also give you two some time together. You might need it."

With Betty Lou, John Harder, and Bob Gary gone, Hawke and Cindy were alone at the table. Hawke lifted his cup to his mouth and looked over the rim at Cindy while he drummed on the table with the fingers of his left hand.

"What?" she asked innocently.

"What do you think?"

"They were talking about us, weren't they?" Cindy asked.

"Yes."

"I wonder why."

"Yes," Hawke said. "I wonder why."

"Are you angry?" Cindy asked.

"Should I be?"

"Hawke, you aren't mad at me, are you?" she said. "I mean, every girl that works here has been wanting to get you to go see the elephant with them. When you agreed to go with me, I . . . well, I just couldn't keep quite about it."

Hawke sighed, then put the cup down, smiled, and shook his head.

"No," he said. "I'm not angry. It's just that I wasn't expecting it to be so public."

"Well, Hawke, we're both in a public business, so to speak," Cindy said. "I mean, you sit down here and play the piano for the public, so all eyes are on you all the time. And anytime I go upstairs with a customer, people know we aren't going up there just to have a nice conversation."

Hawke laughed out loud. "I guess you've got me on that one," he said.

At that moment, about three miles north of town, Clint Jessup stood in his stirrups to relieve the pressure on his seat. Behind him were three thousand head of cattle that he had brought 140 miles down from Cherry County.

The cowboys whistled and called out to the herd as they moved them into a large field. Now and then one of them would break into a gallop as he hurried to redirect a few head of cows back into the herd. Jessup, who owned the Bar-J Ranch, had rented the field from Todd Bailey, the landowner, because it was big enough and had enough grass and water to support his herd until he got them onto the train.

Looking toward Birdwood Creek, which was the source of water, Jessup saw that Poke had parked the chuckwagon on an island in the middle of the creek, in the only grove of shade trees available. The cook was good about choosing the most comfortable place to spend the night. Each day of the drive, Poke would leave immediately after breakfast and proceed to the spot where the herd would be held for the night. That way he'd have supper ready for the outfit by the time they arrived.

The herd had averaged ten miles per day, sometimes taking a circuitous route in order to follow water or to avoid crossing areas where the landowners charged exorbitant tolls. When Jessup factored in all the costs involved—to include wages for twenty men, the cost of the remuda, plus the cost of raising the cows from calves, which he estimated at five dollars per head—he knew he would have to sell his cows at the best possible price in order to realize a comfortable profit.

"The first cows to market will get the best price," his cattle broker had told him.

"I'll be the first one there," Jessup had promised.

"And the fewer the cows that are shipped, the better the price is for those that are shipped."

"What are you telling me?" Jessup asked, confused by the comment. "That I should hold some of my cattle back?"

"No. The trick is to ship all of your cows at the best price, but hope that the other cattlemen can't ship theirs."

"Now, just how is that likely to happen?" Jessup asked.

"Oh, it probably won't happen," the broker had replied. "I was just talking, that's all."

Jessup recalled the conversation as he rode through the creek and onto the island. He had sent a couple of riders out, one to the south and one to the east, to check on other herds that might be coming to the railhead. He expected them back tonight.

As he dismounted in the camp, Jessup saw, and smelled, the stew Poke was cooking in a big, black, iron kettle.

"Hello, Major," Poke said.

"Poke," Jessup replied as he tied off his horse.

"I hope this camp is all right by you. It seemed like the best spot," Poke said. "There's water and shade, and I don't think the creek's going to rise."

"This is fine," Jessup said. "Especially since we are going to be here for a couple of weeks."

"If you don't mind, I'll probably go into town tomorrow right after breakfast and get some supplies," Poke said.

"I don't mind," Jessup replied, filling a coffee cup. "Fact is, I'm going to let the men who take the first batch of cows in spend some time in town after they get them loaded. It's been a long, hard drive and they need to let off a little steam."

"They'll appreciate that, that's for sure," Poke said as he went back to peeling potatoes.

Before Jessup finished his coffee, two of his riders, Deekus and Arnie, showed up. He had sent them out to scout for any other herds that might be approaching.

"Did you see anyone?" Jessup asked.

"Yes, sir, Charley Townes is bringing up the Rocking T herd," Deekus said.

"How many head?"

"Mr. Townes said they started with twenty-five hundred. They lost a few along the way, but not many."

"How long before they get here?"

"Four or five days at the most."

"What about you, Arnie? What did you see?"

"The Slash Diamond is comin' from the west," Arnie said. "Tucker Evans is bringin' about two thousand head."

"Damn," Jessup said. "If that many head are shipped, it's going to drive the price down. I'll do well to break even."

"Sorry, Major. I wish I could've brought you better news," Deekus said.

"Ahh, don't worry about it," Jessup said with a dismissive wave of his hand. "We'll just have to deal with it, that's all."

In Braggadocio, Hawke was sitting at the table nearest the piano. Harder was at the table with him, as was Marshal Matthew Trueblood. The saloon was nearly full but it was relatively quiet. The girls were moving from table to table, smiling and flirting with the men, sometimes taking off a customer's hat and running their fingers through his hair.

Although Cindy had not come over to talk to Hawke, he did catch her looking in his direction several times. He was trying to stay detached, but couldn't help but recall last night, when her nude body lay next to his. His blood warmed and he forced himself to look away in order to get her out of his mind.

Instead he looked toward the bar, where Bob Gary was busy with customers.

"You're doing a pretty good business tonight," Hawke said.

"Yes, it looks like we are," Harder replied. "But everyone seems to be local." He turned to Marshal Trueblood. "Are you sure the Bar-J is here?"

Trueblood nodded. "I'm sure. Todd Bailey is renting them his pastureland. He said they'd be getting in today."

"Well, if they're getting into Bailey's place today, like as not they'll be comin' into town tomorrow," Harder said.

Out at the cow camp the next morning, Jessup addressed all of his riders.

"I'm going to let those of you who take the cows in today

to stay in town for a while. Have a good meal, take a shower, have some drinks. Enjoy yourself, but be back in time to take another bunch in tomorrow."

"All right!" someone said.

"Hey, you reckon they got'ny women in that town?"

"Of course they do, it's a town, ain't it?"

"I don't mean women, women. I mean whores."

The other cowboys laughed.

Jessup held up his hand to get their attention.

"Now, the only way we can do this is to keep some people back to watch the herd. So if five of you want to volunteer, do it now."

Only three volunteered.

"We're goin' to have to choose two more to stay behind," Deekus said.

"Here's how we will do it," Jessup said. "You men form a long line. Poke, you stand out in front with your back to us. I'm going to start walking down the line. When you say stop, whoever I'm in front of will stay behind."

The men formed the line, and Poke stood out in front with his back to them.

"All right, I'm going to start walking now," Jessup said.

Poke waited a second or two, then said, "Stop."

The cowboy selected stepped out of the line and Jessup started walking again.

"Stop."

"Damn!" Carter said as he stepped out of line. "Of all the luck."

"Don't worry," Shorty said. "I'll drink enough whiskey for the two of us, and I'll tell you all about it when I get back."

"Hah," Carter said. "Like as not you'll get so drunk you won't even remember it. Tex, you and Brandt will have to tell me what happened."

"What makes you think we'll be sober enough to remember?" Tex asked.

The others laughed.

Everyone went to the remuda to saddle their horses, those who would be taking the first batch of cows as well as those who would be staying back with the rest of the herd.

"Yeeee ha!" Tex shouted. "Boys, we're goin' to have us a good time tonight!"

Tex's shout, reminiscent of the Rebel yell, gave Jessup a sense of déjà vu. For a moment these weren't cowboys getting ready to take a herd into town . . . these were soldiers, preparing for a raid.

"Men!" Jessup called in his most commanding voice. He saw all his men looking at him, and for a moment he was at a loss for something to say. It wasn't the ranch owner who had shouted, it was the military commander he'd once been, and he surprised himself with the outburst.

There was a long moment of silence.

"Major, you want to say something?" Tex asked.

"Uh, yeah," Jessup replied. "Let's don't be in such a hurry to get to town that we forget why we're going." He pointed to the herd. "Go cut three hundred head out."

The question as to whether the Bar-J had arrived was answered when the first three hundred cows were brought into town and driven down to the railroad. The cowboys whistled and shouted at the cows, often darting quickly up or down the street to keep the cows in line. Dogs ran alongside the cattle, barking at cows and riders alike. Children followed, excitedly, down the street.

As the cowboys passed Pearlie's, the girls who worked for her came out onto the balcony, all heavily made up, with breasts that spilled over the tops of the low-cut dresses they were wearing. Although the two saloons—the Hog Lot and Foley's—employed girls, Pearlie's was the only out and out whorehouse. Her girls were older and somewhat less attractive, and it was the place where the girls wound up after they left the two saloons.

Pearlie's girls leaned over the balcony and waved at the cowboys, some being so brazen as to lift their skirts.

"Hey, all you cowboys!" one of the girls shouted. "Come see us when you can! We'll be waiting for you!"

"Darlin', we been on the trail for a long time," one of the cowboys called back. "You sure you can handle one of us?"

"One of you? Honey, I can handle all of you," one of the girls called back, and while the girls and cowboys laughed, a few who were within earshot of the ribald conversation turned away from the distasteful language.

As the cattle were being driven through town, all other traffic was stopped and wagons and buckboards were forced to the side of the street or into one of the side streets until the cattle passed. That was not unusual. It happened every year as the cows were brought down to the railhead.

A special train, consisting of an engine and ten cattle cars, waited on a side track at the depot. The engineer stood alongside the six-foot-high driver wheels of his locomotive, squirting oil from an oversized oil can with a very long spout into the fittings.

When the cows reached the depot, they were pushed into the loading pens where they were held until they could be driven up ramps and crowded into the cars. It was a noisy operation, with the cattle bawling, the cowboys whistling, shouting, and cursing, gates being slammed shut, and the engine venting steam.

Jessup had come into town with the first batch of cows, and now stood at the loading chute watching as the cattle were loaded.

"How many do you have?" Gene Harris asked as he wrote out a receipt. Harris was the broker that Jessup had hired to sell his herd.

"Three hundred in this batch."

"How many total?"

"I brought three thousand head up," Jessup answered. "What is the going price?"

"Depends on how many head we ship out of here," Harris replied. "Like I told you before, the lower the number, the greater the demand, and that will drive the price up. I'll get the best price I can for you, Jessup, you know that."

"There are two other herds coming."

"How big?"

"One is nearly as large as mine, the other a little smaller."

Harris shook his head. "That's not good," he said. "But like I said, I'll do the best I can. Do they have someone brokering their cattle for them? Or are they just going to ship north for whatever they can get?"

"Hell, this is the first time I've ever used a broker," Jessup replied. "So I'm sure they don't have one. I think they just plan to ship them north and take whatever the rate is on delivery."

"It's good that they don't have brokers," Harris said. "I know I can get you a better price than they're going to get. But it sure would be good if they weren't shipping at all. We could double our asking price, maybe even do better than that."

When the last of the cows were loaded, Jessup returned to the camp. For the cowboys, though, this was their first time to be in any town since they started the drive weeks earlier.

When Shorty, Tex, and Brandt finished the loading, Shorty jumped onto his horse, spurred it into a gallop and shouted to the two men behind him.

"Come on! Let's show this town that we're here!"

Tex and Brandt got on their horses and broke into a gallop as well, and the three dashed down the main street of Braggadocio, laughing at the people who had to scramble to get out of their way. They tied off their horses at the hitching rail in front of the Hog Lot, then pushed through the bat-wing doors.

"The Bar-J is here!" Shorty shouted.

"You boys bring in them cows we seen comin' down the street earlier?" one of the saloon patrons asked.

"We not only brought 'em down the street, we brought 'em halfway down the state," Shorty said.

"Well, welcome to Braggadocio."

"You want to make us welcome? Bring us whiskey and women!" Tex shouted.

Shorty and Brandt's raucous laughter followed Tex's yell.

Chapter 3

~~~

NOT LONG AFTER SHORTY, TEX, AND BRANDT AR-
rived at the Hog Lot, several of the other Bar-J riders came
into the saloon as well, and the atmosphere changed almost
immediately. Unlike the locals, who were generally quiet
and reserved, the cowboys were loud and boisterous. They
were argumentative with the customers and with each other.

"Hey, piano player, play 'Buffalo Gals'!" Shorty yelled.

Hawke complied. He also played, by request, "Oh Su-
sanna," "Dixie," and "Jimmy Crack Corn."

"Hey, piano player, play 'Buffalo Gals'!" Shorty yelled.

Once again Hawke complied, then he played "Trail to
Mexico," "Sally Doodin," and the "Texas Quickstep."

"Hey, piano player, play 'Buffalo Gals'!" Shorty yelled
again.

"Come on, cowboy," Hawke replied with a smile. "I've
played that song half a dozen times. I'm sure people are getting tired of hearing it."

Shorty, who had been standing at the bar with Tex and Brandt, pushed his way through the crowd to confront Hawke.

"You're a piano player, ain't you?" Shorty said.

"I'm a pianist," Hawke replied.

Shorty looked confused for a moment, then laughed and called back over his shoulder to Tex and Brandt, "Did you hear what this here fella just said? He said he was a peein'."

Tex, Brandt, and several of the other cowboys from the Bar-J laughed.

"Mister, ain't you got sense enough to go outside whenever you got to pee?" Shorty asked Hawke.

Again the cowboys laughed, though Hawke noticed that the regulars were beginning to get a little uneasy.

"Now, Mr. Piano Player, if you don't want to get on my bad side, you'll play 'Buffalo Gals' just like I asked you to."

"I'll tell you what," Hawke said. "Suppose you go back over to the bar and have a drink. Tell Mr. Gary the drink is on me." Hawke smiled. "And I'll play 'Buffalo Gals' for you one more time."

Shorty nodded and smiled. "Well, now, maybe you're not as dumb as I thought you was," he said. "You know better than to get on my bad side, don't you?"

Hawke played "Buffalo Gals" once more. The cowboy had irritated him, but he hadn't actually made Hawke angry. It took a lot to make him angry, and he was self-confident enough not to let the annoying prattle of some drunk get to him.

"Hey, piano player!" Shorty shouted when the song was over. "Play 'Buffalo Gals'!"

"Oh, honey, do you want to listen to that song all night?" a woman asked. "Or do you want to have some real fun?"

Looking back toward the bar, Hawke saw that Cindy had stepped in between Shorty and the piano. She was flirting with him, as was her job. And she was suggesting that they go upstairs to her room, which was also her job.

Hawke had been working in the Hog Lot Saloon long enough now that he'd seen Cindy and all the other girls take men up to their rooms scores of times. It was not something he had ever given a second thought. And he knew that the fact that Cindy had been with him last night gave him no proprietorship over her.

But, unexpectedly, he found the idea of her taking this obnoxious cowboy up to her room now particularly disagreeable. For just a moment he thought it was unthinking of her, particularly given that he and Shorty had had words a few minutes earlier. Then he realized that it was just the opposite. She wasn't unthinking at all. She was offering to take him up to her room to prevent any further escalation of the argument that appeared to be developing between him and the cowboy. It was as if she were sacrificing herself for him. And, for some reason, that seemed even worse.

Hawke was playing "I'll Take You Home Again Kathleen" as he watched Cindy lead Shorty up the stairs. Just as they reached the top, Cindy looked back down toward him. The expression on her face seemed to say, *Please forgive me.* She had never looked at him like that with any other man she had taken up to her room. But then, it had never bothered him before.

"What time did you close last night?" Betty Lou asked at breakfast the next morning.

"Well, thankfully, most of the cowboys had a pretty rough day so they were all out of here before midnight," Harder replied. "Bob, what time was it when you served your last drink?"

"Just before one this morning, and that was to a local," Bob answered from his position behind the bar. "It got real quiet after the cowboys left."

"Hawke, what was it with you and 'Buffalo Gals'?" Harder asked. "Seems to me like I heard that song about twenty times."

"It seems that the cowboys like that song," Hawke replied, without getting into the specifics.

Out of the corner of his eye he saw Cindy descending the stairs. She came over to the table and looked down at him.

"Do you mind if I join you?" she asked, her voice hesitant, almost apprehensive.

"Hah!" Harder said. "Since when do you have to ask permission to—" He stopped in mid-sentence when he saw that Cindy and Hawke were looking directly at each other. He saw too the concern in Cindy's face.

"Of course you can join us," Hawke said, getting up to pull out a chair for her.

"Hawke, I—" Cindy started, but Hawke reached across the table and put his hand on hers.

"You came to my rescue last night, and I am grateful to you for it," he said, interrupting her.

"Would you mind telling me what you two are talking about?" Harder asked.

The expression on Cindy's face eased, and she smiled in relief. "Oh, I'm so glad to hear you say that," she said. "I have to go upstairs and wake him up now, but I wanted to just make sure that you understood."

"Wake him up?" Betty Lou said. "Lord, child, you still have someone in your room?"

Cindy nodded. "He was too drunk to . . . uh . . ." She looked pointedly at Hawke. "Well, he was just too drunk last night, if you know what I mean. So I figured that, at the very least, I owed him a place to sleep." She laughed. "I'll just tell him how good he was last night, and he'll never know the difference."

Harder and Betty Lou laughed with her as she started up the stairs.

"Well, I'd better get back to the kitchen," Betty Lou said.

"Bob, how do we stand on liquor?" Harder called over to his bartender.

"Too many more nights like last night, and we'll be dry as a bone," Bob replied.

"I've got a new shipment coming in by train. I just hope we don't run out of whiskey before it does get here. If you think the Bar-J cowboys are hard to handle now, wait until you see them with a thirst and nothing to drink. They are the worst of the lot."

"Are they really the worst of the lot? Or are there just more of them?" Hawke asked.

Harder stroked his chin. "Well, they are the biggest outfit," he said. "But it's not just that. The owner of the Bar-J is a fella by the name of Major Clint Jessup, and he doesn't do much to keep his men reined in."

"Major?"

"Yeah, that's what his men call him. He was a Rebel, I know that. And I think he was a cavalry commander. I just don't understand why he doesn't control them more."

"Maybe he just got a bellyful of command and decided he doesn't want to give any more orders," Hawke suggested.

"Could be, I suppose," Harder said, though it was obvious he didn't buy Hawke's explanation.

Their conversation was interrupted by a scream from upstairs.

"No! No!"

Looking up toward the landing immediately above them, Hawke and Harder saw Cindy running from her room, trying to make it back to the head of the stairs. Shorty was chasing her.

"I wonder what's going on up there?" Harder asked, concern in his voice.

"Come back here, you bitch!" Shorty demanded. He caught up with her just as they reached the top of the stairs.

"Stay away from me! Leave me alone!" Cindy screamed out in fear.

"What did you do with my money?" Shorty demanded.

"Shorty, leave her alone!" Hawke shouted, starting up the stairs.

"You stay out of this, piano player. I'll leave her alone soon as she tells me what she done with my money."

"Shorty, I didn't take your money," Cindy insisted.

"Oh yeah? Well, if you didn't take it, who the hell did? And where the hell is it?" Shorty shouted angrily. He grabbed Cindy and began shaking her hard. "I said I want my money!" he yelled.

Cindy started scratching his face, and he pushed her away from him. Cindy fell back and called out in shock and fear as she tumbled down the stairs, her sharp scream cut short halfway down. She tumbled the rest of the way, then lay sprawled at the bottom of the stairs, right in front of Hawke. Her head was twisted to one side, her eyes open and glazed, and her mouth open, though the scream was now silent.

"Cindy!" Hawke shouted. But even before he bent down to examine her, he could tell that she was dead. And the twist of her head suggested that it was the result of a broken neck.

"Now, you bitch, you ain't goin' nowhere, are you?" Shorty said, staring down the stairs toward her.

Then, suddenly, Shorty's face registered surprise. He'd realized that Cindy was dead. He looked at the others in the saloon; Bob Gary, who was behind the bar washing glasses; John Harder, still standing by the table he had shared with Hawke; Betty Lou, standing in the door of the kitchen; as well as half a dozen customers who had been quietly eating their breakfast. On the landing above, four of the other working girls, drawn by the noise, had come to the railing and now stood looking down at Cindy's still and twisted form on the floor below.

"I . . . I didn't do this," Shorty said, pointing down at Cindy. "You all seen it. It was an accident. She fell down the stairs."

"You were chasing her," Bob Gary said as he put down the

towel and glass he was working on. "She wouldn't have fallen if you hadn't been chasing her."

"I was chasing her because this bitch stole my money," he said, pointing at her prone form.

"Cindy didn't steal your money, cowboy," one of other the girls said.

"Oh yeah? Well, what happened to it?"

"You spent it all last night," the girl insisted. "You didn't even have enough to go upstairs with Cindy until you borrowed some from a couple of your friends."

The cowboy put his hands to his head. "I . . . I . . ." he started, then drew his pistol and waved the gun around, threatening everyone in the room.

"This was an accident," he said. "You all saw it. This was an accident. I didn't mean to kill her, and I ain't goin' to get hung by no lynch mob that doesn't even know what they are doin'."

"I don't blame you," Bob said from behind the bar, speaking in a low, calming voice. "I'll tell you what. Why don't you put your gun away and wait for Marshal Trueblood to get here? I'm sure it can be worked out."

"No! I ain't goin' to jail!" Shorty said. He started down the stairs.

"Cowboy, wait! You're making a mistake," Bob said. "You need to stay and work this out!"

"You go to hell!" Shorty shouted, and shot at Bob, hitting the bartender in the shoulder.

The impact of the bullet knocked Bob back against the shelf of mirrored whiskey bottles, shattering the mirror and sending the bottles tumbling down, to break on the floor.

Hawke had watched the scene quickly deteriorate. Now he pointed his finger at the cowboy.

"Shorty! Put your gun down before you make things any worse!" he ordered.

"Ain't no damn piano player goin' to tell me what to do!" Shorty shouted. He swung his gun toward Hawke and fired, his bullet frying the air no more than an inch from Hawke's ear. Hawke, whose gun had been in his holster, now drew it so quickly that to the witnesses in the room it seemed as if it had appeared in his hand by magic.

Hawke returned fire, and his bullet hit the cowboy high in the chest. With a gasp of surprise, Shorty fell forward, tumbling down the rest of the stairs, winding up on the floor alongside Cindy. He raised himself up on his elbows.

"Kilt by a piano player," he said. "Who would've thought?" Then he fell forward and lay quietly.

Shortly afterward, Trueblood, with pistol drawn, came running in through the front door. He saw Cindy and Shorty lying at the foot of the stairs. Behind the bar, Bob was holding his hand over a bleeding wound in his shoulder. Hawke had already put his own pistol back in the holster.

The marshal stood just inside the door for a long moment, taking everything in.

"Hello, Matthew," Harder said.

"Marshal Trueblood," Bob said.

The calmness of the greetings told Trueblood that everything was over now, so he put his pistol away.

"Someone want to tell me what went on here?"

"It all started with the cowboy there," Harder said, pointing toward Shorty. "He caused Cindy to tumble down the stairs. The fall killed her, then when Bob suggested that he wait for you to come sort things out, the cowboy shot Bob."

"Uh-huh," Trueblood replied. "And who shot the cowboy?"

"I did," Hawke replied.

"You?" Trueblood replied.

"Yes."

"I guess you are some surprised by that," Harder suggested.

"Not particularly," Trueblood replied, looking pointedly at Hawke.

Hawke realized then that Trueblood knew he was more than a saloon piano player. The marshal must have realized that he was a man with skill and experience in the use of handguns.

"By the way, I forgot to tell you," Harder added, "the cowboy also shot at Hawke, *before* Hawke even drew his pistol. It was the damnedest thing I ever saw. Hawke must've been scared to death to draw his own gun that fast."

"I was scared, all right," Hawke said, not taking his eyes off the marshal. He saw that Trueblood did not believe that he had been frightened.

"Uh-huh," Trueblood replied. "Who wouldn't be? We're going to have to get Judge Craig to hold a hearing. I'm sure there won't be anything come from the hearing, but you need to get this cleared up . . . no sense in letting it follow you around. I'd appreciate it, Hawke, if you didn't leave town until this is taken care of."

"I won't be going anywhere," Hawke said.

"When you think we can have the hearing?" Harder asked.

"I don't see why he couldn't do it today," Trueblood answered.

Marshal Trueblood looked over at Bob.

"I'll get the doc to come down to take a look at your shoulder," he said. He nodded toward Cindy. "What about the girl? Does she have family in town?"

By now all the girls from upstairs had come down to be closer to Cindy. All of them were crying.

"I don't think she did have family here," Harder said. "Millie, you were her closest friend, I think. Where was Cindy from?"

"She was from Kentucky," Millie answered in a choked voice. "But she didn't have any family back there either. Her pa was killed in the war, and her ma died shortly after. She didn't have anybody left."

"She has us," one of the other girls said. "We're her family."

"We'll take care of her funeral," Harder said. He looked at the cowboy. "I don't plan to do anything for that son of a bitch, though."

"Is he with the herd that just got brought up?"

"Yes, he's with the Bar-J," Harder said.

"Then I'll send Robert Griffin down for him and the girl. And I'll see to it that the Bar-J pays for buryin' the cowboy," Trueblood suggested.

The marshal didn't have to send for the doctor or the undertaker. Word had already reached both men, and they arrived at about the same time. Doc Urban was carrying a medical bag, while Robert Griffin was wearing the top hat and tails of his profession. The doctor went over to look at Bob, while Robert Griffin stepped over to look down at Cindy. It was always Robert Griffin and never "Bob," because the undertaker believed the diminutive of his name lacked sufficient respect for his profession. And it wasn't just Robert either. He always insisted upon being referred to by both names.

"I want you to take good care of her, Robert Griffin," Harder said.

"I take good care of all my customers," Robert Griffin replied, somewhat haughtily.

"Yes, well, take special good care of her. I'm paying all the expenses."

Robert Griffin nodded, then looked at Shorty. He pulled him some distance away from Cindy and lay him out on the floor. He framed Shorty's body with the thumb and forefinger of his two hands, estimating what he would need for a coffin.

"Would a couple of you gents help me get these two bodies in the back of my wagon?" Robert Griffin asked.

"Uh-uh, no you don't," Harder said.

"I beg your pardon?" Robert Griffin said in surprise.

"Don't you dare put Cindy in the same wagon with the son of a bitch who killed her."

"I have to, John. I've only got one wagon," Robert Griffin said.

"Then make two trips," Harder ordered.

"All right," Robert Griffin agreed. "Some of you help me with the girl. I'll come back for the cowboy."

The hearing over the shooting death of Shorty was held less than an hour after the incident itself. It was quick and un-eventful, and after Judge Craig heard from all the eyewit-nesses, he made his ruling.

"Mr. Hawke acted with prudence and judgment, drawing his gun only in an attempt to disarm the cowboy who, at the time of this hearing, is known only as Shorty. He did so in order to prevent any further injury. Eyewitnesses have all testified to that effect. Eyewitnesses also stated that Shorty fired at Mr. Hawke first, Mr. Hawke's weapon then being sheathed, thus constituting no danger to Shorty's life. It wasn't until after Shorty fired that Mr. Hawke drew and dis-charged his own weapon.

"Mr. Hawke's aim being better than Shorty's, the ball from Mr. Hawke's pistol struck Shorty in the chest, killing him almost instantly. This court finds no fault in Mr. Hawke's action; therefore it is the ruling of this court, and it shall be so published, that no charges be filed now, nor at any time hence. Mr. Hawke, thank you for your attendance. This hear-ing is adjourned."

Judge Craig slapped his hammer on the desk, and those who had come to the hearing began filing out of the court.

"It may not be over," Trueblood said with a sigh.

"Why is that?" Hawke asked.

"Clint Jessup."

"That's the owner of the Bar-J?"

"Yes," Trueblood said. "He's sort of a hard case and we had some trouble with his outfit last year. He's not going to like it that one of his men got shot."

"You heard all the witnesses, Marshal," Hawke said. "I didn't have any choice but—"

Trueblood waved his hand. "Don't get me wrong, Hawke,

I'm not blaming you for anything. I'm just commenting that Jessup may be trouble, that's all. He's a big man up there in Cherry County and I guess he figures that makes him a big man throughout the state."

"Is he native to Nebraska?" Hawke asked. "The reason I ask is, John said he thought he was a Confederate officer during the war."

"Originally I think he is from Missouri or Arkansas, or some such place. And John's right, he did fight for the South. Also, he tends to hire Southerners to work for him. You get a bunch of Rebs in a Northern town, especially if they need to let off a little steam, and there's just bound to be trouble."

"Maybe I didn't tell you, Marshal, but I fought for the South," Hawke said with a smile.

"Yeah, I know you did," Trueblood replied. "But since you've been here, this is the only fracas you've got yourself into, and you didn't start this one."

Trueblood was quiet for a moment. "Hawke, I know who you are."

"I'm Mason Hawke."

Trueblood waved his hand. "I know that. I'm not saying you are using a phony name. I'm just saying that I know who you are."

"I sort of figured you might know about me," Hawke said. "You're a good law officer, Matt. I would think you would want to keep track of people who come into your town. But if you do know about my past, you know that I'm not wanted anywhere."

"Maybe not, but I know that this isn't the first time you've been in a shooting. In fact, you've been in quite a few of them over the last few years. And you've managed to develop yourself quite a reputation in some parts of the country as being particularly good with a gun. I have heard all about you, but, like you say, there are no dodgers out against you. And from all I've been able to find out, you've always been on the right side of every fracas. That bein' the case, I just figured that as long as you kept your nose clean, there was no sense in spreading it all over town. Because the truth is, once a man gets a reputation, it becomes harder and harder to avoid trouble. You always have some fool wanting to try you, wanting to establish a reputation of his own."

"I appreciate that," Hawke replied.

"Besides, you ain't the only one that's had a hard time comin' back from the war. There's quite a few folks who still have devils chasin' after 'em, despite the fact it's been over for better'n ten years."

Marshal Trueblood was talking about the war veterans who had found it nearly impossible to return home and take up the plow, or go back to work in a store, repair wagons, or any of the other things that were the necessary part of becoming whole again.

There were also those, especially who had fought for the South, who had no choice, because they had nothing to go home to. They returned to burned-out homes, farms gone to seed or, worse, taken for taxes. These men became the dispossessed. Unable to settle down, many of them went West, where there would be less encroachment of civilization upon their chosen way of life. Some took up the outlaw trail, continuing to practice the skills they had learned during the war. But most were innocent wanderers with all bridges to their past burned, and the paths to their future uncharted.

Mason Hawke was such a man. When he found that he had nothing to return to, he became a wandering minstrel, playing the piano in saloons and bawdy houses throughout the West. The irony was that few of those who heard him playing "Cowboy Joe" or "Buffalo Gals" realized that he had once played before the crowned heads of Europe, that he had, in fact, been knighted by the Queen of England for his skills and talent.

But there was another, darker side to Hawke.

The same digital dexterity that made him a great pianist also made him exceptionally good with a gun. Hawke did not openly seek trouble, but neither would he back away from it. Hot-headed hooligans would sometimes mistake the piano player for an easy mark.

But like the cowboy who killed Cindy, it was a mistake they only made once.

As Hawke and Marshal Trueblood left the courtroom, they saw another batch of cows being brought in to be loaded on the cars. The cowboys bringing them were as boisterous and animated as those who had brought the cows in the day before.

"Hey, Deekus, you goin' to Pearlie's after we get done here?" one of them asked.

"Not me. I'm headin' for the Hog Lot," the cowboy named Deekus replied.

"What you aimin' to do?"

"I aim to drink me four beers," Deekus replied. "Then, after that, I aim to get down to some serious drinkin'."

The other cowboys who were within earshot laughed.

"It looks like they haven't heard about Shorty yet," Trueblood said.

"Either that or they are shedding no tears over the loss," Hawke said.

As Hawke and the marshal were talking, a man picked his way across the street, carefully avoiding the many dung deposits left behind by the cows. He wore a black suit, a ribbon tie, and a low-crown, wide-brim hat. It was Gideon McCall, the pastor of Holy Spirit, a nondenominational church that was the town's only house of worship.

"Hello, Parson McCall," Trueblood said.

"Marshal, Mr. Hawke," the parson replied.

Hawke nodded at the preacher.

"Marshal, do you have any plans as to the funeral of the cowboy who was killed?" McCall asked.

"Not really," Trueblood replied. "I don't think it's my place to make plans. Seems to me that should be up to Clint Jessup. Why? Are you volunteering for the job?"

"Not exactly," Gideon replied. "Though, of course, I would make myself available. Everyone deserves a Christian burial. I was just curious as to what arrangements are being made. Have you spoken to Major Jessup yet?"

"No," Trueblood admitted. "I was hoping that he would come in with his men today, but it doesn't look as if he did. To tell you the truth, I'm not looking forward to riding out there to tell him that he has to bury one of his men."

"Marshal, if you'd like, I'll ride out there with you," Hawke offered.

Trueblood laughed. "Hell no," he said. Trueblood glanced quickly at the pastor. "Excuse my language, Parson," he said.

"That's quite all right, Marshal, I know you are under a great deal of stress," McCall replied.

Trueblood resumed his dialogue. "Hawke, did you forget that you're the one that shot him? No, I think if I had you with me when I went out to see Jessup, it would just make matters worse. I'll tell him myself."

"Whatever you say," Hawke replied.

"Mr. Hawke, I wonder if I might ask a favor of you," the parson said.

"What is it?"

"The other, uh . . . ladies who are friends of Miss Carey have asked me to conduct her funeral. And they would like for you to play the piano."

"I was under the impression that your wife played the piano for you."

"She does," McCall replied. "But Tamara is self-taught, and it is such a struggle for her that she would gladly put the burden down. I am told that you are quite a good pianist. I am also told that Cindy called you her friend. Is that true?"

Hawke nodded. "That's true, but I like to think that I am the friend of all the ladies who work the bar at the Hog Lot."

"Wealthy is the person whose life is enriched by friends,"

Gideon said. "And generous is the one who shares his friendship with others. Will you play?"

"Of course I'll play," Hawke replied. "I would be honored to play for her funeral."

Gideon smiled. "Thank you. I know she would be pleased. The services will be at ten A.M. on Friday morning. And you are welcome to come try out the piano anytime before then."

Chapter 4

CLINT JESSUP HAD AWAKENED JUST BEFORE DAWN. He rolled out of his blankets, pulled on his boots, then sat staring into the fire. Although Clint was an early riser, he was not the first one up. Poke Travis, the cook, had been up for an hour, and now he stood in the light of his lantern at the lowered tailgate of his wagon, rolling out biscuits for breakfast. He had already made coffee, and the aroma permeated the encampment area.

Just beyond the bubble of light created by the cook's lantern and the campfire, the herd stood in the quiet darkness, watched over by three nighthawks. The rest of the Bar-J riders were still asleep, their snores renting the still, morning air.

Poke brought Jessup a cup of coffee. "Would you be wantin' me to cook you up an early breakfast, Major?" he asked.

"No thanks, Poke," Jessup answered. "Coffee will do for now."

"All right. I'll get back to my wagon, then," Poke said.

Jessup took a swallow of his coffee as he stared into the fire, watching the flames curl around a piece of glowing wood.

His thoughts drifted back to another time and another place.

A dozen fires roared, sending showers of sparks climbing into the night sky, creating glowing red stars to compete with the little blue pinpoints of light that were spread across the vault of black, velvet sky. The raiders were laughing as they rode up and down the street of the little Missouri town of Sikeston, shooting every male over the age of sixteen.

"No! My boy is only fourteen!" a woman pleaded.

"He's old enough," one of the raiders said.

"No! No! He's just a child!" the woman shouted. Her cry was followed by the sound of a gunshot.

"He's old enough now. He's dead, and you don't get'ny older than dead," the raider said with a high-pitched laugh.

There were more screams, gunshots, and laughter as the raiders continued to ride up and down the street, spreading terror to the small town.

Finally the leader called to his sergeant. "That's enough."

"Major, we ain't collected from all the people yet," the sergeant said.

"Did we get the money from the bank?"

"Yes, sir, but there was only a couple hundred dollars was all that was in there."

"If that was all that was in the bank, then that means the people don't have anything; at least, not enough to take a chance on our staying any longer. We've been here an hour, that's long enough. We're pulling out now. Call in the men."

"Yes, sir."

The sergeant fired three shots into the air, and within moments all the raiders were assembled in a formation. A few were holding items they had looted from the homes, a brass candlestick, a clock, a silver cup. One of the raiders even had a woman's dress thrown across the front of his saddle.

"You're going to get all dressed up for the cotillion, are you, Reeves?" the major teased.

The others laughed, and Reeves's face got even redder in the light of the fire that was consuming the town.

"I was just goin' to find me some gal to give it to," Reeves replied.

"Leave it here."

"But, Major—"

"Leave it here," the major said again.

Reeves let the dress fall into the dirt.

"Column of twos," the major said. "Forward, ho." As they rode out of town, a burning timber broke in two, falling in on itself with loud snapping and popping.

One of the larger logs on the fire Jessup was watching broke in two, falling in on itself with loud snapping and popping. The fire blazed up more brightly, bringing Jessup out of his reverie.

Clint Jessup wasn't his real name. If he had used his real name, there was a very good chance he would be arrested and hanged for murder.

The charges did not seem right to him. There were hundreds of thousands who were killed or who died as a result of the war. Why should he be singled out just because the unit he led had never been officially sanctioned by the Confederate Congress? Hell, he thought, the Confederate Congress itself had never been officially sanctioned, so what did it matter whether his little band of guerrillas had been recognized or not? It was war.

Jessup had changed his name two or three times in the first few years just after the war, always staying a few jumps ahead of the authorities. But he had used the name Clint Jessup for the last six years, ever since he bought the Double Bow and changed it to the Bar-J.

He felt reasonably certain now that he would not have to

change his name again. He had been enriched by his wartime activities and had invested that money wisely. He was now a respected businessman.

It was true, the old adage of "hiding in plain sight." Nobody even suspected him. Besides, the intensity with which the authorities were trying to bring men like him to justice had eased up in the last few years. It was as if everyone was ready to put the war behind them.

By now the other riders for the Bar-J were beginning to wake up. They stretched, pulled on their boots, relieved themselves, then began joking and laughing as the cow camp became active.

"Hey," one of the cowboys called. "Where at's Shorty? Tex, you seen Shorty?"

"Not since last night," Tex answered.

"Last night? What do you mean last night?"

Tex laughed. "Oh, that's right, you didn't go into town last night, did you, Carter?"

"You know I didn't. I was one of the ones that was tolled out, remember?"

"Oh, yeah, I remember. Well, you shoulda been with us yesterday," Tex said. "After we delivered the cows, me 'n' Brandt and Shorty went into town, had us a good supper at Lambert's Café, then had us some drinks at Foley's."

"Did you go to Pearlie's?" Carter asked.

"We was goin' to, but Pearlie has only got five girls and they was too many there."

"So we wound up at the Hog Lot," Brandt interjected. "Besides which, the girls is prettier there anyhow."

"So, you two are back. Where's Shorty?"

"Well, that's what we're gettin' at. You know them pretty girls I was talkin' about? Well, Shorty didn't come back 'cause he fell in love with one of 'em," Tex said, laughing loudly.

"What do you mean, he fell in love? Who did he fall in love with?"

"Well, like Tex said, Shorty fell in love with one of them whores at the Hog Lot," Brandt said. "I don't recollect her name, but she sure was a purty thing."

"It was Cindy," Tex said. "Her name was Cindy."

"Yeah, now that I recollect, I believe it was Cindy," Brandt said.

"Tex," Jessup said, interrupting. He had overheard the conversation. "Are you saying that Shorty is still in town?"

"Yes, sir, Major," Tex replied. "It wouldn't do but that he spend the night with his whore. Onliest thing is, he didn't have enough money, so me 'n' Brandt lent him a dollar so's he could stay."

"Yeah, you might say we was Cupid," Brandt added, laughing.

"Well, he better get back here before we take the next batch of cows into town," Jessup said. "Or it'll take more than Cupid to get him out of trouble."

"Don't worry, Major, Shorty'll be here," Carter said. "He's a good man. You know that."

The cook began pounding on a steel ring then, and all the cowboys, with their kits in hand, hurried over to a breakfast of biscuits, bacon, and potatoes.

Throughout the rest of the morning, Jessup forgot all about Shorty as he went about the business of counting out the steers that would be taken in to the railhead for the next shipment. Because lunch for everyone, including Jessup, was jerky, which was eaten in the saddle, the outfit did not gather again, so the subject of Shorty's absence didn't come up until it was time to take in the cows.

"Deekus," Jessup said.

"Yes, sir?"

"If you see Shorty, you tell him for me that he'll be staying behind with the herd for the rest of the time we are here. And if he doesn't like that, he can just ride away with only half his wages."

"Yes, sir, Major, I'll tell 'im," Deekus said.

* * *

It was late that afternoon, while Jessup was out with the herd, that he looked up to see Poke riding toward him. The cook wasn't alone. At first Jessup didn't know who the other rider was, then he recognized him. It was Matthew Trueblood, the city marshal for Braggadocio.

"Major, this here is Marshal Trueblood," Poke said.

"Yes," Jessup said. "I know the marshal. Hello, Marshal."

"Major Jessup," Trueblood replied by way of greeting.

Jessup sighed. "You don't have to tell me," he said. "You've got one of my men in jail. It wouldn't be Shorty McDougal, would it? He went into town yesterday and hasn't come back. I figured it might be something like this."

"I wish that's all it was," Trueblood said.

Jessup frowned. "What else could it be?" he asked.

"I hate to be the one to tell you this, Jessup, but your man, Shorty, is dead."

"Dead? How'd it happen?"

"He was shot," Trueblood said.

"Well, I trust that the son of a bitch who shot him is either dead or in jail," Jessup said.

Trueblood shook his head. "No, sir, it didn't happen that way." Trueblood went on to explain how Shorty had killed Cindy Carey, shot the bartender, then shot at the piano player.

"So, who killed him?"

"The piano player," Trueblood replied.

Jessup looked incredulously at Trueblood, then laughed. "Wait a minute, here. What are you trying to tell me? The piano player? Do you expect me to believe that the piano player shot Shorty?"

"I expect you to believe it, because that is what happened. After Shorty shot the bartender, he turned to shoot at the piano player. The piano player then drew his gun and shot back, killing Shorty."

"Shorty shot at the piano player, *then* the piano player drew his gun and shot back?"

"That's the way it happened."

"Did you see it?"

"No."

"No, I didn't think so. Because even you know that's not true. There's no way a piano player could outdraw Shorty."

"He didn't outdraw him, exactly. I told you, Shorty already had his gun out and shot at the piano player before the piano player even drew his gun."

"Yeah, well, so you say. There is going to be a trial, right? When is the trial? I plan to be there. I want to hear, firsthand, the story of how Shorty lost a gunfight to a piano player."

"We've already had the trial," Trueblood answered. "Actually, it wasn't a trial, it was a hearing. The judge listened to all the witnesses and found that the piano player acted in self-defense. That's the end of it. There will be no trial, because no charges are going to be filed."

Jessup shook his head. "My men aren't going to like that," he said.

"Well, Major Jessup, I expect you to keep your men in line. After all, they do work for you. And you've had experience commanding men, haven't you?"

"I'll do what I can," Jessup said. "But Shorty McDougal was very popular with the men. In fact, I liked him myself. He was a good hand, dependable and trustworthy. By the way, where is his body?"

"It's with the undertaker, Robert Griffin. He has a place behind the hardware store."

"I hope Robert Griffin does him up nice," Jessup said.

"Well, that's one of the reasons I came out here," Trueblood said. "If nobody steps up to pick up the funeral expenses, the city is going to have to bury him. And anyone who gets buried at city expense gets no more than a wooden box."

Jessup shook his head no and made a waving motion with his hand. "No, no, I want him done up right," he said. "You tell Robert Griffin that I'll be in town tomorrow when we take our next batch of cows to the depot, and I'll take care of it then."

"All right, I'll tell him," Trueblood said, then turned and started back.

"Marshal?" Jessup called.

Trueblood turned around. "Yes?"

"What about the whore?"

"I beg your pardon?"

"The whore," Jessup said. "Didn't you tell me Shorty killed a whore?"

"Yes, he did."

"Tell Robert Griffin I'll pay for her funeral too."

"Thank you, that's decent of you. But her friends are taking care of that," Marshal Trueblood replied.

Jessup paused for a moment, then nodded. "All right," he said. "I just thought I'd make the offer."

"Major Jessup," Trueblood said. "You know there will be other herds coming in, in the next few days."

"Yes," Jessup said.

"Well, you might want to hold your boys back a bit."

"What do you mean?"

"The folks in town aren't all that friendly toward cowboys as it is," Trueblood said. "Too much trouble and they might just tell the railroad to move their shipping operation somewhere else. There's been some talk about that already. Now that might not bother you all that much, you've already started shipping and would probably be finished by the time they got the loading pens shut down. But it could make it hard on the other cattlemen, and I don't figure you want to do that."

"No," Jessup said. "I wouldn't want to make it hard on the others."

"I'll be getting back into town now," Trueblood said. "I'm sorry about your man. But, like I said, he brought it on himself."

"So you said," Jessup replied flatly.

* * *

Three of the cowboys who had stayed back with the herd learned what happened to Shorty from Poke. They were discussing it as they were riding perimeter around the herd.

"I can't believe they just let the son of a bitch go," Cracker said.

"They let who go?" Brandt asked.

"The piano player, that's who. The son of a bitch that shot Shorty. They had a hearing, and they let 'im go free."

"According to what the marshal said, Shorty shot at the piano player first," Tex explained.

"The hell you say," Cracker said.

"Yeah, and not only the marshal," Brandt added. "Ever'one that spoke at the trial said that's what happened."

"But it wasn't no real trial," Cracker said. "It was just a hearing. Even the marshal said that. And let me ask you, was any of our people there when they had the hearing? I mean we was all three in town yesterday, but we wasn't there when it happened."

"It happened this morning, after all the rest of us had come back," Tex said.

"So, what does that tell you?" Cracker asked.

"What do you mean, what does that tell us?"

"That means that the only folks doin' the talkin' at that hearing was town folks. And if you think any of them damn Yankees is goin' to find one of their own guilty for killin' a cowboy, then you just ain't thinkin' straight."

"Cracker, you know yourself that Shorty had a temper," Tex said. "He could get all worked up over the least little thing."

"Do you think he actually killed that whore?" Cracker asked. "You seen how he was takin' on over her last night, same as me."

"Yeah, I think he might have killed her," Tex admitted. "I don't think he done it of a pure purpose, but I ain't got no doubt but what it happened pretty much like the marshal said it did. I mean, even the marshal said it was sort of an accident."

"Well, if it was an accident, then nobody had any right to kill Shorty, did they?"

"You know, Tex, Cracker's right," Brandt said. "And there's somethin' else nobody seems to be considerin'."

"What's that?"

"They're sayin' that the fella who kilt him was the piano player, right?"

"Right."

"Well, don't you remember that him and Shorty seemed to get into it while we was there?"

"Yeah," Tex said. "Yeah, now that you mention it, there was words passed between them."

"That's right," Cracker said. "I remember that too. The piano player wouldn't play the song Shorty was askin' him to play, and they come near to getting' in a fight over it."

"Yeah," Tex replied. He laughed. "But I tell you the truth, I was just as glad the piano player didn't play it anymore. I was gettin' plumb tired of listenin' to 'Buffalo Gals.' But you're right there was cross words that passed between them."

"Well then, there you go," Cracker said.

"There you go, where?"

"That's how he come to kill Shorty. It didn't have nothin' at all to do with Shorty killin' that whore, because even the marshal said that was an accident. I think the piano player kilt Shorty 'cause him and Shorty got into an argument."

"Well, what if it was?" Tex replied. "Everyone still says that Shorty drew first."

"So what you're sayin' is, we ought not do anything about it," Cracker said.

"Just what do you think we could do about it?" Tex asked.

"I don't know," Cracker admitted. "But there ought to be somethin' we could do. I mean, what if it was one of you lyin' up there dead? Wouldn't you want your pards to do somethin'?"

"Well, we could go into town and get drunk and celebrate," Tex suggested.

"Celebrate? What are you talkin' about? You mean celebrate that Shorty's dead?"

"Sure, the Irish do it all the time," Tex said. "It's called a wake."

"Well, I ain't no Irishman."

Tex smiled. "No, but Ian McDougal was."

"Ian McDougal?"

"Yeah," Tex said. "You didn't think Shorty was his real name, did you?"

"I guess I never thought about it."

Brandt laughed. "Do you believe folks think that Cracker is your real name?"

"Yeah," Cracker said. "Yeah, I see what you mean. A wake, huh?"

"Yep."

"And you think Shorty would like this? I mean us having a wake and gettin' drunk 'n' all?" Cracker asked.

"Oh, yeah, I think he'll be lookin' down from heaven, just smilin' at his old pards," Tex said.

Brandt laughed.

"What are you laughin' at?"

"Knowin' Shorty, he's not smilin' down from heaven. Like as not, he's lookin' up from hell, wishin' he had just one drop to cool his tongue."

The others laughed at Brandt's observation.

"What is it you called that celebratin' thing, now?" Cracker asked. "Us gettin' drunk and all?"

"It's called a wake," Tex said.

"A wake, huh? Well, I sure hope it don't wake him up," Cracker said.

"What do you mean? I thought Shorty was your friend," Brandt said.

"Yeah, he was my friend. But he's dead now, and I'd just as soon anyone that's dead, stay dead."

"Ooooooh," Brandt said, putting his hat over his face.

"Stop that," Cracker said.

"Oooooh, Cracker, this is Shorty, comin' back from the dead. Oooooh."

"Stop that, I said," Cracker said irritably. "That ain't no way funny."

When the cowboys took the third bunch of cows into town to the railhead the next day, Jessup rode with them. He was halfway through town when he saw what he was looking for.

There was a sign, in the shape of a hand, suspended from the overhanging awning that covered the boardwalk in front of Robison's Hardware Store. The finger pointed to the rear of the building. Hanging from the hand was another sign:

ROBERT GRIFFIN
UNDERTAKER
FINE COFFINS
OFFICE IN BACK

"Deekus," Jessup called.

"Yes, sir?"

"You take charge till I get down there. I'm going to see about Shorty."

"Yes, sir," Deekus replied.

Jessup turned away from the others and rode over toward the mortuary. Dismounting, he followed the sign around back.

A bell, attached to the door, jangled when Jessup stepped into the room. The room smelled strongly of formaldehyde. This was obviously a showroom for coffins, because there were three on display. There was a door leading from this room into another room, but a hanging curtain prevented anyone from looking into the back room.

Hearing the bell, Robert Griffin stepped through the

curtain, drying his hands as he did so. He was wearing a white apron which was stained with blood, old and new.

"Yes, sir, what can I do for you?" Robert Griffin asked.

"I'm Clint Jessup," Jessup said. "I own the Bar-J. I believe you have one of my men."

"You are talking about the cowboy who was involved in the trouble at the Hog Lot?"

"Yes."

"Yes, I have him."

"I'd like to see him," Jessup said, starting toward the curtain.

Robert Griffin stepped in front of him. "I'm sorry, sir, but I don't allow anyone in the embalming room."

"You think you can keep me out?"

Robert Griffin shook his head. "No, sir, I don't suppose I could if you wanted to force your way in. I would hope, though, that you would have enough respect for the dead not to do that."

Jessup paused for a moment, then nodded. "All right, I'll give you that," he said. "I guess I'll be able to see him soon enough. I'm here to make arrangements for him. I want to pay whatever your costs are, and I want to pick out a coffin."

"What kind of coffin?"

"A good one," Jessup said. "Your best one."

"Oh, then I think you would like this one. It is particularly nice," Robert Griffin said, pointing to a highly polished, black and silver casket. "It is called the Eternal Cloud, and it is guaranteed for one thousand years."

Jessup laughed.

"I beg your pardon, Major Jessup, but have I said something humorous?" Robert Griffin asked, surprised by the ranch owner's unexpected response.

"Yeah," Jessup said. "You think you're going to live for a thousand years?"

"No, of course not."

"Then, suppose I dig this coffin up in a thousand years and it's rotted out. You'll be dead, who the hell am I going to collect my guarantee from?"

"Well, it's a substantial company, I'm sure there will be someone who can . . ." Robert Griffin started, then paused. "Sir, you won't be here in one thousand years either."

"That's my point," Jessup said. "So, don't tell me about the one thousand year guarantee. It doesn't matter."

"I see what you mean," Robert Griffin said, somewhat crestfallen from the exchange. He ran his hand across the smooth, glossy black surface. "However, I am sure you are discerning enough to understand what a wonderful piece of workmanship this is."

"I'll take it," Jessup said.

Robert Griffin picked up his account book and wrote: *One Eternal Cloud coffin to Major Clint Jessup.*

"I presume you'll have the late Mr. McDougal's body shipped somewhere?"

"Yes," Jessup said. "But first I want him put on display."

"I see. You want to arrange for a visitation and viewing so you —"

"No," Jessup interrupted. "No visitation."

"But I don't understand. I thought you said you wanted him to be on display."

"That's exactly what I said, and that's exactly what I mean."

"How can there be a display without a visitation and viewing?"

"I want you to dress him up in a suit, then I want you to open up the top half of that fancy casket I just bought and set him in the front window of this hardware store. I want everyone in town to see him if they happen by the store window."

"I don't know if Mr. Robison would agree to that. He owns the hardware store."

"Find out how much it costs to make him agree," Jessup said. "I want Shorty displayed in that front window."

"Very good, sir," Jessup said. "I'll make the arrangements."

"And I want you to have the sign painter paint a sign to put on the coffin."

"You want a sign buried with the coffin?"

"Not buried with it," Jessup said. "I want the sign put on the coffin while it's on display in the window, so that everyone who happens by will be able to read it."

"What shall the sign say?" Robert Griffin asked.

"This is what it will say," Jessup said, handing a piece of paper to the undertaker.

Leaving the mortuary, Jessup rode down to the railroad depot where the cows his men had just brought in were being loaded. Deekus was standing with the broker, watching as the cows were led up the ramp and into the car. As each car was filled, the train would move forward slightly, then the next car would be filled, thirty cows to each car.

"How's the count going?" Jessup asked.

"Three hundred today, three hundred yesterday," the broker said.

"Eight more days and we'll have them all loaded," Jessup said.

"Unless the town runs us off," the broker said.

"What do you mean, unless the town runs us off?"

"Some of the folks in town are talking about closing the cattle shipping facilities here."

"Yes, Trueblood said something about that yesterday. But I'm not worried. They aren't going to do that. They'd lose too much money."

"Maybe not. There are more farmers around Braggadocio than there are ranchers. If they closed the cattle pens, they could build more grain elevators. They say they don't have as much trouble with the farmers as they do with the cowboys. That was one of your riders killed yesterday, wasn't it?"

"Yes," Jessup answered. He nodded back toward the center of town. "As a matter of fact, I just stopped by to make arrangements with the undertaker."

"You going to bury him here?"

"No, I'm going to ship him back to Iowa," Jessup said. "But first, I want the people of the town to have an opportunity to see him."

The broker looked up in surprise. "Why in heaven's name would you want that?"

"Let's just say that it is my way of reaching out to the town," Jessup said.

By mid-morning nearly half the town had wandered by Robison's Hardware Store, where Shorty's body lay on display in the front window. All talked about the beautiful black coffin with the bright, silver accouterments, and the cowboy who was dressed more elegantly in death than he had ever been in life.

But the thing that got everyone's attention was the neatly painted, hand-lettered sign that perched on the bottom half of the coffin.

**YOU SEE HERE THE MORTAL REMAINS OF
IAN "SHORTY" MC DOUGAL
A GRIEVING MOTHER'S SON
GATHER 'ROUND YE DEMONS OF BRAGGADOCIO
TO LOOK AT WHAT YOU HAVE DONE**

Chapter 5

~~~~~~

**SHOOTOUT IN THE HOG LOT SALOON
TWO KILLED, ONE WOUNDED
COWBOY SHOT DEAD BY ACCURATE
SHOOTING
COWBOY HAD KILLED A WOMAN
BARTENDER WOUNDED IN FRACAS**

THE ISSUE OF THE *BRAGGADOCIO JOURNAL* THAT told of the shootout came out on the day before Cindy's funeral, and it sold more copies than any paper Vernon Clemmons had ever printed. He had to go back to the Washington hand press several times, eventually turning out over 250 copies. Nearly everyone in town got a copy of the paper, and in the saloons and cafés of the town, the incident, and the article in the paper, were the prime subjects of conversation.

"Who would have thought that a piano player would be able to best a cowboy in shooting?"

The questioner was George Schermerhorn, owner of Schermerhorn Wagon Freight. The two men with him were James Cornett, who owned the general store and was also the mayor of the town, and Jubal Goodpasture, owner of the livery stable. They were having lunch at Lambert's Café.

"Well, have you ever paid much attention to this piano player?" Goodpasture replied.

"Not in particular. I mean, he's just a piano player. Who pays attention to a piano player?" Schermerhorn asked.

"Mason Hawke is a pretty good one, though," the mayor said. "You two might remember the one Harder had working for him before he hired Hawke. Sifferman, I think his name was. His piano playing sounded like a peddler's wagon banging across the prairie."

The other two laughed at the mayor's description of the previous piano player's talents.

"Yeah, but I'm not talkin' about his piano playin'," Goodpasture said. "I was in the Hog Lot a few weeks ago when a drunk pulled his pistol and threatened to shoot ol' Bob Gary, claimin' that he watered the drinks."

"Hell, Gary does water his drinks," Schermerhorn said, and the other two laughed.

"Maybe," Goodpasture said. "But there was that drunk, waving his gun around, threatening to shoot anyone who came close. That didn't stop Hawke, though. He walked up to him, just as calm as you please, picked up a bottle and hit him over the head."

"I remember that. But the man was drunk," Schermerhorn said.

"I was there, Schermerhorn, you was there, there was maybe a dozen more in there. But Hawke was the only one who had nerve enough to walk up to him and disarm him."

"Yeah, that's true, now that you mention it. I reckon it did take some nerve to do that," Schermerhorn admitted.

"I'm tellin' you," Goodpasture said, "I think there's more to this fella Hawke than meets the eye."

"Are either of you goin' to the girl's funeral?" the mayor asked.

"I am," Schermerhorn said. He chuckled. "I wasn't, I figured my wife would give me hell for goin' to a whore's funeral. But she's been readin' the paper and she's got so interested that she's wantin' to go."

"I think Karen wants to go," Cornett said. "But she's wondering how it will look to the good folks of the city if they see their mayor at a whore's funeral."

"Hell, Mayor, how's that going to be any different from you sittin' down at the Hog Lot havin' drinks while whores is walkin' by, pattin' you on the head?" Goodpasture asked.

"They may pat me on the head," the mayor said. "But I've never patted any of them on the behind."

Goodpasture, and even Schermerhorn, laughed at the observation.

"What about you, Goodpasture?" Schermerhorn asked. "You goin' to the funeral?"

"Yeah," Goodpasture answered. "And unlike you two, I don't have a wife to answer to."

"Hell, Goodpasture, you don't have to tell us you don't have a wife," Cornett said. "What woman would be dumb enough to marry you in the first place?"

The jibe was good natured, and everyone, including Goodpasture, laughed.

The church was filled to capacity for Cindy Carey's funeral. As people continued to file in, Tamara McCall, the parson's wife, was standing just inside the pastor's study, looking through the crack in the barely opened door at the crowd gathering in the sanctuary.

"I had no idea so many people would be here," she said.

"The newspaper article attracted a lot of attention," Gideon said. He was tying and retying his tie. "I can't get this thing tied," he said in frustration.

"Here, let me do that," Tamara said, stepping up to tie it for him.

"I don't deserve you," Gideon said.

Tamara smiled. "No, you don't," she agreed. "But you've got me."

"And Lucy," Gideon added. "Is she out there, by the way?"

"Oh, yes. She's sitting in the front row, right next to Mrs. Rittenhouse."

Gideon chuckled. "There is no accounting for that child's choice of friends. I don't know how she can stand that woman."

"Gideon," Tamara scolded. "Please remember that you are a man of the cloth. I'll admit that Mrs. Rittenhouse can be cantankerous from time to time."

"Can be? Tamara, that woman's normal disposition is cantankerous. What you mean is, she can be normal from time to time." He sighed. "But somehow, Lucy seems to bring that out of her."

"Lucy is a sweet child who brings out the best in everyone," Tamara said with pride.

There was a small knock on the back door of the study, and Tamara walked over to open it. The visitor was Mason Hawke.

"Mr. Hawke," Tamara said, smiling pleasantly. "How wonderful of you to agree to play for the funeral."

"Well, Cindy . . . that is, Miss Carey . . . was a friend of mine," Hawke said. "I'm very pleased to be able to play for her, and honored that you would ask."

"Do you play by music, or by ear?" Tamara asked. "The reason I ask is, so many saloon piano players play by ear. But I'm told by those who have heard you that you are quite good."

Hawke smiled. "I play by music . . . or by memory," he said. "And by ear," he added.

"Well, I have some sheet music if you would care to use it. It's from the hymnal."

"Thank you," Hawke said. "I will play the songs you have picked out for me. But I also brought some sheet music that I would like to play as well. That is, with your permission." He showed the music to her.

" 'Joseph Haydn's Mass in G,' " Tamara said, reading the title. "Oh, my, that sounds quite . . . ambitious."

"I thought it might make an appropriate prelude," Hawke said. "So if you don't mind, I'll just go get started."

"Please, by all means," Tamara said, leading him to the door that opened onto the sanctuary. "Be my guest."

Hawke walked out to the piano and looked down at it. It was a Haynes Square piano, rosewood, with octagon curved legs and mother-of-pearl inlay on the name board. He had been told that it was a good piano, but had no idea it was this good. He was pleasantly surprised by the quality of the instrument, and when he depressed a few of the keys, he was rewarded with a rich, resonant tone.

Hawke sat on the bench, put his music on the ornately carved lyre before him, then looked out over the congregation. Every seat in the church was full, and a long line of mourners stretched along one side of the church as the men and women filed silently by to view the open coffin that sat just below the sacristy.

Hawke couldn't see Cindy's body from where he sat and was just as glad. He preferred to remember the young woman the way she was the last time he'd seen her, when she was drinking coffee with him, laughing and flirtatious.

Then he began to play.

Many in the congregation had heard him in the saloon, but most never had. They thought that, at best, it would be little more than a saloon piano player, selected for the service only because the decedent was one of his own. They were totally unprepared for what they were about to hear.

The music filled the church and caressed the collective

soul of the congregation. If they did not know of his talent and ability before now, it took but a few bars of music to convince even the most skeptical that they weren't hearing a mere saloon piano player. They were listening to a concert pianist of great skill.

Not one person in the congregation had read the story in the *London Times*, written by a British music critic, about Mason Hawke. But if they had, they would have agreed with every word:

> His music was something magical. The brilliant young American pianist managed, with his playing, to resurrect the genius of the composer so that, to the listening audience, Mason Hawke and Ludwig Beethoven were one and the same.

They merely would have substituted the name Joseph Haydn for Ludwig Beethoven.

Even before the music finished, the coffin was closed and those who could find a place to sit did so. Those who could not find seats stood along the walls on each side and at the rear of the church. Even the narthex was filled, and several more waited out front, ready to accompany the funeral cortege to the graveyard.

Gideon McCall had come out of the study during the prelude, and sat quietly in his chair in the sacristy until the music ended. Then he stepped up to the pulpit, looking out over the congregation. A couple of people in the congregation coughed. At the rear of the church someone opened a window. Not until there was absolute quiet did Gideon begin to speak. His voice was richly timbered, and it resonated throughout the room. Every eye was turned toward him, every ear attuned.

"I begin today with a reading from the Book of Matthew," he said.

He looked at the Bible on his pulpit and began to read:

*Jesus said, "Verily I say unto you, that the publicans
and the harlots go into the kingdom of God before you.*

*"For John came unto you in the way of righ-
teousness, and ye believed him not: but the publicans
and the harlots believed him: and ye, when ye had seen
it, repented not afterward, that ye might believe him."*

Gideon looked up from the Bible. "Here endeth the lesson," he said.

"Thanks be to God," the congregation responded.

Gideon closed the Bible.

"Cindy Carey was a harlot."

There were several gasps from the congregation, but
Gideon held out his hand as if asking for a moment to explain.

"Cindy was a harlot," he repeated. "But do not believe that
because she was a harlot she was abandoned by our Lord. In
our reading, Jesus told us that a harlot who is good at heart
will be welcome into the Kingdom of God. And those who
knew Cindy have all attested to the fact that she was a woman
with a good heart, truly, a child of God. Therefore we can re-
joice with Cindy, because I can tell you with Biblical authority," he held up the Bible, "that Cindy is in heaven today.

"The hymn I have chosen today speaks eloquently of
God's grace for all sinners."

At a nod from Gideon, Hawke began playing the music that
Tamara had selected for him. The congregation began to sing:

> *There's a wideness in God's mercy
> Like the wideness of the sea . . .*

When Cracker, Tex, and Brandt rode into town with the
next batch of cows for delivery, they passed by the church.
The area in front of and immediately around the church was
filled with wagons, buckboards, and tethered horses. The
hearse was parked in front, back up against the steps. The

team of horses was in black harness, and black bunting draped the windows of the hearse.

In addition to the horses and vehicles, there were several men and women just outside the church, some of whom were standing by the open windows so they could hear the eulogy and the music from inside.

> *There is welcome for the sinner*
> *And more grace for the good . . .*

"What's goin' on in there, you reckon?" Cracker asked. "Why are they havin' church on a Friday morning?"

"There's a hearse," Tex said. "That means it's a funeral."

"Shorty's funeral, do you reckon?"

"Nah, Shorty ain't goin' to have a funeral here. The major is shippin' him back to Iowa. I expect this is the whore's funeral," Tex said.

"Who woulda thought they'd have a whore's funeral in a church? And who woulda thought there would be that many folks comin' to the funeral of a whore?" Cracker said.

"You think Shorty is still lyin' in the window of the hardware store?" Brandt asked.

"I expect he is," Tex answered. "Leastwise, that's what Deekus said."

"After we deliver these here cows, I think we should go down there 'n' pay our respects," Cracker said. "Especially if we're going to have us that wake you was talkin' about."

Once the cows were delivered to the train, the three cowboys left the depot and rode down the street toward the hardware store. Because of the funeral, the street was nearly empty and there was no one standing in front of the store. As a result, they could see Shorty's coffin from two blocks away . . . propped up at a forty-five-degree angle for better viewing. It created the illusion that Shorty was staring back at them from the far end of the street.

"Damn," Brandt said. "That's kind of spooky, ain't it? I mean, seein' ol' Shorty down there like he's lookin' back at us."

Cracker stopped.

"What is it?" Tex asked.

"I don't want to go."

"Well, hell, you was the one said you wanted to go in the first place."

"Yeah, I know, but I didn't know it would be so damn spooky."

"Ooooooh," Brandt said, teasing Cracker.

"Cut that out!" Cracker said.

Tex and Brandt laughed.

"It's Shorty, remember?" Tex said. "Even if he is a spook, he ain't goin' do nothin' to his ol' pards."

"Yeah, I guess you're right," Cracker said.

The three men rode to the end of the empty street, then dismounted and stood in front of the window, looking at Shorty.

"He looks kinda pasty-faced, don't he?" Cracker said.

"He's dead," Tex replied. "Dead folks tends to get pasty-faced lookin'."

"He sure is dressed up nice," Brandt said. "Wonder where-at he got them fancy clothes?"

"Like as not the major bought 'em for 'im whenever he bought that fancy coffin," Tex said.

The three cowboys stood for another minute, then Tex cleared his throat. "Let's go get somethin' to drink," he said.

"I'm for that," Brandt agreed.

The men rode back to the Hog Lot Saloon, but as they were dismounting, Cracker said, "What the hell? It don't look like there's nobody here."

"It's closed," Tex said.

"How do you know?"

"That's what the sign says."

"Oh. I can't read. What else does it say? I know that closed is only one word, and there's more words than that."

"It says, 'Closed for the funeral of Miss Cindy Carey, a lovely flower, plucked from our midst by a deranged cowboy,' " Tex said, reading the sign.

"Deranged cowboy? What does that mean?" Brandt asked.

"It means crazy."

"Hell, Shorty wasn't crazy," Cracker said. "I mean, he could get crazy mad sometimes. But he wasn't crazy."

"We could go down to Foley's," Brandt suggested. "It ain't as nice as the Hog Lot . . . can't get no food there."

"That's okay. They got liquor and whores at Foley's," Cracker said.

Foley's was just across the street and down about fifty yards from the Hog Lot. It was open, but there were only two customers in the place when the three cowboys pushed through the bat-wing doors to step inside.

"Damn, this place is empty," Cracker said. "Where-at is ever'body?"

"Purt' near the whole town has turned out for the funeral," the bartender said, coming down the bar to meet them. "What'll you gents have?"

"Three whiskeys," Tex said, putting a coin on the bar.

"And we'll have the same," Brandt said, putting his own coin down. Cracker joined him.

"Where-at's your whores?" Cracker asked.

"If you mean the young ladies who work here, they are at the funeral as well."

"Why'd they go? I mean the whore they're buryin' worked at the Hog Lot, didn't she?" Cracker asked.

"Hell, Cracker," Tex said, "whores all stick together, like cowboys do."

"Yeah, I reckon that's right. I 'spect even the girls from Pearlie's is over there. I guess I just never figured on seein' so many people go to a whore's funeral," Cracker said.

Nine glasses were put before the men, then filled from the bar bottle.

"By the way, the cowboy that kilt her got hisself kilt too," the bartender said. "You can see him in the window down at Robison's Hardware."

"Yeah, we seen 'im," Cracker said. "But I still don't know why the whole town would turn out for a whore's funeral."

"Could be Vernon Clemmons's doin'," the bartender suggested.

"Who is Vernon Clemmons?"

"He's the publisher of the *Journal*. Yes, sir, we got us a real good paper, and ol' Vernon wrote a dandy article as to how the whore was really a good girl at heart, and how the cowboy was as evil as ol' Satan hisself. I reckon it was that article that got folks all riled up so. And goin' to the woman's funeral was about the only thing they could do about it."

"You got one of them papers?" Tex asked.

"Sure do, but it'll cost you a nickel."

"A nickel? Hell, you can get a paper in Kansas City for two cents," Tex said.

"Well, you ain't in Kansas City, cowboy," the bartender replied. "You're in Braggadocio."

"Ain't you got a paper that somebody's done read that I can have?"

"Yep."

"I'll take that one."

"It'll cost you a nickel," the bartender said.

Growling his displeasure, Tex put a nickel on the bar and the bartender reached under the bar to take out a newspaper and hand it to him.

"Let's go over to the table and sit a spell," Tex said. He tossed down all three whiskeys, then called to the bartender. "We'll take a whole bottle."

"That'll be a dollar and a half."

The three cowboys came up with fifty cents apiece, then Tex grabbed the bottle and they moved to a table.

* * *

When the services in the church were completed, the congregation filed outside. They formed up on either side of the steps as the pallbearers brought Cindy's body through the front door, then placed it in the back of the highly polished, black, glass-sided hearse. The bell of the church began tolling as Robert Griffin, wearing striped pants, cutaway coat, and high-topped hat, climbed up on the seat, then started driving the matched team of black horses toward the cemetery.

The mourners followed the hearse, not only those who were coming from the church, but the ones who had been waiting outside as well. John Harder, his bartender Bob Gary, whose arm was in a sling, Mason Hawke, and the soiled doves who worked at the Hog Lot, all rode in a wagon directly behind the hearse. They were accorded this honor because they were as close to family as Cindy had. The girls from Foley's and Pearlie's rode in the next wagon behind.

The grave had already been opened and the grave digger stood over to one side of the cemetery, sweating and dirty from his labors. He stayed out of the way so as not to intrude into the graveside services.

Down at Foley's, Tex, Cracker, and Brandt were separated from the funeral by distance and disposition. The bottle, which was full when they carried it to the table, was now three-quarters empty. As they drank, they shared stories about Shorty.

The other two customers in the saloon were at an adjoining table.

"Are you three gents from the Bar-J outfit that's sittin' just outside town, here?" one of the two men asked.

"Yeah, how'd you know?" Brandt replied.

"You was talking about the dead cowboy that's lyin' in the window down to Robison's Hardware Store, wasn't you?"

"Yeah, we was," Brandt said.

"I thought you was. And when I heard the way you was talkin' about him, why, I figured you was friends of his. I'm sorry he got hisself kilt."

"What I can't figure is what kind of town would let someone just murder someone and get away with it," Cracker said.

"What do you mean?"

"This here piano player. He kilt Shorty, didn't he? Only he ain't in jail, is he?"

"It wasn't like that," the bar patron said. "It was a fair fight. Your friend shot at the piano player first. Fact is, the piano player didn't even have his gun drawed."

"I don't believe it really happened that way," Cracker said. "If Shorty had shot first, the piano player would be dead."

"Oh, it happened that way, all right," the patron said.

"How do you know?"

"'Cause I was there, and I seen it."

"I don't believe you."

"Are you callin' me a liar?" the patron asked.

"Ike," the bartender called to the patron.

"What?"

"Go home now."

"What?"

"Go home," the bartender said. "I don't want no trouble in here."

"Well hell, Mica, he's the son of a bitch that started it," Ike replied.

"Do me a favor and go home now, will you?" Mica replied. "Don't worry about your bar bill. I'll pay it."

The expression on Ike's face eased, and he nodded. "All right, Mica," he said. "If it'll make you feel any better." Ike and his friend stood up and started toward the door.

"Yeah, run away from me, you coward," Cracker called toward him.

Ike turned back quickly, but he heard the double click of a

double-barreled shotgun being cocked. Looking toward the bar, he saw that Mica was pointing the shotgun toward the table where the cowboys sat.

"On second thought, Ike, you can stay," Mica said. "But you sons of bitches are going," he added, raising the shotgun to his shoulder.

"What the hell?" Tex said. "Why are you kicking Brandt and me out for somethin' Cracker said?"

"Let's just say I'm being cautious," Mica said. "Ike, you 'n' Pearson get over here behind me until these gents is gone."

Scowling, Tex, Cracker, and Brandt left the saloon, taking their bottle with them.

"Where now?" Cracker asked.

"Well, we could go down to the Nebraska House and get us some supper," Brandt suggested. "That is, if you don't shoot off your mouth an' get us kicked out again."

"I didn't like the way that son of a bitch was talkin'," Cracker said.

"Yeah, so we gathered," Tex said. "Come on, let's get something to eat."

The three walked down to the Nebraska House, where they had a meal of ham, eggs, potatoes, and biscuits. Tex continued to read the paper as they ate.

"Listen to this," he said, and read an excerpt.

The cowboys who come into our fair town with the transient herds are a necessary evil in that they do provide economic benefit to our community. But, make no mistake about it, they represent the evil part of the term "necessary evil."

The late cowboy, Ian McDougal, is not an exception to the cowboys. Unfortunately, he is typically representative.

They haunt our saloons, turning gentlemanly drinking establishments into dens of inequity. They

*become drunk and disorderly, they carouse the streets
so that no decent woman dares to go about her daily
business without being escorted by a male member of
her family.*

*It has been suggested that we eliminate this blight
on our fair community by removing the cattle pens and
provided services only to the area farmers who, history
has shown, are much more productive and peaceful
citizens.*

*That solution seems a little drastic, and while this
newspaper is not ready to support that, we would support an alternate proposal. The cowboys, long on the
trail and absent from the ameliorating effect of civilization, should be required to report to the marshal's
office immediately upon entering town. And therein,
they should surrender their firearms, not to be re-
claimed until they leave town.*

*This paper supports that recommendation, and
adds to it. This paper believes strongly that the law-
abiding citizens of Braggadocio should be exempt
from such a requirement. For only if the citizens of
the town are armed, and the cowboys disarmed, will
there be peaceful coexistence between the two ele-
ments.*

Tex looked up from the paper. "How do you like that?
This son of a bitch wants us to give up our guns, but he
wants the people of the town to be exempt."

"What does 'exempt' mean?" Cracker asked.

"It means he doesn't think they should have to give up
their guns."

"Piss on that," Brandt said. "If the people in town don't
give up their gun, I sure as hell ain't goin' to give up mine."

"I ain't goin' to give up my gun, period," Texas said. "No
matter what the people of this town do."

"Yeah," Cracker said. "I ain't plannin' on givin' up my

gun either. I mean, look what happened with Shorty. It was a town person who kilt him, wasn't it? A town person with a gun?"

"Yeah, it was," Tex said. He poured the last of the whiskey into the three glasses. "Drink up, boys. I've got a plan."

Chapter 6

AS THE TOWNSPEOPLE WERE RETURNING FROM THE funeral, they heard the loud crash of breaking glass, followed by raucous laughter. Looking toward the newspaper office, they saw something thrown into the street.

"Marshal Trueblood!" Harder called. "Marshal, something's going on down at the newspaper office!"

"At my office?" Vernon Clemmons shouted, running up quickly. "What is it?"

As they got closer, Clemmons recognized what was going on before anyone else. "My type!" he said. "That's my type in the street!"

Two other trays of type came hurtling through the broken window, and Trueblood, with his gun drawn, ran toward the newspaper office.

"Cracker, you 'n' Brandt get ahold of the other side of this thing," Tex was saying as he started toward the press. "We'll throw this out in the street with his type. I'd like to see him print a paper out there," he added, laughing.

At that moment Trueblood stepped in through the front door.

"Hold it!" he shouted. "Get your hands up!"

The three cowboys who had been trashing the newspaper office stopped and lifted their hands.

"Oh, now, Marshal," Tex said, laughing. "You had to come along and spoil our fun."

"Fun? You call this fun?" Clemmons said angrily, coming up then. He looked down at his type, scattered in the dirt. "Why would you do such a thing?"

"Are you the newspaper fella?" Cracker asked. "Are you the one that says cowboys are evil?"

"Is there any doubt?" Clemmons said. "You've proven my point." He waved his hand over the mess. "It'll take me all day to put this together again."

"No it won't," Hawke said. By now he and much of the rest of the town were present. "A town can't be without a newspaper. We'll help you put it back."

"Wait a minute," Tex said, looking at Hawke. "I know you. You're the piano player, aren't you?"

"No," Hawke said.

"No? What do you mean no? I was there the same night Shorty was there. I saw you playing the piano. Are you going to say that wasn't you?"

"That was me."

Tex looked confused. "So what is it? Are you the piano player that killed Shorty or not?"

"I am the *pianist* who killed Shorty," Hawke said.

"I'll be damned," Tex said. "Who would've thought that a good man like Shorty would be killed by a sissified dandy like you?"

"That's enough, mister," Trueblood said. "You three are going to jail now."

"No, I don't think we are," Tex said. He put his hands down, and the other two cowboys, seeing that, put their hands down as well. "We don't want no more trouble here, so I think we'll just go on back out to the herd. Newspaperman, you just tell us how much it's going to cost you to put the window back and we'll pay for it."

"Oh, you'll pay for it, all right," Trueblood said. "But first you're going to jail."

The expression on Tex's face hardened. "I say we aren't. Unless you really are going to shoot us over something like this. And I don't think you're willing to do that."

"I am," Hawke said.

"You are what?" Tex asked.

"I'm willing to shoot you," Hawke said.

There was no anger in Hawke's voice. There was no fear, and no hatred. There was no expression of any kind, other than a cold statement of fact.

"Hah!" Cracker said. "You think 'cause you got lucky with Shorty that you can—"

"Shut up, Cracker," Tex said sharply. He continued to stare at Hawke. "The son of a bitch means it. Marshal, you heard him. He just threatened to kill us, and he ain't no lawman. I demand that you arrest him."

"Mr. Hawke, raise your right hand," Trueblood said.

Hawke did as Trueblood asked.

"You are hereby appointed as a temporary deputy," Trueblood said.

"You can't do that," Tex said.

"I can, and I just did. Now, drop your gun belts," Trueblood ordered.

Tex hesitated.

"Now!" Trueblood repeated, this time reinforcing his order by pulling back the hammer of his pistol. It made a deadly click as it engaged the sear.

First Tex and then the other two cowboys unbuckled their pistol belts and let them fall to the floor.

"Now step back away from them," Trueblood ordered.

"Look here, Marshal, this is gettin' a little out of hand now," Tex said. "Like I told you, me 'n' the boys was just havin' us a little fun. We didn't hurt nobody. So we're just going to go on about our business. Come on, boys." Tex and the other two started toward the front door.

"Stop!" Trueblood called. "Stop!"

"You want us, we'll be out at the cow camp," Tex said.

There was the sound of a gunshot, then a mist of blood sprayed from Tex's left ear. Shouting in pain, he slapped his hand to his ear and spun around. He saw Hawke holding a smoking pistol in his hand.

"You son of a bitch!" Tex shouted in shock and anger. "You shot off my ear!"

"I just nicked it," Hawke said. "If I had wanted to shoot off your ear, I would have done so. Now, you do what the marshal tells you to do or I *will* shoot it off."

"Come on, Tex," Brandt said. "This son of a bitch is crazy. I believe he really would shoot your ear off."

The three cowboys started toward the marshal's office, then Tex turned and pointed at Hawke with a hand that was red with blood from his wounded ear.

"We'll be meeting again," he said with an angry snarl.

"I'm sure we will," Hawke said, then bent down to help Clemmons pick up his scattered type. Several of the other townspeople joined in, and by the time Trueblood had the three cowboys in jail, nearly all the type had been recovered.

"Would you really have shot off his ear?" Clemmons asked as he squatted beside Hawke to retrieve his type.

"For starters," Hawke said easily.

"Damn," Clemmons said. "Remind me never to make you mad."

The next day, after Tex, Cracker, and Brandt were taken to jail, another three hundred cows were brought into town. Although Clint Jessup had nothing to do with actually driving the cows in, he arrived with them, as did Deekus and Arnie. Deekus was driving a wagon, and they stopped in front of Robison's Hardware Store.

"You two wait here," Jessup said as he swung down from his horse. "I'll get with the undertaker, then we'll take Shorty's body down to the depot and have him shipped back to Council Bluffs."

"All right, Major," Deekus said, setting the brake on the wagon. He pulled out a plug of chewing tobacco, cut off a piece, and offered it to Arnie, who turned it down. Deekus shoved the cut into his own mouth while he waited.

Robert Griffin was polishing the hearse in the barn behind his shop when he saw Jessup go into his office. He hurried back, and stepping inside, saw that Jessup had wandered into the embalming room, where he was standing by the table.

"Is there something I can do for you, Major Jessup?" Robert Griffin asked.

Jessup pointed to the table. It was covered with galvanized tin, and slanted at a slight angle toward a catch basin. There was a pole to one side of the table, with a tube hanging down from it.

"Is this where you embalm the bodies?" Jessup asked.

"Yes."

"So before you start, do you take all the blood from the body?"

"As much as possible," Robert Griffin answered. "One can never get it all. Major Jessup, could we go up to the front office?"

"Why? You don't have any bodies back here now," Jessup said.

"No, I don't."

Jessup looked at one of the tubes, and at a small valve. "The stuff that you put in them, the embalming flood, it comes down through this tube?"

"Yes," Robert Griffin said impatiently. "Major Jessup,

please, I don't like people back here. Is there something I can do for you?"

"Yes, I'm here to pick up Shorty," Jessup answered. He nodded toward the front of the building. "I figure the town has had a chance to see what they did in killing a fine young man. I want you to close his coffin and let my men load him on the wagon. We're shipping him home today."

"Yes, sir," Robert Griffin replied. He didn't add, but he thought, *Thank God.* Although having the cowboy's body on display in the front window of the hardware store had been good advertising for how well he could make a body look, he was ready for it to be taken away.

Concluding his business, Jessup stepped back outside. Deekus and Arnie were waiting in the wagon parked just in front of the hardware store. They were watching a young woman who was walking along the board sidewalk. As they watched, they carried on an unsubtle conversation about her.

"What do you reckon a pretty young woman like that is doing downtown all by herself?" Deekus asked.

"I don't know. If I had a filly like that, I'd keep her chained to the bed," Arnie replied.

"Hell, I'd keep her chained to me and the bed," Deekus said, and both men laughed, loudly.

The young woman, obviously able to hear what they were saying, blushed, and lifted her skirt high enough to allow her to walk more quickly.

"Deekus, Arnie," Jessup said.

Neither man had heard Jessup return, but they turned toward him at the sound of his voice.

"Yes, Major?" Deekus said.

"Get Shorty in the wagon and take him down to the depot." He gave Deekus a piece of paper. "This is the bill of lading. Give it to the freight master. Shorty's passage has already been paid for."

"Yes, sir."

"When you're all finished there, come down to the Hog Lot Saloon. I'll buy the drinks."

"Yes, sir!" both Deekus and Arnie answered enthusiastically.

Bob Gary, still wearing the sling from his encounter with Shorty, moved down to the end of the bar where Jessup was standing.

"Yes, sir, can I help you?"

"You the fella that Shorty shot the other day?" Jessup asked.

"I am."

"I'm Clint Jessup, owner of the Bar-J. Shorty McDougal rode for me."

"Yes, sir, Major Jessup, I know who you are," Bob said. "I remember you from last year."

"I apologize for you being shot."

"No need for you to apologize," Bob said. "You didn't shoot me, and the man who did do it is dead."

"Yes," Jessup said. "Killed by your piano player, I'm told."

"Don't let Hawke hear you say that," Bob said. "He's some kind of particular about what folks call him. He likes to be called a pianist."

"A pianist? Isn't that what you call someone with concert training?"

"I reckon it is."

"That's sort of taking on airs, isn't it? I mean somebody who plays piano in a saloon calling himself a pianist. Is he that good?"

"He's good," Bob said. "I don't have any way of tellin' just how good he is. I mean, I haven't heard that many pianists. But he's sure the best one that I have ever heard."

"Well, I'd like to hear him sometime."

"Stick around, he'll be in shortly. It's nearly time for him to start playing. Now, what can I get you?" he added, indicating that he had talked to Jessup as much as he cared to.

"Give me a bottle," Jessup said. "And three glasses."

"Three?"

"A couple of my men will be joining me soon."

Bob nodded, got a full, unopened bottle and three glasses and put them on the bar. Jessup paid for them, then took them to a table where he sat quietly and watched as business gradually picked up in the saloon.

When Hawke came downstairs, Jessup didn't have to be told who he was. He could tell by the way he was dressed.

"You look like someone who would call themselves a pianist," Jessup said under his breath.

As Hawke walked by, Jessup called out to him.

"Would you be Mr. Hawke?"

Hawke stopped. "I am. Do I know you?"

"The name is Jessup. Clint Jessup. But most people call me Major Jessup."

"Why would they do that?" Hawke asked.

Jessup was somewhat taken aback. He was used to exuding authority, both from his military background and, more recently, as the owner of a very large ranch. And by the content and tone of Hawke's question, Jessup could see that he did not fit the pattern of those who were quickly impressed with him.

"I guess it has to do with the rank I held during the war," Jessup replied. "What about you, Mr. Hawke? Were you in the war?"

"I was."

"Which side?"

"There was no side," Hawke said. "The entire war was insane."

"I might agree with you on that point," Jessup said. "Well, no matter which side you were on, that's all behind us now. Here we are, I'm a successful rancher and you are a . . ." Jessup paused before he said the word. ". . . pianist."

"Something I can do for you, Major Jessup?"

Jessup drummed his fingers on the tabletop for a moment before he replied.

"I'm told that when you killed Shorty, you didn't even draw your gun until after he shot at you. Why is that? Are you that arrogant? Or are you that good?"

"I didn't have my gun drawn because I didn't have any intention of shooting him," Hawke replied. "But when he shot at me, I had no choice."

"Yes, well, not all of my cowboys believe that someone like you could do that to Shorty. Shorty had a reputation of being very good with a gun."

"I suspect his reputation was a bit overblown," Hawke said. "He wasn't all that good."

"I would think you would want Shorty to have the reputation of being good with a gun," Jessup said.

"Why? What difference does it make?" Hawke asked.

"Well, if he was good with a gun, and you killed him, it would make you all the more heroic."

"Killing someone doesn't make anyone heroic," Hawke replied.

"No, I . . . I suppose not," Jessup said. "It's just that the cowboys are young and impressionable, and they are having a hard time believing you are that good."

"And what about you? Do you believe it?" Hawke asked.

"I don't know. I don't know how good you really are," Jessup said. "I think I would like to see you sometime, to judge for myself."

Hawke stared at him but made no reply.

"Play the piano, I mean. I'm told you are a very good pianist. I really would like to see that."

"I am sure you will have the opportunity to find out for yourself sometime."

"Yes, I'm sure," Jessup said.

Deekus and Arnie came into the saloon just as Hawke was walking away.

"Hey, that there's the piano player, ain't it?" Arnie asked as the two of them sat down at the table.

"No. He's the pianist," Jessup answered.

"You mean that ain't the one who kilt Shorty?"

"Yes, that's the one," Jessup said without explaining his pianist remark. "What took you two so long? Did you have some trouble at the depot?"

"No, they're goin' to put Shorty on tonight's train," Deekus said. "Major, you remember we was wonderin' why Tex, Cracker, and Brandt didn't come back last night? Well, we don't need to wonder about it'nymore. They got 'em all in jail, right here in Braggadocio."

"Why are they in jail?"

"Beats me," Deekus said. "I think they broke a window or something."

"Are you telling me they put them in jail for breaking a window?"

"That's what it sounds like," Deekus said. "Ain't that the way you heard it?" he asked Arnie.

"Yep. They broke out the window over at the newspaper office, and the sheriff—"

"He's not a sheriff, he's a town marshal," Jessup said.

"Yeah, well, the marshal, he put all three of 'em in jail."

Jessup stood up, and when his two riders started to stand as well, he held up his hand. "No, I'm going to see about Tex and the others. You two stay here and finish the bottle."

"All right," Deekus said enthusiastically.

"And don't get into any trouble. I've got one dead and three in jail now. I can't afford to lose any more men."

Leaving the saloon, Jessup walked down the street to the jail. He stopped just outside the marshal's office and looked in the window. Instead of the marshal, he saw a deputy leaning back in a chair, his feet propped up on the desk.

When Jessup went inside the little building, the deputy took his feet down and sat up quickly.

"Major Jessup," the deputy said, flustered that he had been caught napping.

"You know who I am?" Jessup asked.

"Yes, sir, just about ever'one in town knows who you are."

"Except the piano player. He didn't know who I was."

"You're talking about Mr. Hawke? Well, he's new to town. Mr. Hawke has only been here a couple of months, so he's never been around durin' cattle-shipping time."

Tex and Brandt were sleeping off their drunk on cots in the cell. Only Cracker was awake, and seeing Jessup, he called out happily.

"Major! I knew you wouldn't let us rot in here. Tex, Brandt, wake up! It's the major come to get us."

"I'll settle with you men later," Jessup said, his voice showing his displeasure with them. He turned to the deputy. "What's your name?"

"I'm Truman Foster. I'm a deputy here."

"Well, Foster, where's Trueblood?"

"Trueblood ain't here," Foster answered.

"I can see that. Where is he?"

"He took the train down to Plumb Creek this morning," the deputy said. "He'll be back in tomorrow mornin'. Is there somethin' I can do for you, Major?"

"Yes," Jessup answered. "You can tell me what the fine is for my men, so I can pay it and get them out of here."

"See that, fellas!" Cracker said. "I told you the major wouldn't let us down."

Again Jessup frowned at the three cowboys, but this time he said nothing.

Deputy Foster shook his head. "No, I'm sorry but I can't do that," he said.

"You can't do what?"

"I can't let you pay their fine and get them out."

"I know there are damages. A broken window, I think? I'll pay that as well."

Again Foster shook his head. "I can't."

"What do you mean, you can't? It's not like they killed someone. All they did was get drunk and break out a window. Why the hell can't I just pay their fine and damages?"

"Well, for one thing, I don't know what the fine is, or how

much the window is going to cost," Foster said. "Marshal Trueblood said they was too drunk to go before the judge yesterday. They're going tomorrow."

"You mean it's going to be three days before they even get charged?"

"Yes, sir, it looks like it," Foster said.

"Then how about releasing them to me until tomorrow?" Jessup said. "I'll have them back in time for their trial, then I'll pay whatever cost and fines there are."

"I can't do that," Foster said. "Maybe Marshal Trueblood could do that if he was here. But I can't. I don't have the authority to do that."

"Are you going to take that from him, Major?" Cracker called out from his cell. "Make him let us out."

"Shut up, Cracker," Jessup replied. "You three have caused enough trouble already."

"I'm sorry, Major, but there's nothing I can do," Foster said.

"Yes," Jessup said. "Well, I thank you for your time."

Chapter 7

BY EIGHT O'CLOCK THAT EVENING THE HOG LOT was reasonably full. There were several cowboys in the saloon, and for the most part they were fairly well behaved. Some were a bit more effusive than others, but there were no fights or even loud arguments.

Hawke kept lively music going throughout the night, and from time to time one of the patrons would come over to put money in a glass bowl that sat on the piano.

The four bar girls moved about the room attending to their business, but it was obvious they were all thinking about Cindy. The cowboys were so absorbed with having fun that none of them noticed anything in the girls' demeanor. But Hawke could tell that the girls' smiles were a bit more forced and their expressions more detached.

Millie came over to stand beside Hawke. She leaned against the piano for a moment, and, extending her lower lip, directed a stream of air to blow an errant tendril of hair away from her forehead. She was sweating from the heat of the night and from the exertion of always having to be on her feet and constantly on the move, going from table to table.

"If you don't mind, I'm just going to take a break for a moment," she said.

"I don't mind at all," Hawke replied, looking up. "I'm glad for the company."

Millie picked up a fan lying on top of the piano and waved it in front of her face a few times.

"You ladies are working particularly hard tonight," Hawke said as he continued to play.

"So are you," Millie said. She turned the fan and started fanning Hawke. The breeze she generated felt good to him.

"Thanks," he said. "I feel honored," he added. "I'll bet you aren't fanning any of the cowboys."

"No," Millie replied. "But I know I've told every cowboy in here, at least a dozen times, how thrilling it must be to bring up a herd of cows." Millie mimicked herself. "Oh, my, just feel those muscles. You are so strong. Can I bring you another drink from the bar?" She laughed.

"It appears to be working," Hawke said. "Mr. Harder is doing quite a brisk business tonight."

From somewhere in the saloon a cowboy's loud, raucous laugh was followed by the high-pitched squeal, and then the laughter of one of the other bar girls.

"Listen to Trudy," Millie said. "She is so good at this. I'll bet she's sold more drinks than anyone except Cindy, who—" Millie stopped in mid-sentence. She was quiet for a moment, and as the tears began to flow, Hawke finished the song and handed her his handkerchief.

"Thanks," she said, dabbing at her eyes.

"I'm always willing to come to the rescue of a damsel in distress," Hawke said.

Millie returned his handkerchief. "Oh, all the girls wanted to thank you for playing at Cindy's funeral yesterday," she said. "It was beautiful."

"I was honored to be asked," Hawke said.

"She liked you, you know."

"She was a sweet girl."

"No, I mean, she really liked you."

Hawke looked up at her as he began to play his next song, but he didn't say anything.

Millie gave a little self-conscious laugh. "I know, girls like us have no right to like anyone, uh, in that way," she said. "But we all have our dreams, and sometimes those dreams, impossible as they may seem, are all that keep us going."

"Everyone has a right to their dreams," Hawke replied.

"Even if there is no chance that those dreams will ever come true?"

"Who is to say what would or would not have happened?" Hawke replied. "As I said, Cindy was a very sweet girl."

"Then you did like her, didn't you?" Millie asked, and the expression in her voice showed that she very much wanted it to be true.

"Yes," Hawke said, nodding. "I liked her very much."

"I knew it," Millie said enthusiastically. "I just knew it. Oh, the tragedy of it all."

"We will all miss her," Hawke said.

"Hawke, would you play her song? I mean, just for her? Her favorite song was—"

" 'Lorena,' " Hawke said, giving the title before Millie could.

"Yes, 'Lorena.' Would you play it?"

"It would be my pleasure," Hawke answered.

"As soon as you are finished with this one, I'm going to make everyone be quiet for her song," Millie said.

"I'm finished now," Hawke said, playing the closing bars.

Millie turned toward the crowded saloon room. "Ladies and gentlemen," she called, but nobody paid any attention to her.

"Let me help," Hawke said. He played a very loud riff. As a result, all conversation halted and everyone turned toward the piano to see what was going on. "All right," Hawke said. "You've got their attention."

"Ladies and gentlemen—" Millie started again.

"Ha! What do you mean, ladies? There ain't no ladies in here!" one of the cowboys shouted. "Ain't nothin' in here but whores."

"There ain't no call for you to be talkin' like that, Deekus," one of the other cowboys said. "Let the lady speak."

"All right, all right, speak," Deekus said. He stood up and bowed toward Millie, and a few laughed.

Millie continued. "As you all know, one of the girls who worked here was killed recently. We had her funeral yesterday. But now, to honor her, I've asked Mr. Hawke to play her favorite song. And I'd like to ask all of you to please be quiet while it's playing."

"Wait a minute," Deekus called out. "Before you play that whore's song, I want you to play 'Buffalo Gals.'"

"Hold on, mister," Bob Gary called from behind the bar. "Miss Millie was first. Besides, what's so great about 'Buffalo Gals'?"

"What's so great about it?" Deekus replied. "I'll tell you what's so great about it. That was the favorite song of our pard." Deekus walked over to the piano. "I'm talking about Shorty McDougal. You all know who he was. He was the fella this here piano player kilt." Deekus pointed at Hawke.

"As you say, I am the one who killed him," Hawke replied calmly. "It was unfortunate, and I wish it hadn't happened, but it did. And, that being the case, I do not think it would be appropriate for me to play a song in his honor. So, Mister . . ." Hawke paused for Deekus to provide him with a name.

"Deekus," Deekus said. "No Mister, just Deekus."

"All right, Deekus, if you will just take your seat now, I'll play 'Lorena.'"

Deekus pointed to Millie. "Mister, did that whore pay you to play this here song you're a'fixin' to play?"

"No."

Deekus stuck his hand in his pocket, pulled out a dollar, and dropped it into the bowl.

"Well, this here's a whole dollar. And I'll thank you to play 'Buffalo Gals' before you play that whore's song."

Hawke stood up, took the dollar from the bowl, and gave it back to Deekus.

"Keep your dollar. I'm not playing the song," he said.

"Mister, you need to learn your place. I told you to—" Deekus said angrily, going for his gun as he spoke.

What happened next happened so fast that few in the saloon could even follow it. As the gun was clearing the holster, Hawke grabbed Deekus's hand and jerked it up. Deekus hit himself in the chin, while at the same time losing his pistol. As he stepped back with his eyes open in shock and anger, he realized that Hawke was now holding the pistol, and pointing it at him.

"I would appreciate it if you would keep quiet while I play the song the lady requested," Hawke said. He removed the cylinder from Deekus's gun, then walked over to the bar and dropped it into a half-full spittoon.

"Why, you son of a bitch!" Deekus shouted. Picking up a chair, he raised it over his head and started toward Hawke, but stopped when he saw Hawke's own gun suddenly appear in his hand.

"There are ladies in this room," Hawke said. "I suggest you apologize for your language."

"What?"

"I said apologize for your language."

"The hell you say," Deekus replied. "They're all whores. You think they ain't never heard language like that before?"

"I said, apologize to the ladies," Hawke said again.

Deekus stared at the pistol. "I . . . I apologize," he said.

"To the ladies," Hawke said, coaching him.

"To the ladies," Deekus repeated.

"For my language."

"For my language."

"Good. Now, I want you to stand over there where I can keep an eye on you while I'm playing," Hawke said.

Deekus started to lower the chair, but Hawke raised his pistol.

"No," he said. "Keep the chair up over your head."

"The hell you say. I'm not going to keep this chair up here."

Hawke pulled the hammer back on the pistol, and in the room, which had become very quiet for the unfolding drama, the double click sounded loud and ominous.

"I want you to stand over there where I can keep an eye on you," Hawke repeated, slowly and deliberately. "And I want you to hold the chair over your head until I say otherwise."

"You're crazy if you think I'm going to do that," Deekus said blusteringly.

"And you are dead if you don't," Hawke replied, his voice deadly calm.

"Hah! Don't listen to any damn piano player, Deekus," Arnie said. "There's no way he would shoot you just for lowering that chair. That would be cold-blooded murder."

"What do you say, Deekus?" Hawke asked. "Are you going to take a chance that your friend is right? Or are you going to listen to me when I tell you that I will kill you if you lower that chair so much as one inch."

By now a patina of sweat had broken out all over Deekus. His eyes were open wide in fright, his pupils dilated, and he licked his lips nervously.

"You ain't afraid of a piano player, are you, Deekus?" Arnie asked. "There's no way he is going to—"

"Shut the hell up, Arnie! I'm lookin' into his eyes and you ain't!" Deekus said. "And I know that the son of a bitch means it when he says he'll kill me."

"Well, Deekus," Hawke said. "You are a little smarter than you look."

Hawke sat down at the piano then and looked over at Millie. She had been joined by the other three girls, and they were looking at him with as much shock and surprise as everyone else in the saloon. No one had ever seen him like this before. Yes, he had killed Shorty, but everyone was sure that was a fluke. After all, he was only a piano player.

Hawke began playing, and never had that scarred and stained piano produced such beautiful music. As the melancholy music of "Lorena" poured out from the piano, the four bar girls wept openly, and there were even some wet eyes here and there among the men who were regular customers and knew Cindy.

When Hawke finished the song, he looked over at Deekus, who by now was showing the strain of having held the chair over his head for so long.

"You can put the chair down," Hawke said, and with a loud and groaning sigh, Deekus put the chair on the floor, then almost collapsed into it.

"My arms feel like they're about to fall off," Deekus complained.

"Yes, well, think about that the next time you plan to hit somebody with a chair," Hawke said.

Deekus returned to his table, while Hawke continued to play music.

"Ha," Arnie said. "You sure looked dumb, standin' up there, holdin' that chair over your head like that."

"Shut up," Deekus replied. "You!" he shouted to Trudy. "Bring me a drink."

Trudy looked at him a moment, then went over to the bar and got a whiskey, which she brought back to Deekus. Without so much as one word, she put the drink on the table in front of him.

"What? That's it?" Deekus asked. "You ain't goin' to tell me how good lookin' I am or anything?"

"You asked for a drink, here it is," Trudy said coldly.

Deekus laughed. "And here, the way you was talkin' to me earlier tonight, I thought you was wantin' to go get married," he teased.

The others at the table laughed with him as Trudy turned and walked away.

Back at the cattle encampment, Jessup sat on a log near the chuck wagon, drinking a cup of coffee. He had been thinking about the discussion he'd had with the cattle broker.

At first he was concerned that perhaps Braggadocio would close their cattle loading facilities. But the more he thought about it, the more he realized that they probably would not get it closed until all his cattle had been shipped. The only ones who would be hurt by the closing would be the Rocking T and the Slash Diamond outfits, who had not yet begun to ship their cows, and would not be able to ship any until after he was through.

If that happened, he would wind up getting top dollar for his cows, making this a very profitable year. And all he'd have to do to bring that about would be to convince the town that they should close the loading pens.

He'd have to do that in a way that would not expose his real motive. But he believed he had an idea that just might accomplish that very thing.

It was nearly ten o'clock, and some of the cowboys who had been in town were back.

"Carter," Jessup called. "Did you just get back from town?"

"Yes, sir," Carter replied.

"Any trouble in town tonight?"

"No, sir, not really," Carter said. "Except . . . well, that wasn't really no trouble. Not for anyone but Deekus at any rate."

"What are you talking about?"

"Deekus got to raggin' the piano player in the Hog Lot. You know, the one that kilt Shorty?"

"Yes, I know. Go on, what happened?"

"Well, Deekus got to raggin' him, and the next thing you know, well, Deekus was going for his gun."

"Did he shoot the piano player?"

"Lord, no. It wasn't even close," Carter said. "It's the damnedest thing I ever seen, Major, but one second Deekus is goin' for his gun, and the next second, well, I don't know how the hell he done it, but Deekus's gun was in the piano player's hand."

"So the piano player shot Deekus?"

"No, sir." Carter went on to describe the events that left Deekus holding the chair over his head. "This here ain't no ordinary piano player, I can tell you that."

"I agree," Jessup said. "Maybe you boys will learn better than to keep messing with him. Now, I want you to do something for me."

"Yes, sir, whatever you say."

"I want you to ride back into town. Go into the Hog Lot, Foley's, Pearlie's whorehouse, wherever you have to go, but I want you to get our men out of there."

"Hah," Carter said. "That's not goin' to make 'em like me all that much."

"Get Deekus and Arnie first. They rode with me during the war," Jessup said. "I want you to tell them that we're going to have us a little foray into town tonight. They'll know what you are talking about, and they'll help you bring the others back."

"A foray? What is that?"

"You'll find out tonight," Jessup said. "I don't intend to let any jerkwater town keep my men in jail for nothing more than a broken window."

"We're goin' to break 'em out, ain't we?" Carter asked, a big smile spreading across his face.

"Just do what I said," Jessup replied. He drained his coffee. "In the meantime, I'm going to take myself a little nap. Wake me when you return."

Chapter 8

THE DREAM CAME AGAIN.

Because of the ebb and flow of the battle, the dead and wounded were scattered over a wide area. The fighting had left many casualties on both sides, and during the night their moans and cries could be heard above the thunderous drumming of the rain and the incessant boom of artillery. The sound was heartrending even to the most hardened ears.

Most of the wounded were calling for water, so Jesse Cole collected a couple canteens and started out onto the battlefield. Fortunately, the rain stopped shortly after he went out, but the night was still dark and overcast, without moon or stars to light the way.

Jesse wasn't the only one who went out, and because the night was so dark, many of the men who prowled the battleground were carrying lanterns to help them distinguish the wounded from the dead. As a result, the battlefield looked like a great meadow filled with giant fireflies, as the lanterns, carried knee high, bobbed about from point to point.

A breeze came up, carrying on its breath a damp chill. Jesse pulled his coat about him and continued on his mission of mercy, picking his way across the roads and fields, now littered with the residue of battle: weapons, equipment, and, among the discards, the dead and dying.

"Water," a weak voice called, and Jesse halted. "I beg of you, sir, be you Union or Reb, if you are a God-fearing man, you'll give me water."

"Yes," Jesse said. "I have water." Moving quickly to the soldier, he saw that it was a Yankee officer, an infantry lieutenant. He uncorked the canteen and knelt down by the officer, then lifted his head.

"Here you go, Yank," he said.

"Bless you," the wounded soldier replied.

Jesse heard the metallic click of a pistol being cocked.

"You give that Yankee one swallow of water and I'll kill you for the traitor you are," a cold voice said.

He looked toward the man who had issued the challenge. It was a Confederate officer, though not anyone he recognized. That was understandable; there had been thousands of men from both sides committed to this fight, and there was no way he could know everyone.

"I'm not going to deny this man a drink of water just because he is a Yankee," Jesse said.

"I'll shoot you if you so much as give him one drop of water," the Confederate officer replied. "As far as I'm concerned, he and all the rest of the Yankee trash out here can die of thirst."

"If you are going to shoot, go ahead and shoot," Jesse said resolutely. "But this man's going to die with water on his lips." Once again he offered the canteen up to the Yankee officer, and the wounded man began drinking thirstily.

"You son of a bitch! I warned you!" the Confederate officer shouted. That was as far as he got. An instant before he could pull the trigger, there was a loud thump as someone came up behind him and hit him over the head.

"Did you kill him?" Jesse asked. There was a nonchalance to his voice that belied the situation.

"No, sir," his sergeant said, kneeling down beside the man he had just hit. "He's still alive. He's going to have one hell of a headache when he wakes up, though."

"Thank you," the wounded Yankee said as he took his fill of water. "You are a true gentleman."

"Major, we'd better get back," the sergeant said.

"In a minute," Jesse answered. "Where are you hit?" he asked the Yankee.

"In the leg."

Jesse held the lantern down toward the wound as he and the sergeant examined it. "What do you think, Sergeant Kincaid?" Jesse asked.

"I think if he can get back to his surgeon and have the bullet taken out before it festers, he'll be all right," Kincaid said.

"You think you can walk?" Jesse asked.

"I don't know. I'll try."

"I'll help."

"Major, leave him be," Sergeant Kincaid begged. "They's Yankees all over out here."

"You go on back, Kincaid. I'll handle it from here," Jesse said.

Kincaid shook his head. "No, sir. If you're a'goin' to take him to his lines, I'm a'goin' with you."

With Jesse on one side and Sergeant Kincaid on the other, the two Rebel soldiers got the wounded Yankee officer on his feet, then began walking him toward the Union lines.

"My name is Reader," the young officer said. "Lieutenant Lou Reader. Who might you gentlemen be?"

"Just a couple of good Samaritans," Jesse said.

"Are you men with General Sterling Price?"

"In a manner of speaking. Our group just joined with him for this battle. We are irregulars."

Reader gasped. "Irregulars?" After a moment's silence he continued. "Maybe you should leave me here," he suggested. "I can make it the rest of the way on my own."

"We'll take you a little closer," Jesse said. "What's the matter? Does it bother you because we are irregulars?"

"Yes," Reader admitted. "But I'm worried for you, not for me. You may not know this, but the orders are out. If any irregulars are captured—"

"We are not to be treated as prisoners of war, but as criminals," Jesse said. "Yes, I've seen the orders."

"But, don't you understand? If you are captured tonight, you'll be dead by sunup. They'll hang you."

"They haven't caught us yet," Sergeant Kincaid said.

"Shhh," Jesse whispered. "We're nearly to the Yankee lines. No sense in announcing our presence."

Jesse's warning was too late. From the darkness in front of them, two Yankee soldiers suddenly appeared. Both were carrying rifles, and holding them at the ready position.

"Halt!" one of them called. "Who is there?"

"Yankee pickets," Sergeant Kincaid said under his breath.

"Soldiers, I am Lieutenant Lou Reader, of the Seventh Illinois," Reader said.

The soldiers looked at Reader. His uniform clearly announced who he was, but neither Jesse nor Sergeant Kincaid were wearing uniforms.

"Who are these men? They don't look like Union soldiers to me," one of the pickets challenged.

"They are Missouri irregulars," Reader said.

"Missourians! By God, they are bushwhackers!" one of the soldiers exclaimed.

Jesse and Kincaid looked as if they had been betrayed, and they tensed to make a break. But Reader's next words stopped them.

"No!" Reader said. "Remember, Missouri is a border state! They have as many men fighting for the North as they do for the South."

"You mean, these fellas are on our side?"

"Thank you very much for your help," Reader said to Jesse and Kincaid, ignoring the soldier's question. "But I expect you two had better get on back to your own unit now."

"And what unit would that be?" one of the pickets asked, still curious.

"This is no place to stand around gabbing, soldier," Reader said. "Why don't you two men help me back to the aid station?" Reader put his arms around their shoulders. "I have a minié ball in my leg and it's going to have to come out."

With their attention diverted, Jesse and Kincaid were able to go back across no man's land.

"I'm sure glad that Yankee lied for us," Sergeant Kincaid said. He put his finger in his collar, then pulled it away from his neck. "I wouldn't have taken too highly to hanging in the morning."

"He didn't lie for us," Jesse replied.

"What do you mean, he didn't lie for us? He said we was Missouri irregulars, fighting for the North."

Jesse chuckled. "No, what he said was, we were Missouri irregulars—which we are—and that there are as many Missourians fighting for the North as there are fighting for the South. He never did say which side we were on."

"I'll be damned," Kincaid said. "I didn't think about it, but you're right. Why would he do that?"

"Because I think he truly is a man of honor," Jesse said. "I don't think he could tell a lie even if it was militarily expedient to do so."

"Major? Major Jessup? You wanted me to wake you up when I got back."

Jessup opened his eyes and saw Carter squatting beside his bedroll.

"Did you get the men?" Jessup asked.

"Yes, sir, they's all here," Carter said. "Ever man jack

that's a'ridin' for the Bar-J. 'Cept Tex, Brandt, and Cracker. And they're in jail."

"Gather the men around the chuck wagon," Jessup ordered. "I want to talk to them."

"Yes, sir."

As Carter walked away and went to gather the men, Jessup pulled on his boots, strapped on his gun, and put on his hat. By the time he walked over to the chuck wagon, all of his riders were gathered there, illuminated not only by the lantern that Poke had sitting on the tailgate, but also by the full moon, which was exceptionally bright.

"Poke, is there enough coffee for everyone?" Jessup asked.

"Yes, sir, I made up a bunch, just like you asked."

"Good. We're going to need it tonight. Men," he called out to the others. "Get yourself a cup of coffee and then come on back here. I've got something to say."

Poke brought a cup to Jessup, and he held the warm mug in his hands, smelling the aroma for a moment before he took a swallow, slurping it in through extended lips in order to cool it.

It took a moment for everyone to get their coffee and return, and then they stood in a semicircle, looking toward Jessup to see what he wanted with them at this hour of the night.

"Men," Jessup began. "We started this drive together. We've been through lightning-spooked cows, heat that would fry an egg on your skin, bone-aching tiredness, bad water, drenching rain and dust storms where you couldn't see two feet in front of your nose. We even had to deal with some rustlers, and we left two of 'em hanging from an old oak tree.

"But, through it all, we stuck together."

There were a few grunts of agreement as the men listened and nodded.

"Then we reached this place," Jessup said. "A place where we thought we could relax, have a few drinks, and enjoy ourselves while our cattle are being shipped back East."

Jessup paused for effect.

"But that's not the way things have turned out here. Instead of a place that's cordial to cowboys, we find a place where the drinks are overpriced and watered, where even the very goods we buy in the stores cost us more than it does the people who live here."

Jessup held up a newspaper. "And, if you have read this newspaper article, the city council of Braggadocio is making plans to disarm every cowboy who comes into town. They want to take away our guns, but let the townspeople continue to wear theirs."

"What?" one of the cowboys said. "That ain't right. That ain't right at all."

There were others who reacted as well, and Jessup waited a moment for his men to grow quiet again.

"One of the men who started this drive with us has already been killed. Shot by a piano player."

"Major, you ain't never seen a piano player like this fella," Deekus said. "He ain't your ordinary piano player."

"Yes, Deekus, I heard of your encounter with him. That makes it even more unfair that they want to leave a man like him armed, while making us surrender our guns when we go to town. This piano player, Mason Hawke, has already proven himself to be not only a killer, but a man with a quick temper.

"So, where do we stand? We have had one of our number killed, three of our friends are now rotting in jail for nothing any more serious than breaking a window, and Deekus was humiliated in front of his friends by an armed bully."

Jessup held up his finger and wagged it back and forth.

"Now, let me ask you boys something," he said, speaking so quietly that they had to strain to hear him. Then he bellowed out the next words. *"Are we just going to sit back and take this?"*

"No!" the cowboys shouted, the word erupting as one from thirty lips.

A big smile spread across Jessup's face. "Good," he said. "Now, I want all of you to get mounted. We are going to take a ride into town."

"All right!"

"Yahoo!"

"Here we come!"

The cowboys whooped and shouted in excitement as they hurried to the remuda to saddle their horses.

Jessup looked over at Poke, who, with his arms folded across his chest, was leaning against the chuck wagon. Poke had watched the whole thing, and smiling now, he applauded quietly.

"I tell you true, Major, you still got it in you," he said. "I ain't heard a rip snorter like that since the war, and the speech you give us before we raided Norwood."

It was three o'clock in the morning, and Jessup had thirty men with him, spread out on the military crest of a hill, meaning they were just below the actual crest, so as not to form silhouettes against the night sky. The leaves of a nearby tree caught the full moon and, waving in a gentle breeze, sent slivers of silver scattering into the night. Below them the town of Braggadocio lay shimmering as the roof of every building gleamed in the glow of the full moon.

It was no coincidence that the riders resembled a military unit about to launch an operation, because that was exactly the way Jessup planned it. And although he had led many such operations during the war, this was the first time he had done anything on such a scale since then.

Jessup rode a few feet in front of his men, then turned to speak to them.

"Do you men understand what I want you to do?" he asked. "I want you to ride through the town making as much noise and disturbance as you can. I don't want you shooting at anyone in particular, but it is important that you make enough noise to cause everyone to pay attention to you."

He turned to Deekus.

"Deekus, while the rest of the men are creating the diversion, you and Arnie will be with me. We're going to the jail to break out Tex, Cracker, and Brandt."

"Major, you said don't shoot at anyone, but what if someone comes out and starts shooting at us?" Carter asked.

"In that case, shoot back," Jessup answered. "All right, men, follow me, but don't open fire until you hear my signal shot."

The riders started forward, beginning with a brisk walk, then breaking into a trot, and finally a full gallop. The horses' hooves were raising a thunder as they swept toward the edge of town.

"Now!" Jessup shouted, shooting his pistol into the air.

By coincidence, Gideon McCall had awakened just a few moments earlier. He lay in bed, feeling a momentary sense of detachment as a troubled dream slipped away and body and soul rejoined in this place and at this time.

He examined the moon shadows on the wall of the bedroom as his thoughts drifted back to the funeral he had conducted for Cindy Carey. He knew there were a few in his congregation who resented the fact that he had conducted a funeral for a whore. But it was not something he could turn his back on, even if it meant he would lose his entire congregation.

Gideon's sermon had been long on the Lord's forgiveness of sins. Forgiveness of sin was the keystone of his personal Christian faith. Sometimes, though, he couldn't help but ask himself just how generous God really was with His forgiveness. Was Cindy truly forgiven? Would God accept someone like her, a whore? Would He accept those who had lied and stolen? Would He forgive someone who had killed?

He knew that within his congregation he had sinners of every stripe. He wondered just how much comfort he could give them and still serve the Lord.

Tamara lay sleeping in the bed beside him, and he could hear her deep, even breathing. Lifting himself up on one elbow, he looked down at her, marveling at how lucky he had been to find such a woman.

Like many in his congregation, Gideon was a sinner. He was a repentant sinner, but a sinner nevertheless. There had been a time when he fell away from the faith, and during that time he had wandered about, lost and without direction.

Then he met Tamara. It was as if she were an angel sent by the Lord to show him the way. And, in his mind, there was no greater proof of the forgiveness of the Lord than that he had been blessed in such a way.

Tamara and Lucy were the light of his life, and thinking of them calmed the restlessness that had awakened him. He lay back down and closed his eyes. That was when he heard the first gunshot.

Across town from the parsonage, separated not only by distance, but by social mores, was the Hog Lot Saloon. In his room above the saloon, Hawke, at the sound of the first gunshot, was out of his bed with his gun in hand. Moving to the window, he saw the riders coming into town, firing their weapons. The muzzle flares lit up the night like flashes of summer lightning.

By now there were so many guns being fired that the shooting made one sustained roar, and in addition to the sound of the gunfire, Hawke could also hear the buzzing of bullets as they whistled down the street. One crashed through his window, and he saw other windows being shot out as well.

Hawke didn't know who the raiders were, why they were doing this, or even how many were out there. But from the number of flashes and the rapidity of the firing, he knew there were quite a few.

He chose one of the flashes and fired just to the right of the flame pattern. He saw the rider clasp his hand over his chest, then tumble from his saddle. A second later a riderless horse dashed by just under his window.

Bullets continued to whistle through the night. Many of

them made little fireballs as they struck stone, then whined off as dark, deadly missiles. The firing continued very intensely for nearly a full minute.

Jessup, Deekus, and Arnie had broken off from the main body just as the group swept into town. Now, with each of them leading a mount, they rode to the back of the marshal's office. Leaving Arnie to hold the horses, Jessup and Deekus ran alongside the jail. When they reached the front, they saw Deputy Foster, gun in hand, standing on the front porch, shooting toward the riders. Jessup slipped up behind the deputy and brought his gun down sharply on his head. The deputy dropped to the porch.

"Inside," Jessup said to Deekus.

When the two men stepped inside the jail, Jessup called out, "Tex, Brandt, Cracker? Are you in here?"

"We're back here, Major," Tex answered.

"What's all that shootin' about, out there?" Cracker asked.

Jessup didn't answer. Instead, he got the keys off the hook, then opened the cell door. "Get your guns," he ordered. "Let's get out of here."

The three men did as told. As they stepped outside, they saw Foster lying in a crumpled heap on the porch.

"Is he dead?" Tex asked.

"I don't know if he is or not," Jessup answered. "We don't have time to see. Hurry up! The horses are around back. We've got to get out of here."

"Who is it that's doin' all the shootin'?" Cracker asked again.

"It's our outfit," Jessup said. "They've created a diversion so we could break you out of jail. Now hurry up, I can't keep them out there too long."

The five men ran to the back of the jail, then mounted.

"Deekus, take them to the encampment," Jessup said. "I'm going to call our men back."

"Come on, boys, let's go," Deekus said.

Bending low over his horse, Jessup galloped toward his men. When he got close enough to them, he called out.

From his room over the saloon, Hawke heard a commanding voice shouting from the darkness.

"Men, pull back! All riders withdraw!"

The shooting stopped almost instantly, and the riders turned, then galloped back to the far end of the street, leaving town in the same direction from which they had come.

With the gunfire over and the hoofbeats receding, other sounds now filled the early morning: barking dogs, crying babies, and men calling to each other in the darkness.

"Who were those people?"

"Anybody hurt?"

"There's someone down here! Help me, somebody, there's a man down in the street!"

From where the call was coming, Hawke knew that the man down was probably the one that he had shot.

Hawke dressed quickly, then hurried downstairs, his way illuminated by the moonlight that spilled in through the front windows. By the time he reached the street, there were two dozen or more armed citizens of the town milling around, their oversized shadows projected onto the false-fronted buildings by the wavering yellow light of the torches many of them were carrying.

Because several were also regulars at the Hog Lot Saloon, Hawke recognized many of the men. John Harder was one of them. George Schermerhorn was there as well, and so were Jubal Goodpasture and James Cornett.

He was not surprised to see any of them, but was surprised to see that Gideon McCall was among the men who had turned out to see what was going on. The parson and Bob Gary were standing over to one side engaged in quiet conversation, and Hawke couldn't help but think of the juxtaposition of a parson and a bartender as a coda on what was already an unusual morning.

"Good morning, Bob . . . Parson McCall," he said.

"Good morning, Mr. Hawke," Gideon replied.

"Hello, Hawke," Bob said.

"Who were those men who came riding through here this morning?" Cornett asked the assembled group. "Did any of you recognize any of them?"

"It was too dark and it happened too fast," Jubal answered.

"My best guess is that it was a bunch of drunken cowboys out on a tear," Harder suggested.

"Were they Bar-J riders, do you think?" George Schermerhorn asked.

"They could have been," Harder agreed. "But there are a couple more outfits here now, just waiting their turn to start shipping their cows. Could've been one of them, or a combination of them."

Gideon shook his head. "No, Mr. Harder, I think you are wrong there. This wasn't a bunch of cowboys out on a drunk. This was an organized raid."

"An organized raid?" Cornett asked. "What makes you think so?"

"Didn't you notice the military preciseness of their maneuver? They came into town in a column of twos, and they maintained column integrity until they were withdrawn. And they *were* withdrawn, Mr. Mayor, they didn't just suddenly tire of the game and run away."

"The parson's right," Schermerhorn said. "I heard someone callin' out for the others to fall back."

"Yes, well, planned or not, here's one of them that didn't get away," the mayor said. He nodded toward the man lying in the street. Doc Urban was squatting beside him. "How is he, Doc?"

Doc Urban shook his head. "He's dead, that's how he is."

Cornett pointed to the man on the ground. "Well, what about this man?" he asked the others. "Now that we can get a close look at him, have any of you ever seen him before?"

"Jubal, hold your torch down by his face so we can all get a look," Harder said. "Maybe someone will recognize him."

The livery owner complied, holding the torch down so the man's face could be seen. He examined him closely, then shook his head.

"Nope. He's not anyone I've ever seen," Jubal said.

"Me neither," Schermerhorn said.

"Well, he's never been in my store," Cornett said. "So he's not from around here."

"Maybe he's one of the cowboys from the Bar-J," Schermerhorn suggested.

"I don't know," Harder said. "What about you, Bob, you're behind the bar. I expect you've seen every Bar-J rider who's ever come in. Is this man one of them?"

Bob looked at him for a long moment, then shook his head. "If he is, he's never been in the Hog Lot. What about you, Foley? Have you ever seen him in Foley's?"

"No, I don't think so," Foley answered.

"Who the hell is he?" Cornett asked. Then remembering that the parson was with them, he touched the brim of his hat. "Beg pardon, Reverend McCall, for my language."

"Quite all right," Gideon answered.

Robert Griffin came up then. Even in the middle of the night, he had taken time to put on his top hat and jacket. He looked down at the dead man for a moment, then back at the assembled town's people. "Any other decedents?" he asked.

"Not unless somebody in one of the houses is hurt," Foley said.

"Oh, damn, I hadn't even thought about that," Cornett said.

"Where's Truelove? He ought to be going around checking all the houses now," Foley said.

"He's in Plumb Creek," Cornett said. "He won't be back till tomorrow. But now that you mention it, where is Deputy Foster? Where was he when all this happened?"

"You could ask him yourself," Hawke said. "Here he comes."

Deputy Foster came walking up then, rubbing the back of his head as he approached.

"Are you all right?" Doc Urban asked.

"I don't know," Foster answered. "Yeah, I guess I am all right, but I got hit in the back of the head."

"Let me take a look," Doc Urban said. He examined the back of Foster's head, then reached up to touch it.

Foster winced with pain. "Damn, Doc, that hurts."

"That's a nasty bump. It's a wonder you don't have a skull fracture," Doc Urban said. "What happened?"

"I don't have any idea," Foster replied. "One minute I was standin' on the porch, shooting at that bunch of riders, and the next thing I know, I was wakin' up. I never saw what hit me."

"Was it a ball that hit him, do you think?" Cornett asked.

Doc Urban shook his head. "No, this wasn't a ball. The wound is too broad. It looks more like someone hit him on the back of the head with some kind of club or something."

"That could be," Foster said. "Like as not, it was one of the three cowboys I had in jail. After I come to, I went back inside and saw that the door to the cell was open. I reckon one of them coulda hit me, then used all the confusion in order to get away."

"Didn't you have the cell door locked?" Hawke asked.

"Yeah," Foster said, still gingerly rubbing the back of his head. "Yeah, I had it locked."

"Then how did one of them get out to hit you?"

"You've got me on that one, Mr. Hawke. I don't have the slightest idea."

"Perhaps their escape is the answer as to why these men rode through here," Gideon suggested. "It could be that the raid was nothing but a diversion, conducted for the sole purpose of freeing your three prisoners."

"Could be," Foster said. "Though it don't seem all that likely, since the only thing them three was being held for was breakin' out a window. And I know for a fact that Marshal Truelove was goin' to set 'em free tomorrow, soon as they paid their fine and paid Mr. Clemmons for a new window. And if that's the case, why would someone bother to break 'em out of jail tonight?"

"Deputy, before you came up here," Cornett said, "we were just saying that maybe we ought to go around from house to house to house, just to make sure nobody else is hurt."

"Yeah," Foster replied. "Yeah, that's a good idea. Uh, does anybody want to help? It'll be daylight before I get to all the houses if I do it by myself."

"I'll help," the mayor offered. "I've got a lot of experience going house to house when I'm campaigning."

"This ought to work out well for you, James," Schermerhorn said. "You can see if anyone is hurt, and ask for their vote at the same time."

"Yeah, the only difference is, with all the shooting, folks might still be scared," Jubal said. "They may shoot right through the door."

"What?" Cornett said. "Uh, listen, now that I think about it, maybe I should get back to the store. Karen will be worried. You can handle it, can't you, Deputy? After all, it's what we pay you for."

"I'll help you, Deputy," Bob said.

"Thanks, Mr. Gary. You take that side, I'll take this side. Knock on every door and yell out that you're a special deputy. I don't think there will be any trouble. Let me know if you find anyone hurt."

"All right," Bob agreed.

"Robert Griffin, how long will it be before you get this body out of here?" Schermerhorn asked. "He's goin' to be gettin' ripe pretty soon, and I don't want him smellin' up my place of business."

"I'll be right back for him, soon as I hitch a team to my buckboard."

"No need for you to go all the way back for your buckboard," Schermerhorn offered. "If you'll give me a minute, I'll get a horse out here and we can just throw this fella belly down over him."

"Oh, I can't treat a body that way," Robert Griffin replied. "It wouldn't be proper."

"Maybe you can't, but I can," Schermerhorn said. "I don't want the son of a bitch lyin' here any longer than he has to. You go on back, I'll bring him down to you and you won't have anything to do with it."

Robert Griffin nodded. "All right," he said. "If you say so."

By now the crowd that had gathered was breaking up to return to their own homes. As it worked out, only Hawke and Gideon remained on the scene.

"I have to confess, Parson, I didn't expect to see you out here," Hawke said.

"Why not? I was awake," Gideon said. "And with all the shooting, it seemed likely that some of our people might have been hurt, or killed. I thought someone might need me."

"You're a good man," Hawke said. "Most of the town stayed inside." He paused for a minute, then added, "Not that I blame them. By the way, how do you know about such things as maneuvering, column integrity, diversions, and the like?"

Gideon smiled. "I wasn't born wearing a parson's cloth, Mr. Hawke. I could ask you how a man who plays piano in a saloon could perform Joseph Haydn's Mass in G so beautifully."

Chuckling, Hawke nodded. "Touché, Parson," he said. "I guess the truth is that, although we just present a part of ourselves at any given time, we are all the sum of our parts. I imagine that more than a few of us have pasts that are drastically different from what we show."

"How true, Mr. Hawke, how true," Gideon said. "Well, I suppose I'd better be getting back. I'm sure Tamara is worried."

Hawke watched the preacher walk back up the street toward the parsonage, which was located at the far end of the street just beside the church. That left him alone with the corpse of the man he had shot.

"No need to stand watch over him, Mr. Hawke. He's not going anywhere," Schermerhorn said, returning and leading a pack mule. "But as long as you're here, will you help me put him up on the mule?"

"Of course," Hawke said.

The two men put the body, belly down, on the mule, and then, as Schermerhorn led the animal toward Robert Griffin's mortuary, Hawke returned to the Hog Lot.

When Hawke stepped inside the saloon, he saw Harder standing in front of the piano, examining it by the light of a lantern.

"Hawke, maybe you had better come over here and take a look at this thing," Harder suggested.

Responding to Harder's invitation, Hawke went to the piano. It was full of bullet holes, and there were wires hanging from the soundboard and keys that were completely shot away.

"Damn," he said.

"Looks like our nighttime visitors aren't music lovers," Harder said.

"So it would appear," Hawke said.

"Can you fix it?" Harder asked.

Hawke shook his head. "John, I don't think Mr. Steinway himself could fix this thing."

"Too bad," Harder said. He sighed. "So, what kind of job do you want now?"

"I beg your pardon?"

"I hired you to be a piano player, but I no longer have a piano. You could help Bob Gary out, I suppose, by tending bar and sweeping floors. I couldn't pay you anything but room and board."

"No," Hawke said. "Thanks for the offer but I don't think

I would care to do that. I'll find some other place to play the piano."

"There's not another piano in town, except the one at the church."

Hawke chuckled. "That sort of limits my choices, doesn't it?"

"I guess so."

"That is a good piano, though," Hawke said. "An exceptionally good piano. I was surprised to see that a church in a town this size could afford a piano like that."

"Oh, the church didn't buy that piano. The parson bought it."

"The parson bought it? Well, that's rather unusual."

Harder shook his head. "Yeah, well, the parson is what you might call an unusual man."

Hawke thought of the conversation he and Gideon McCall had held in the street a few minutes earlier.

"Now that you mention it, he is a little different from your average preacher. Have you known him long?"

"A couple of years, is all. He and his wife and little girl came to town about two years ago, right after the old parson died. The church had stood empty for six months, and to tell the truth, I didn't think Parson McCall would be able to get it started up again. Bob said he would, but I didn't believe him. Turns out, Bob was right."

"Bob? Are you talking about Bob Gary?"

"Yeah, Bob and the parson are great friends."

"That's a rather unusual friendship, isn't it? A parson and a bartender?"

"Well, it's like I said, the parson is an unusual man," Harder replied. "I tell you what, I feel bad about you bein' out of a job and all. What happened here wasn't your fault. You can keep your room till the end of the month. Maybe by then you'll have an idea about what you're going to do."

"Thanks, John, I appreciate that," Hawke said.

"It sure is a shame, though. I never cared much for music

before now, but I have to confess that, sittin' back there in my office, listenin' to you playin' the piano out here . . . well, sometimes that was just real pleasant."

Hawke chuckled. "Well, if I've made another music lover in the world, then my time here wasn't wasted."

"Good night," Harder said. "Or what's left of it."

"Good night," Hawke replied.

Hawke was a man who lived his life on the edge, and, like all such men, he had developed a sixth sense, and that sense gave him a feel for when something wasn't quite right. That feeling hit him as soon as he opened the door to his room.

He drew his pistol, then stepped quickly away from the wedge of light that was created by the open door.

"Who's there?" he said into the darkness, cocking the pistol as he called out.

"No! Don't shoot!" a frightened woman's voice replied.

Hawke recognized it. "Millie?"

A match was struck, and the lantern lit. Millie raised the match to her lips and blew it out. She was wearing a thin cotton sleeping gown, the nipples of her breasts prominent against the cloth.

"What are you doing in here?" Hawke asked.

"I heard all the shooting and I got frightened," Millie said. "Somehow, I felt safer in your room. But now that it's over, I, uh, guess I could go back to my own room. That is, if you think I should," she added.

Millie put every ounce of seduction she could muster in her voice, and she thrust her hip out to one side, accenting her curves. It was planned to be a provocative pose, and it was.

Hawke holstered his pistol. "Or, you could just blow out the lantern," he suggested.

Smiling, Millie pulled her sleeping gown over her head, then stood naked before him.

"I was hoping you would say that," she said.

Chapter 9

FOR THE SECOND TIME IN LESS THAN A WEEK, A corpse was put on display in the front window of Robison's Hardware Store. This time, though, it was displayed in a plain pine box, rather than the highly polished, elegant, Eternal Cloud coffin that Robert Griffin had sold to Clint Jessup. And whereas Shorty had been dressed in a suit and tie, this corpse was wearing the same denim trousers and red shirt he had been wearing at the time of his death.

The corpse's eyes were open and opaque, and his mouth was drawn to one side as if in a sneer. When the viewers looked closely enough, they could see that, although Robert Griffin made a notable effort, he had not been able to get rid of all the blood from the repaired bullet hole in the shirt.

A sign was hanging around the corpse's neck.

**KILLED IN THE RAID ON OUR
TOWN LAST NIGHT.
DO YOU KNOW THIS MAN?**

While Hawke was standing in front of the window looking at the corpse, Mayor James Cornett came up with Elmer
Keith. Keith owned a picture studio, and he was carrying the
tools of his trade with him.

"Can you get a picture of him through the window?" Cornett asked. "Or do I need to go ask Robert Griffin to move
him outside?"

Keith set up his camera and tripod, draped the hood over
himself and sighted through the camera. He made a couple
of adjustments, then came out from under the shroud.

"I can get him through the window with no problem," he
said.

"With me in the picture, don't forget," the mayor said. "I
don't intend to pay for it, unless you've got me in the picture
with him."

"I will be able to get you in the picture," Keith promised.

"Excuse me, Mr. Hawke," Cornett said. "But would you
mind steppin' to one side for a moment?"

"No," Hawke answered. "Not at all."

The mayor moved to stand in front of the window, then
pulled his pistol and held it across his chest. He stared at the
camera.

George Schermerhorn came across the street from his
freight yard.

"James, what in the world are you doin'?" he asked.

"I'm getting my picture took with this here raider that I
kilt last night," the mayor answered. "It'll be good publicity
for my next campaign."

"You killed him?"

"Yes."

"How do you know you killed him?"

Cornett sighed. "All right, I don't know that I kilt him, but I don't know that I didn't either," he replied. "I was shootin' at them as they rode through town. So I figure I come as likely to killin' him as anyone."

"Well, he was lyin' in front of my place," George said. "How do you know I didn't kill him?"

"I don't know," Cornett replied. "But I aim to have my picture took with him, no matter who did it. We know that one of us did it. He didn't kill hisself."

"Would you like your picture taken with him as well, Mr. Schermerhorn?" Keith asked. "I'll print you up a nice copy for only twenty-five cents."

"I—" George started, then stopped, thought about it a moment and grinned. "Yeah," he said. "Why the hell not? If I'm not the one who killed him, I was sure shootin' at the son of a bitch. And like the mayor says, it could have been any of us. Let me go back and get my pistol."

"No need to go back to get your gun, George," Cornett said. "You can use mine. Nobody will be able to tell the difference in the picture anyway."

"All right, James, thanks," George said.

George stood by while Keith took James's picture, then he posed for one of his own. That brought others around, so that within a few minutes Keith had photographed half a dozen of the citizens of the town, all standing beside the coffin of the dead raider, holding a pistol across their chest. By now, not only was Keith making money from the operation, but so was Cornett, who was charging those who didn't have a pistol ten cents to hold his.

Smiling and shaking his head, Hawke walked away from the picture session, then wandered down to the newspaper office. The window that the three cowboys broke out had not yet been replaced, but it was now boarded over. And, not to be deterred by the broken window, Clemmons had painted a sign on the boarded-up window:

THE BRAGGADOCIO JOURNAL
AN ORGAN OF TRUTH
NOT TO BE DETERRED BY HOOLIGANS
VERNON CLEMMONS, PUBLISHER

Clemmons was setting type, and he looked up as Hawke
stepped inside.

"Good morning, Mr. Hawke," Clemmons said. "That was
quite some excitement we had last night, wasn't it?"

"I suppose you could call it exciting," Hawke agreed. "Are
you writing a story about it?"

"Indeed I am. Would you like to hear the headline and
subheads?"

"Sure."

Clemmons stood back from his set type, and, despite
the fact that it was backward, read it easily: "Midnight
Raid on Braggadocio. Cowboys believed the culprits. One
outlaw shot dead in the streets. Town must act to disarm
cowboys."

"What do you think?" he asked, looking up from the type.

"I think you'll sell some more papers," Hawke said.

"Mr. Hawke, how would you like to work for me?" Clemmons asked as he went back to setting his type.

The question surprised Hawke.

"I beg your pardon?"

"How would you like to work for me?" Clemmons repeated. "I know that you will not be able to play the piano
anymore. Not since it was destroyed last night. That means
you are going to be looking for work."

Hawke chuckled. "How did you know that?"

"I'm a newspaperman, Mr. Hawke. I have my fingers on
the pulse of this community," Clemmons answered. "I am
right, aren't I? You are looking for a job."

"I suppose I am," Hawke admitted. "But what makes you
think that I would be a good newspaperman?"

"You are smart and you are educated," Clemmons said.

"And, there is more to you than meets the eye. I have a feeling that you have seen a lot of this old world, Mr. Hawke. That gives you a sophistication that plays well in the newspaper business."

"I thank you for the offer, Mr. Clemmons," Hawke said. "I—"

"Wait," Clemmons said, interrupting him. "Don't dismiss the offer out of hand. At least think about it."

Hawke nodded. "That's just what I was going to say, Mr. Clemmons. I will think about it."

At the Bar-J encampment, Jessup went over to the suspended coffeepot to pour himself a cup. Carter was standing nearby.

"Major, it ain't right that we left Frank Miller lyin' in the street back there," Carter said.

"Then you should have picked him up and brought him back," Jessup replied.

"We didn't have time to pick him up," Carter said. "That's why I think we should go into town now and claim him, the way we done for Shorty."

"Deekus told me Miller had not been into town yet."

"That's true, not till last night he hadn't."

"That means that nobody in town will recognize him," Jessup said. "And if they don't recognize him, they won't be able to connect him with us. It would be foolish to go in and claim his body now. That would just be admitting that we were the ones who rode through town last night, shooting it up."

"Well, hell, they goin' to know it was us," Carter said.

"Not necessarily," Jessup replied. "There are two other outfits here now, and they are nearly as big as the Bar-J. As far as the people in town know, he could be one of their riders."

"Maybe. But still, I hate leavin' Miller back there, lyin' in the street like that."

Jessup sighed. "Well, if it is any consolation to you, I'm positive that he is no longer lying in the street. They've got him in a coffin by now. Probably a cheap one, but you can rest assured that it makes no difference to Miller. He's dead."

"I still don't know why we don't go in and get him. I ain't afraid to let them sons of bitches know it was us that rode through their town. What can they do to us?"

"It isn't what they can do to us if they know who we are," Jessup replied. "It's what we can do as long as they don't know."

"What do you mean?"

"You've never studied military strategy, have you, Carter?"

"No, sir, not that I recall."

"Well I have, and the most powerful weapon any army has is surprise."

"Are you sayin' we're goin' to ride through the town again?"

"I'm saying I want to keep our options open," he said.

"Yeah," Carter said. "Yeah, I think I see what you mean."

Deekus was also nearby, and he overheard the conversation between Jessup and Carter. When Carter walked away, Deekus chuckled.

"What do you find to laugh about?" Jessup asked.

"I was just thinkin', that's all, Major. Don't mind Carter, he don't know about things. He wasn't with us durin' the war."

"This remind you of the war, does it, Deekus?"

"A little," Deekus replied. "I was thinking about Galena. You remember that raid, don't you?"

"Oh yes," Jessup said. "I remember. I remember it as if it were yesterday."

Jessup took a swallow of his coffee as he recalled Galena.

"The scouts are back, Major, and they found the Yankees," Deekus reported.

Just as Jessup wasn't using the name Jessup then, his sergeant wasn't using the name Deekus at that time.

"Where are they?" Jessup asked.

"They're just ahead in Galena. They got their camp set up

in an empty lot between the livery and the leather goods store."

"Wait a minute. Are you telling me they've closed themselves in between two buildings? They aren't out where they can control the street?"

"No sir, they've got themselves in a box, neat as a rabbit in a trap," Deekus said.

"I almost feel sorry for those poor men, having a leader who is that incompetent. We'll be on them before they know what hit them."

"Yes, sir," Deekus said. "That's pretty much the way I was figuring it."

"Tell the scouts they did a good job."

"We goin' to hit Galena?"

"Yes."

"When?"

"First light tomorrow morning."

As Jessup planned the operation, he couldn't help but wonder what his old professor in military tactics would think. It would be a textbook attack, taking advantage of surprise, speed, and firepower.

As he knew it would, the raid caught the Yankee soldiers by complete surprise. Many were at their morning toilet when the raiders swept into the little town from both ends. Jessup's men converged in front of the large empty lot where the soldiers were encamped.

"Rebs!" one of the Yankees shouted, and he stood up and tried to run, though as his pants were down around his ankles, running was impossible.

Ironically, the very thing that prevented the Yankee soldier from running also saved his life, because he tripped and lay facedown on the ground while bullets whizzed by over his head.

For the Rebel raiders, it was like shooting ducks in the water. Most of the Yankees were wandering around unarmed, because their officers had insisted that the weapons

be stored in two or three neatly organized weapons' stacks.
The raiders not only shot the soldiers, they also rode into the
encampment and set fire to the tents, wagons, and ammunition storage. There were three ammunition storage dumps,
all containing several barrels of black powder. The resultant
explosions rocked the town.

Not until the raiders had nearly expended all their ammunition did Jessup call them back. They rode out of town exactly as they had come in, exiting by both ends. They left
behind them a grisly scene of dead and wounded Yankee
soldiers, and a completely destroyed encampment.

As Jessup recalled that incident, he thought of the raid he had
conducted on Braggadocio last night. It was not the same
kind of raid as the one in Galena, since he had no intention to
kill anyone. It was a diversionary tactic only, designed to allow him to get Tex, Brandt, and Cracker out of jail.

Though he had not shared his thinking with any of his
men, he knew that the raid was not necessary. He would
have been able to get the men out of jail today simply by
paying for the broken window. But as far as his men knew,
the raid had gone exactly as planned, in that Tex, Brandt,
and Cracker were out of jail. Of course, nobody had counted
on one of their own getting killed in the process.

The real purpose of the raid was not to free his men, but to
prod the townspeople into closing the cattle loading pens
and prevent any further rail shipment of cattle.

It was a finesse, because he was betting that they would
not be able to close the pens before his shipment was completed. On the other hand, he was gambling that they would
be able to close it before the Rocking T or Slash Diamond
could ship their cows.

Whether or not the raid accomplished its purpose remained to be seen.

Chapter 10

TWO DAYS AFTER THE RAID, MAYOR JAMES COR-
nett and the city council of Braggadocio called for a town
meeting, and since the only place in town large enough to
hold the meeting was the Hog Lot Saloon, the mayor asked
John Harder if he would make his establishment available.

"Sure, I'd be glad to," Harder replied. He smiled. "Hell,
that has to be good for business."

"I'm also going to ask that you close the bar during the
meeting," Mayor Cornett said.

"Now wait a minute, James," Harder answered. "First you
ask me to let you use my place for a meeting, which is fine
by me. But then you tell me I can't serve any drinks. If I do
that, we're going to have some mighty upset and thirsty
people."

"If they are that thirsty, they can go to Foley's."

"Fine, now you are giving my business to my competi-
tion," Harder complained.

Cornett sighed. "If you'd like, I'll issue an executive order closing Foley's until the town meeting is over."

"No," Harder said. "No, don't do that. Foley and I get along pretty well. I don't want to do anything that would make it bad for him. Just get the meeting over with as soon as you can."

"Look on the bright side of it, John," Cornett said. "You'll have people here who have never set foot in your place before. You might wind up getting some new customers out of this."

Harder smiled. "Yeah," he said. "Yeah, I hadn't thought of that, but you're right. Hey, maybe I'd better get the place spruced up a bit before everyone shows up."

True to his word, John Harder had his saloon sparkling clean by the time the people began showing up. Millie and the other girls, who normally dressed as provocatively as possible, were wearing demure clothing, and they acted not as bar girls, but as hostesses, serving coffee and helping the visitors find seats for the meeting.

Even though extra chairs and benches were brought in, there still wasn't enough seating for everyone, so many were standing along the walls. The mayor and city council took their places behind a table set up just in front of the piano. If a reminder of the midnight raid was needed, the bullet-scarred piano served that purpose.

Hawke was standing alongside the piano, leaning against the wall with his arms folded across his chest. He saw Gideon McCall come in, and wondered if this was the first time the preacher had ever been in a saloon. Then he recalled the conversation he and McCall had on the night of the raid. It was strange and enlightening to see them conversing, and as Hawke thought back on it, he realized that this might not be his first time after all.

Parson McCall's wife and daughter were with him, and Hawke was pleased to see that a couple of men got up to offer their seats. Gideon seated his family, then came over to stand beside Hawke and looked at the piano.

"I'm sorry about your piano, Mr. Hawke," he said. "It certainly looks beyond repair."

"Yes, well, in a way, it's hard to tell, because it wasn't that much of a piano to begin with," Hawke joked.

"Mr. Hawke, I know how it is with people like you."

"People like me?"

"Yes, people like you who have God-given talent. I'm talking about artists, writers, musicians," Gideon continued. "You do what you do not merely to make a living, but because it is something you have to. You might call it a divine discontent. So anytime you feel that you must play the piano, please know that you are free to come play the one at church."

"Thanks, Parson."

"Gideon," McCall said. He smiled. "I had a name before I had a title."

Hawke chuckled. "Gideon, sometimes I get the impression that you had a lot before you had a title."

Before Gideon could reply, Cornett banged his gavel on the table to call the meeting to order. "Folks," he called.

"How long is this meeting going to last, Mayor?" someone asked.

"Not too long," Cornett answered. He banged the gavel again. "If you folks will quiet down a bit, we'll get this meeting started."

"Mayor," someone called from the audience, "some of us want to know . . . where was Marshal Truelove while all this was goin' on the other night?"

Truelove was sitting at the table with the city council. "I was in Plumb Creek," he said.

"Well, you shoulda been here. What were you doin' in Plumb Creek, anyhow?"

"I'll answer that, Matthew," Cornett said to Truelove. "For your information, Mr. Lewis, Marshal Truelove was in Plumb Creek testifying at a trial."

"Yeah, well, he should've been here, protecting us," Lewis said.

"Lewis, what did you expect the marshal to do? Stand out there at the edge of town and face them down all by his own-self?" one of the others asked.

"Please," Cornett said. "If you will all just be patient, we'll get to the questions later. Now, it's time to get the meeting started."

Again Cornett banged his gavel.

"I'm going to open the meeting by calling on Vernon Clemmons."

"Wait a minute," Lewis said. "How come he gets to ask the first question?"

"Because he isn't asking a question, he is making a proposal," Cornett said. "Now, Lewis, if you don't settle down, I'm going to have to ask you to leave."

"Mayor," Lewis said, "the other night, while my wife and me was sleeping, a bullet come through the window and hit the headboard not more'n two inches from my wife's head. So you can see why I'm mighty interested in what's going to be done."

"Well, there ain't nothin' goin' to be done, Lewis, unless you shut up and let 'em get on with it," one of the others said.

There were a few nervous chuckles.

"Thank you, Mr. West," Cornett said. "All right, Mr. Clemmons."

The newspaper reporter came up to the front to address the others.

"Mr. Lewis, I understand your concern," Clemmons began. "I've heard similar stories from others in town, and I think we are fortunate that no one was killed. That's why I think the ordinance that my newspaper has proposed is more important now than ever before. I think—"

Clemmons stopped in mid-sentence and stared toward the front door. Others, seeing him do so, looked around as well. They saw Clint Jessup enter with two men.

"Please," Jessup said when he saw everyone looking at him. "Don't stop on our account."

"Major Jessup, the bar is closed," Cornett said. "If you must have a drink, Foley's is open."

"We're not here for a drink," Jessup said. "As you know, I own the Bar-J. These two gentlemen own the two other cattle companies that are here now. How come you didn't send word that you were having a meeting?"

"I didn't send word about it because this is a town meeting," Cornett said. "It is for citizens of Braggadocio only."

"It may be a town meeting," Jessup said, "but it concerns us, so I figure that gives us the right to sit in."

"Well, you figure wrong."

One of the men on the city council said something to Cornett then, speaking so quietly that nobody but Cornett could hear him.

"Are you sure?" Cornett asked.

The council member nodded.

Cornett cleared his throat, then spoke again. "Very well, Major Jessup," he said. "Our city attorney says you folks may attend."

"Thank you."

Clearing his throat, Clemmons continued his report.

"The men who rode into our town the other night, shooting wildly and raising hell, were cowboys."

"You don't know that they were cowboys," Jessup called out loud, interrupting Clemmons's presentation.

"Well, Major Jessup, we know they weren't a group of store clerks," Clemmons said.

The others at the meeting laughed.

"They were," Clemmons continued, pausing for a moment while he considered his statement, "in all probability, cowboys. I'm not saying that they were Bar-J riders. Although there has been a suggestion that the raid was a diversionary effort in order to facilitate the jail break of three of your riders."

"They are young and reckless," Jessup said. "They saw the opportunity to leave and they took it. That doesn't mean it was a raid to free them."

"Major Jessup, one simply has to put two and two together. There was a midnight raid and your three men escaped."

"If you think about it, Clemmons, it simply makes no sense," Jessup said. "The three men would have been released the next day when I paid for your window. And by the way, I did pay for your window yesterday, did I not?"

Clemmons cleared his throat. "Yes, you did," he admitted.

"Then I think we can dismiss that as a reason for the raid."

Clemmons looked at the representatives of the other cattle companies. "Regardless of the reason, the fact remains that the raid did happen, and it was conducted by cowboys. They could have been any of the outfits, or they could have been a combination of several cowboys from all the companies. The point is, they came into town shooting indiscriminately, and we were lucky not to have any of our people killed.

"That's why I feel that the ordinance I'm suggesting would prevent anything like this from ever happening again."

"Do you have a motion for us to consider, Mr. Clemmons?" Cornett asked.

"I do," Clemmons replied. "Mr. Mayor, I propose that the city of Braggadocio enact an ordinance that would require all cowboys who wish to visit us to surrender their weapons as soon as they come into town."

"Hear! Hear!" someone shouted, and the others in the audience applauded.

"Mr. Mayor, Mr. Mayor, may I say something?" Jessup called.

"Major Jessup, you haven't shut up since you arrived. I told you, this is a meeting for citizens of the town. And since you are not a resident, you have no voice."

"Mr. Mayor, that isn't exactly true," Gideon said, speaking for the first time.

"I beg your pardon?" Cornett replied. "What do you mean it isn't exactly true?"

"There are no provisions in our city charter for a town meeting, as such. You can declare an executive session of the city council in which everyone is barred except members of the council. Or you can declare an open session of the city council which bars no one. And it certainly should not bar anyone who has a vested interest in the outcome, which Major Jessup and the other cattlemen certainly have."

"Webber," Cornett said to the city attorney. "Is the parson right?"

Webber nodded. "I'm afraid he is, Mayor."

"All right, Jessup, you can speak," Cornett said.

"Thank you, Parson," Jessup said to Gideon. "Mayor Cornett, members of the city council, before you vote on any proposal that would take away the guns of the cowboys, I would like to remind you of something. Since we arrived here for the express purpose of shipping our cattle east—an operation, I might add, that is vital to the economy of this town—two men have been killed by gunfire."

Jessup paused for a moment, and it had just the effect he was looking for, because every eye in the building was looking directly at him, and every ear was attuned to his words.

"The two men who were killed were Ian McDougal and the poor unfortunate soul you have on public display right now. Ian McDougal was a cowboy, a fine young man who worked for me. And I think it is generally assumed that the corpse you are now displaying is also a cowboy. Both, I remind you, were killed by citizens of your town.

"Not one citizen of your town has been killed by a cowboy's gun. And the one, unfortunate incident that took the life of a young lady who worked in this very establishment was an accident. All who witnessed it agree upon that.

"So, what do we have? We have three dead." Jessup held up three fingers. "The first, a young lady who was not murdered, but who died in a tragic accident. Ian McDougal, a fine young man from an upstanding Iowa family who was shot and killed by Mr. Hawke, and the young man who had hurt no one, but was merely engaging in an act of youthful exuberance, shot down in the street two nights ago by an armed citizen of Braggadocio.

"And yet in the wake of these three deaths, what do you do? You propose to pass a law that would disarm the cowboys but leave the citizens of your town armed. Before you vote, I ask you to consider the fairness of that."

Jessup sat down.

"Thank you, Major Jessup," Cornett said. He looked at Clemmons. "Mr. Clemmons, do you have a response for Major Jessup?"

Clemmons applauded softly, almost sarcastically. "Bravo, Major Jessup," he said. "You made a brilliant presentation of your case . . . unburdened by any obligation to the truth, but brilliantly presented, nevertheless.

"Your suggestion that the tragic death of Cindy Carey was an accident borders on the ludicrous. Miss Carey did fall down the stairs, but only because, in fear for her life, she was running from an enraged Ian McDougal. Mr. Hawke did shoot McDougal, but not until McDougal had already shot Bob Gary, and shot at Mr. Hawke.

"And, as for the—how did you put it? A poor unfortunate soul?—I would remind everyone that the poor unfortunate soul you are lamenting was a member of a large and rowdy band of riders who galloped into town at four in the morning, not to enjoy any of our amenities, but to shoot up the town. In fact, one could almost say it was reminiscent of the heinous bushwhacker bands who, during the late war, spread violence and terror among innocent citizens."

Clemmons pointed to Lewis. "And, as Mr. Lewis can attest, barely two inches separated an act of . . . *youthful exuberance*," he set the words apart, "from a tragic killing.

"I urge the town council to pass and to enforce a law that

would take away the cowboys' pistols as soon as they come into town. Thus disarmed, we will enthusiastically welcome them to visit our drinking establishments, enjoy our restaurants, shop in our stores, and enjoy all that our beautiful city has to offer the peaceful visitor."

"Does anyone else wish to speak?"

"I would like to speak," a large-framed, white-haired man said. He was standing with the other cowboys.

"And you are?"

"You know me, James. I've been bringing cows to Braggadocio ever since the railroad arrived."

"I know you. But for the record, please."

"I'm Charley Townes, I own the Rocking T. We got here a couple of days ago. I don't know what kind of trouble you've been having with the Bar-J, but you've had no trouble with the Rocking T, nor have you ever had trouble with any of my men. If you pass this law disarming cowboys, you are lashing the shoulders of many to get to a few. And if you do that, you may wind up causing more problems than you solve."

"What do you mean by causing more problems?" Cornett asked.

"Come on, James, you know how cowboys are. They are young, proud, and exuberant." He paused and looked directly at Clemmons. "Yes, Mr. Clemmons, I said exuberant young men. They don't have that many personal possessions, and what they do have, they guard very jealously. The possession they are most proud of is their pistol. Take that away from them, and you are bound to have trouble."

"Do you have anything to add?" Cornett asked the other man who had come with Jessup and Townes.

"My name is Tucker Evans," a bandy-legged, raw-boned man said. "I own the Slash Diamond outfit. I don't know what's been going on here before we arrived, but I assure you, not one of my men has caused any trouble in this town. The only thing we want to do is get our cows on the train, then go back home. The boys will be comin' in to have a few drinks, and enjoy your town in a peaceable way. You got no call to take their guns away from 'em."

"Mr. Mayor, I would like to make a proposal," George Schermerhorn said.

"Chair recognizes George Schermerhorn."

Schermerhorn stood to face the rest of the audience. "I agree with the cattlemen that we're just goin' to cause more trouble by takin' their guns away from them."

"What are you sayin', George? That you are on their side?" Jubal asked.

Schermerhorn held up his hand. "Not exactly," he said. "I'm just sayin' that we are whistlin' Dixie if we think takin' away their guns is going to take care of the problem. The only way we are going to be able to take care of it is to close the cattle loading pens, so that the cowboys have to go somewhere else to ship their cows."

"Why would we want to do that, George?" Harder asked. "That's cutting off our nose to spite our face, isn't it? I know the cowboys are difficult to deal with, but they do bring money into the town."

"I know it would be hard for you, John. You and Foley get most of their money because they spend it all getting liquored up. But when you think about it, that's part of the problem. They get all liquored up, then they start causing trouble. In the long run, it would be better for the town if we closed the cattle loading pens and built grain elevators instead. That way the farmers—and there are a lot more farmers than there are ranchers—would use us as a place to store and ship their product. That means more business for the stores and shops of the communities—"

"And for you, since you would be hauling their produce into town," Foley said.

"Yes, for me," Schermerhorn admitted. "And for you, Mayor Cornett, and for the hardware store, apothecary, the mercantile, just about every business you can name except the saloons and Pearlie's. The farmers are all hardworking folks, not nearly as wild as cowboys. We wouldn't be having the kind of trouble we've been having with the cowboys."

"Mr. Mayor," Jubal Goodpasture said.

"Yes, Jubal."

"My business isn't affected either way," Jubal said. "So I figure I can talk about this without takin' sides."

"All right, we're listening."

"I think we should leave things the way they are now. I mean, go ahead and disarm the cowboys like we've talked about, but don't stop the cattle shipments unless there's any more trouble. If there's any more trouble, then we could take another look at stoppin' the cattle shipments."

"That makes sense to me," Cornett said. "I'm going to shelve this proposal for the time being. We've discussed this enough, I think it's time to hear the proposal that's before the council. Mr. Webber, would you please read the proposal?"

The city attorney nodded, then began to read: " 'Whereas armed cowboys have caused civil disorder and endangerment of life and property, and whereas the citizens of Braggadocio feel the need of arms to protect life and property, be it hereby resolved that a law be enacted, to wit: That while citizens of Braggadocio shall be allowed to keep their arms, no armed cowboy will be allowed inside the city limits of Braggadocio, and those who come bearing arms shall be divested of said arms.' "

"Thank you, Mr. Webber," Cornett said. "The proposal is now before the council. All in favor, say aye."

"Aye," the town council said as one.

"All opposed?"

No one spoke.

"The ayes have it, the act is passed. Marshal Truelove, you may begin immediate enforcement of this law."

"Very good, Mayor," Truelove said.

Cornett brought his gavel down sharply. "This meeting is adjourned."

Even as the meeting was ending, another group of cows was being herded down Malone Avenue, as the main street was called.

Evans and Townes came over to talk to Jessup.

"How many head have you moved?" Townes asked.

"Some over two thousand with this bunch coming through today," Jessup said.

"So you are two-thirds done?"

"A little better than that."

"It wouldn't matter much to you whether they close the loading pens or not, would it?"

"I wouldn't want to see them closed," Jessup said.

"Yeah," Evans said sarcastically. "I'm sure you wouldn't. Of course, the fact that you'd get more for your cows if we can't get ours shipped wouldn't matter to you, I don't suppose."

"I don't know what you are talking about," Jessup said.

"Major, we've been checking around," Townes said. "Neither one of us plan to say anything about it, but that cowboy who was killed the other night was one of your men."

"Yes, he was," Jessup said.

"In fact, the whole crazy bunch of cowboys who rode into town, raising hell, were all your men, weren't they?"

"They were," Jessup admitted.

"What was the purpose of all that? Why do you want to stir up trouble?" Townes asked.

"They're the ones who started the trouble," Jessup replied. "Do you want to just let the town run over us? You saw what they just did. Passing that law about disarming the cowboys when they come into town was a slap in the face of all of us."

"It's no slap in my face," Townes said.

"Mine either," Evans added.

"So, you plan to just sit back and let the town run roughshod over you?"

"We didn't come here to be in no pissin' contest," Evans said. "We come here to get our cows shipped up to Chicago."

"That's what I'm here for as well. Look, I can't be weak, not even for one moment. Do you think I was born with that ranch down there? I worked hard to get it, and I don't plan to lose it because I'm not strong enough to do battle when it's forced on me."

"You should learn to choose your battles," Townes said. "How many more head you got to ship out?"

"About nine hundred or so," Jessup replied.

"I just pray to God you get them all shipped before a full-scale war breaks out between the cattlemen and the town," Evans said.

"Yeah," Jessup said. "That's exactly what I want."

Jessup's response was purposely ambiguous. When he said that was exactly what he wanted, that was exactly what he meant. He wanted to get all of his cattle shipped . . . then wanted a full-scale war to break out between the cattlemen and the town. That would close the cattle pens, and his cows would go for top price.

Chapter 11

~~~

"HAWKE, MY INVITATION FOR YOU TO PLAY THE piano is still open," Gideon told Hawke as the meeting ended.

"I hate to impose."

"Nonsense, you aren't imposing at all," Gideon said. "Come on down and play it now. That is, unless you intend to hide your candle under a basket."

"I beg your pardon?"

Gideon chuckled. "That's a Biblical reference," he said. "It means that if you do come down and play the piano, that I hope you won't mind if I listen."

"No, I wouldn't mind at all," Hawke said.

"So, you'll come play now?"

"All right," Hawke said. "I'll be glad to. And I thank you, very much, for the opportunity."

As the two men walked toward the church, they continued their conversation.

"You know, Hawke, I can't help but wonder why you are wasting your talent by playing in a saloon. You have been classically trained to play the piano, haven't you?" Gideon asked.

Hawke didn't reply right away.

"I'm sorry," Gideon said. "I had no right to butt into your personal affairs like that. You don't have to answer, if it is uncomfortable for you. It was more of an observation than a question, anyway."

"That's all right," Hawke said. "Everyone is entitled to a little curiosity. Yes, I have been classically trained."

"Have you ever used that training?"

"I toured as a concert pianist for a while. Both here and in Europe."

"That seems like a noble enough profession," Gideon said. "I mean, music is one of God's greatest gifts to mankind. I can't help but wonder why you gave it up."

"You are a preacher, Gideon. You, of all people, should know what it is like for a man to lose his soul."

Gideon was quiet for a moment before he spoke. "Are you talking about the war?" he asked.

"Yes."

"The war is a collective sin, Hawke. No one man is responsible for it, and no one man can lose his soul because of it. I serve a just, loving, and forgiving God. Believe me, your soul is still intact. All you have to do is claim it."

"I wish I could believe that, Gideon. I truly wish I could believe it."

Gideon put his hand on Hawke's shoulder. "Hawke, my friend, I'm not speaking as a preacher. Like you, I have agonized over my own soul. But I have found peace with the Lord."

"I'm glad it's working for you, Gideon," Hawke said.

By now the two men had reached the church. When they stepped inside, Hawke walked down to the front to examine the piano.

"This is your personal piano?" Hawke asked.

"No, this piano belongs to the church."

"Oh. I must have been misinformed. I was told you bought this with your own money."

"You weren't misinformed," Gideon replied. "I did buy it. But I gave it to the church."

"That's a very generous gift," Hawke said. He depressed a few keys. "It's very well tuned."

"We have a man who comes by train from Omaha to tune it."

Hawke sat down and played a few bars of music.

"Chopin's Sonata Number One," Gideon said, recognizing the tune. "Beautiful."

"You know your music."

"You are surprised?"

"No," Hawke replied with a chuckle. "I'm finding less and less about you that surprises me. What surprises me is that I played it well enough for you to recognize it."

Gideon laughed. "False modesty is not becoming, Hawke. You are an exceptionally gifted pianist, and I'm sure you know that."

Hawke continued to play.

"How would you like to come here anytime you wish?" Gideon asked.

"Anytime I wish? I don't understand."

"It's easy enough to understand," Gideon said. "You are free to come here to the church and play the piano anytime you want."

"That would be exceptionally kind of you."

"Not kind," Gideon replied. "Practical."

"Practical?"

"Yes, practical. After all, as the church pianist, you would need access to the instrument in order to pick out the hymns for Sunday services, and to practice them."

Hawke stopped in the middle of a bar of music and, for a

second, the strings continued to resonate with the last chord he'd played.

"Wait a minute," he said. "Are you asking me to become the church pianist?"

"Yes."

Hawke laughed.

"You find that funny do you, Hawke?"

Hawke realized by the expression on Gideon's face and his tone of voice that the preacher was hurt by his response.

"No, I don't find it funny, I find it very flattering," Hawke said. "I just thought you were teasing, that's all. Especially given the fact that I play piano in a saloon."

"Well, you aren't playing the piano in any saloon in this town," Gideon replied. "You saw what happened to the piano in the Hog Lot, and I'm told that there is no piano in Foley's. I don't know if there is a piano in Pearlie's or not."

Hawke laughed. "Well, now, if you knew that, I really would be surprised," he said. "But to answer your question, no, there is no piano in Pearlie's." Hawke started playing again.

"Bach, Vivaldi, Beethoven, so many wonderful composers wrote their music to the glory of God," Gideon said. "Could you not do them the honor of playing their compositions for the glory of God?"

Hawke played a passage from a Bach Toccata and Fugue, then Vivaldi's Four Seasons, and finally Beethoven's Ninth Symphony.

"You are weakening, I can tell," Gideon said with an engaging smile.

"It is a good piano," Hawke said again.

"You are a practical man, aren't you, Hawke? Consider this," Gideon said as he continued to try and recruit Hawke. "I know what the saloon was paying you, and I can't pay as much. Also you won't be able to put a beer mug on the piano for tips. On the other hand, you can play the music you want to play, anytime you want to play it, and you won't have to sweep floors or put up with drunks."

Hawke played the first four notes of Beethoven's Fifth fortissimo, then smiled up at Gideon.

"Parson, if you preach as well as you argue your case, you must give some rip-snorter sermons," he said. "All right, Gideon, you've got yourself a pianist."

"Wonderful!" It was a woman's voice, and Hawke, surprised, turned to see that Gideon's wife Tamara had come into the church while they were talking.

He quickly stood. "Mrs. McCall," he said. "Oh, wait a minute, you are the church pianist, aren't you? Look, I don't want to cut you out of your job."

"I'm not the church pianist, Mr. Hawke. I was the church piano player, and you, of all people, know the difference. I am thrilled that you have agreed to take Gideon's offer."

"I'm glad you don't mind," Hawke said. "Oh, by the way, speaking of offer, what is the offer?"

"Thirty dollars a month," Gideon said. "You can sleep in the spare room over in the parsonage and take your meals with us."

"No," Hawke said, holding up his hand. "I'll accept your offer to play, but I don't want to put you out. I've got another month of room and board coming from the Hog Lot. I'll stay there."

"You are going to stay at the Hog Lot?" Tamara asked in surprise. "Oh, I think—"

"That would be fine, if that's what you want to do," Gideon said, interrupting Tamara in mid-sentence.

"But, Gideon—" Tamara started.

Gideon waved her protest aside.

"Is my staying at the Hog Lot going to cause trouble?" Hawke asked. Then he answered his own question. "Of course it will, I guess I just wasn't thinking."

"Don't worry about it, Hawke," Gideon said. "A few of my parishioners will get themselves in a stew over the fact

that you are playing piano for the church while living in a saloon. They are the same ones who question my friendship
with Bob Gary. And they are the same people who will be
upset about my hiring you in the first place. We'll just have
to win them over."

"Do you think we can do that?"

"I think we can."

"As I said, I don't want to cause you any trouble," Hawke
repeated.

"Believe me, when they hear you play, they'll forget any
reservations they may have had over my hiring you. And if
they don't come around, they can always go to another
church."

"Gideon, the next nearest church is thirty miles from
here," Tamara said. "Even by train, that's almost two hours
away."

Gideon smiled. "Yes," he said. "Isn't it?"

Leaving the church, Hawke walked back to the Hog Lot. At
the end of the street he saw Marshal Truelove at work, disarming the cowboys who were bringing in another bunch of
cows to the railhead. Although it was obvious that they
didn't appreciate having to give up their weapons, the cowboys were doing it without causing any trouble.

When he returned to the Hog Lot, Hawke saw that it was
back to normal. The tables, which had been taken outside to
make more room for the town meeting, were now back inside, and the girls were once again dressed to entice the customers to buy more drinks. A couple of card games were in
progress, and several men stood at the bar. Many of them
had empty holsters.

John Harder was sitting at his usual table, which was just
outside his office door, and Hawke walked back to him.

"Pull up a chair, Hawke, and join me," Harder said. He
poured a drink for Hawke and slid it across the table.
"What with your piano playing and all, we've never had the

opportunity to just have a nice, social drink together before now."

"Thanks," Hawke said.

Harder held his glass up by way of a toast. "To lusty women everywhere," he said.

Smiling, Hawke touched his glass to Harder's, and the two men drank.

"Have you decided what you are going to do?" Harder asked.

"First, are you serious about letting me stay here for another month?"

"I am."

"Then I'd like to take you up on that offer. And I don't expect you to furnish room and board free, so, I'll tend bar or sweep the floor or—"

Harder waved his hand. "No need for that. With all the cattle companies camped just outside of town, there are going to be some rowdy cowboys from time to time. And even though they are all supposed to be disarmed, there's no way of being sure that they haven't snuck a gun in. So if you are interested, you could act as a private guard for the saloon."

"A private guard?"

"Well, in a manner of speaking you would be private. I've talked to Truelove. He will make you a deputy marshal. That will give you some legal authority, but the city won't be paying you. I will."

"I don't know," Hawke said. "I guess I'd have to think about that for a while."

"It was the girls' idea," Harder said. "Look, Hawke, I've seen you in operation. I've never seen anyone who could handle themselves under pressure the way you do. I'd not only be willing to furnish you with room and board, I'd also pay you the same thing I was paying you when you were playing the piano."

"I've taken another job," Hawke said.

"You have? Well, whatever they are paying, I'll pay more."

"You've already offered more than they are paying," Hawke said. "I've taken the job as pianist for the church."

Harder laughed out loud. "You?" he said, pointing. "You are going to play piano for the church?"

"Why not?" Hawke asked.

"The question isn't why not? The question is, why would you? I mean, Hawke, come on, you in church? Aren't you afraid the walls might come tumbling in?"

"Have you ever been to church?" Hawke asked.

"Well, yeah, I was in church just a few days ago. Hell, you remember that. It was for Cindy's funeral."

"I mean, other than that."

"When I was a kid, I went to church."

"It might be good for you to go again sometime."

"Ha!" Harder said. "The walls really would come tumbling down if I went to church." Harder was quiet for a moment. "Let me get this straight. You plan to play piano for the church, but you want to keep your room here?"

"Yes."

"And you are willing to work for your room and board?"

"Yes."

"All right, we don't have a problem. You can play the piano in church on Sunday and be a private guard here the rest of the time."

"It's a deal," Hawke said.

Sunday morning Hawke was standing on the front stoop of the church when Gideon arrived, having walked over from the parsonage, which was just next door.

"Well, good morning," Gideon greeted. "Beautiful morning, isn't it?"

"I suppose it is," Hawke said. He chuckled. "But then, I don't have anything to judge it by. It's been a long time since I was up this early."

Gideon laughed as well. "You have a key to the church, don't you?"

"Yes, you gave me one."

"You don't have to stand out here and wait for me, you can go in anytime you want."

"Thanks."

Hawke stood by as Gideon opened the door, then followed him in. As soon as they were inside, Gideon took a long pole with a little hook on the end and began pulling the very tall windows down from the top, then lifting them up from the bottom. Seeing another pole, Hawke started doing the same with the windows on the other side of the church.

"Gideon, I've taken another job at the saloon," Hawke said, speaking loud enough for Gideon to hear him from across the room.

"Yes," Gideon replied as he continued setting the windows. "Bob told me you had. But he also said that it wouldn't prevent you from playing piano for us on Sunday."

"I will play for you if you don't have a problem with the fact that I'll be working in the Hog Lot during the week."

"Why should I have a problem with that? Bob Gary is one of my closest friends. He works at the Hog Lot, and it hasn't affected our friendship."

"You know, I've been wondering about that. How did it happen that a preacher and a saloon barkeep became such friends?"

"Bob wasn't a barkeep when we met," Gideon said. "And I wasn't a preacher," he added.

Working their way forward, the two men finished opening all the windows, allowing for a cooling cross breeze.

"There," Gideon said, standing the pole in the corner. "That should keep the congregation cool enough when I start speaking of fire and brimstone for the sinners."

Hawke chuckled.

"So, what are you going to play for us today?" Gideon asked.

"I thought I'd do Bach for the prelude and postlude, but I was hoping Mrs. McCall would select the hymns for me."

"I'm sure she would love to do it," Gideon said.

There were several gasps of surprise from the congregation when they arrived later that same morning to see the saloon piano player setting at the piano bench. Their whispers could be heard as they commented on it from their pews, but when Hawke began to play, all conversation halted, the congregation lost in the beauty of the music.

The ensuing service went peacefully, as it always did. "May the Lord bless you and keep you, and may His countenance shine upon you. Go, now, in peace, to serve one another and to love the Lord," Gideon said at the conclusion.

As Hawke began playing the postlude, Gideon hurried to the front door to greet the departing congregation.

"It was a wonderful sermon today, Reverend McCall, one woman gushed. "And the music was lovely, just lovely."

There was one woman, however, who was so adamant in her disapproval that she demanded a meeting of the church board.

"Her name is Evelyn Rittenhouse," Gideon explained when he told Hawke about it. He sighed. "I think God gives every church someone like her just to see how far the pastor's patience can be tried. And Lord knows, this woman has taken me to the end of my patience more than once."

"When is the meeting?" Hawke asked.

"Tomorrow afternoon," Gideon said. "Hawke, please don't feel that you have to attend. This is my problem, not yours, and I'll handle it. Besides, I'm afraid your presence might make her even more entrenched in her opposition."

"If you say so," Hawke agreed.

As Hawke left the church, he saw a few cowboys in town, and as they rode by he saw that none were armed. Apparently, word was getting around.

Chapter 12

WHEN HAWKE DROPPED BY THE NEWSPAPER OFFICE the next day, Vernon Clemmons was standing at the composing table, setting type.

"Good morning," Hawke said.

"Which sounds better?" Clemmons asked without looking up. " 'We must balance the economic benefit derived from our visiting cattle herds *with* the safety of our citizens,' or, 'We must balance the economic benefit derived from our visiting cattle herds *against* the safety of our citizens'?"

"I think 'against' is better," Hawke said.

"Why?"

"It's a more dynamic word, don't you think?"

Now, Clemmons looked up and at Hawke. "See! See! I knew you would make a good newspaperman," he said. "Who else but a natural newspaperman would consider a word because it is dynamic?"

Hawke chuckled. "Why do I get the feeling you were just testing me?"

"Perhaps because you have a newspaperman's intuition," Clemmons said. "And you are right. If you look here, you will see that I have already set that word."

"Where is the story you are setting it from?" Hawke asked.

"What do you mean?"

"Don't you write your stories before you set the type?"

"No, why should I? That's just a wasted step. I write it as I set the type," Clemmons replied. "I've been doing this for so long that I can set type as quickly as I can write the story on paper."

"I'm impressed," Hawke said as he watched the newspaper publisher's hands fly from type box to plate. "But, about the job you offered me—"

"I know. You are coming by to tell me that you are turning it down."

"Uh, yes. I did think about it, but—"

"You decided to play piano for the church instead," Clemmons said, finishing Hawke's response for him.

Hawke chuckled. "How did you know that? You weren't in church yesterday."

"I know that, my boy, because I am a newspaper editor. And it is my business to know everything. And as far as seeing me in church, that's not likely to ever happen."

"You have a score to settle with God, do you?" Hawke asked.

"No, not at all. In fact, I like to think that God and I get along pretty well. I just don't want some organized religion to come between us."

"What do you have against organized religion?"

"Do you have to ask? You've had one day there now. That should be enough for you to pick out a few of the more holier-than-thou members."

"You mean like Evelyn Rittenhouse?"

"Ah, yes, so you have met the grand dame of the Army of the Republic, have you?"

"I haven't actually met her, but she has come to my attention. What do you mean by the grand dame of the Army of the Republic?"

"Evelyn Steffe Rittenhouse is the sister of John William Steffe. It is said that he is the one who came up with the tune for 'John Brown's Body.' Later, of course, Julia Ward Howe added different words, and that became—"

"The 'Battle Hymn of the Republic,'" Hawke said, interrupting. "That is an interesting piece of information to know."

Clemmons tapped himself on the temple. "That's me. I'm a walking repository of interesting, though often totally worthless, bits of information."

"Maybe not as worthless as you think," Hawke said.

There were six voting members of the church board, all of whom were men, and four nonvoting members of the ladies' auxiliary. Not only did the ladies' auxiliary have no vote, but they could speak only if they were invited to do so. That did not stop Evelyn Rittenhouse, who, by the power of her personality, treated her membership on the auxiliary as if it were a full-fledged voting position on the church board. She didn't wait to be invited to speak, she addressed the board as if she were the head deacon.

"I am very disappointed in you, Reverend McCall," she said. "It was bad enough when you conducted a funeral for a common harlot. But now, right here, in my church, you have invited the piano player, from the same saloon that employed that woman, to play for us."

"Your church?" Gideon said. "That's funny, Mrs. Rittenhouse, and here, all this time, I thought it was God's church."

"Of course it is God's church," Evelyn said, fuming. "But that makes it even worse. I mean, the very idea of a sinner like that man, a killer even, mingling with us during our worship. What sort of impression do you think it will make on our children to have a murderer playing piano for us?"

"He isn't a murderer. He killed in self-defense," Gideon said.

"It doesn't matter why he killed, the point is, he did kill. He took another person's life."

Although Hawke had not come into the pastor's study where the meeting was being conducted, he had come to the church, and now stood just outside the door, in the sanctuary, listening to the discussion.

"Mrs. Rittenhouse," Jubal Goodpasture said. "I've killed. So have several others in the church."

"What?" Evelyn said in a shocked tone of voice.

"It was during the war," Jubal said.

"Oh, well, that's different."

Hawke walked over to the piano and sat down. He began playing, very softly. There was a somber elegance to the music.

"Yes, ma'am, it is different. You see, Mr. Hawke killed a man who was not only trying to kill him, but who had already shot another innocent person . . . to say nothing of the fact that McDougal was responsible for a young woman's death. And I believe that, had Mr. Hawke not killed him, McDougal might well have killed someone else.

"In my case, the sin is greater, because I killed good men who were God-fearing family men, who had never committed a crime against anyone. Their only guilt was that they were wearing a gray uniform. So if you want people to leave this church because they have killed another human being, regardless of why or how they killed, then I'm afraid I would have to leave."

"So would nearly half the men who are members of this church," Gideon added. "We have many veterans of the war in our congregation, men who served on both sides."

"Well, of course I didn't mean that," Evelyn said. "My own husband was a veteran of the war."

The music Hawke was playing slowly built in intensity.

"But regardless of whether the killing was justified or not, it still leaves the fact that he plays piano in a house of prostitution."

"He *played* piano in the Hog Lot," one of the other board members said. "He plays it no longer. Besides, it is a saloon and restaurant; it is not a house of prostitution."

"Call it what you want, I still say—" Evelyn started, then heard the music. By now the "Battle Hymn of the Republic" filled the church, with each bar distinctive and resonating within the souls of all who could hear it. Evelyn looked back toward the sanctuary.

"What?" she said in a quiet voice. She pointed toward the sound of the music. "What is that?"

"That's Mr. Hawke," Gideon replied. "I imagine he is just practicing. If you wish, I'll go tell him to stop playing until after our meeting."

"He is playing my brother's song."

"Is he?" Gideon asked, turning his head toward the sanctuary. "I hadn't noticed, but now that you mention it, I believe he is."

Evelyn got up from the meeting table and started toward the door that led into the church.

"As I said, I'll tell him to stop." Gideon stood and started toward the door.

"No," Evelyn said. "Wait." She went out into the church and saw Hawke, leaning over the piano, coaxing every note from the song, making each bar a concerto all its own.

Evelyn walked over to the piano and stood there, listening to the music. Her eyes welled and glistened, then tears began sliding down her cheeks. She stood, completely mesmerized, until the last note hung regally in the air.

It wasn't until then that Hawke looked up and saw her there.

"Oh," he said. "I beg your pardon. Did my playing disturb the meeting? If it did, you have my most sincere apology. I'll leave and come back later."

"No!" Evelyn said, sticking her hand out to touch him on the arm. "Please, would you play it again?"

"The 'Battle Hymn of the Republic'? Of course I will." Hawke chuckled. "That is a Yankee song, and I fought for the South. But now it belongs to all of us, and I am glad. I have always considered myself a musician first and foremost, and I believe that to be one of the most beautiful tunes ever written."

"Thank you," Evelyn said.

"Thank you?"

"My brother wrote the music that you just played."

"Steffe? You are related to John William Steffe?"

"You know about John? Most people only know about Julia Ward Howe. How is it that you know of my brother?"

"Because I am a musician, Mrs. Rittenhouse. Without the music, Mrs. Howe's words would be mere poetry. With the music, it becomes the greatest patriotic anthem in the history of our Republic."

"Yes! You are so right! My brother has never received the credit he deserves. I am so glad that you know his name and recognize what he has done."

Hawke stood, took her hand, and bowed to kiss it. "Mrs. Rittenhouse, your brother has my utmost respect and admiration. I have played music of the masters, but for sheer impact from simplicity of style, I have played nothing that compares with this masterpiece."

"You are too kind," Evelyn said, flattered by the attention Hawke was bestowing upon her.

"Please, sit here," Hawke said, drawing up a chair and seating her. "Let me play it again, this time just for you."

By now the other members of the board, which included the other ladies of the auxiliary, had come out into the sanctuary. They took seats to listen as well.

The first fifteen notes of the song were played as individual notes, clear, bell-like, uncluttered tones. Then he brought in harmony and bass, counter melody and trills, enriching the tone and tint of the music until it was full, thunderous, and majestic. And yet, through it all, woven like a golden thread in a beautiful and elegant tapestry, was the continuing, bell-like notes of the melody.

Then, as the last crescendo reverberated back from the walls and stained-glass windows of the church, Gideon presented his handkerchief to Evelyn Rittenhouse. There was a moment of silence before Gideon cleared his throat.

"Yes, well, we must get back to our meeting. The discussion at hand is whether or not we should continue to use Mr. Hawke as our pianist."

"Reverend McCall," Evelyn said in a choked voice.

"Yes, Mrs. Rittenhouse?"

"I know that I have no legitimate voice nor vote in this matter, but I would like to urge, as strongly as I possibly can, that Mr. Hawke be retained." She smiled at Hawke through tear-glistened eyes.

"Anyone who has a God-given talent like this should use that talent in God's house."

"Hear, hear," Jubal said.

"Well, then there's no real need to return to my study is there?" Gideon asked. "We can put it to a vote right here. Shall we retain Mason Hawke as pianist for the Ecumenical Church of the Holy Spirit? All in favor say aye."

"Aye," the board said as one.

"Very good," Gideon said. "Thank you, ladies and gentlemen, for coming."

"And thank you, Mr. Hawke," Evelyn said, "for the most beautiful rendition of my brother's song that I have ever heard. *C'était vraiment musique joué pour les anges.*"

"I believe all music is played for the angels," Hawke responded. *"Et c'était un honneur et un privilège jouer pour vous, madame."*

"Oh, my! You speak French. Mr. Hawke, you are a man of surprising depth," Evelyn said, almost flirtatiously.

"And you, madam, are a woman of grace and charm."

Evelyn blushed under the compliment. "Reverend McCall, if you ever let this magnificent pianist get away, I will be extremely upset."

"I will endeavor to hold on to him," Gideon replied.

Not until Evelyn and the other board and auxiliary members left did Gideon break out into laughter.

"My French is a little rusty, but did you actually say that it was an honor and privilege to play for her?"

"Yes."

"I'll give you this, Mason. You certainly know how to flatter and cajole a person. You have won her over, and that is something I haven't been able to do ever since I came to this church."

"That's because I can lie easier than you can," Hawke said, and both men laughed.

As Hawke was leaving the church he saw Marshal Truelove and his deputy, Truman Foster, stopping two cowboys who were just coming into town.

"What the hell do you mean you're a'goin' to take our guns?" one of the cowboys shouted angrily. "They didn't nobody take away our guns when we come here last year."

"It's a new city ordinance, just passed this year," Truelove said to the cowboy.

The cowboy pointed toward Hawke, who was standing close by, watching the drama unfold.

"He's a'wearin' a gun," the cowboy said. "Why don't you take his gun?"

"He is a citizen of the town. Only the cowboys coming into town have to give up their guns. You can pick it up again when you leave town."

"I ain't givin' no one my gun! You want my gun, you're goin' to have to take it!" the cowboy shouted, pulling his pistol.

"Kerry, no, don't do it!" the other cowboy yelled.

Truman Foster was holding a shotgun, and as the cowboy started for his pistol, the deputy shouted out as well.

"No! Leave it be!"

"The hell you say!" the cowboy replied, continuing to draw his gun.

Foster waited until the cowboy brought his gun up and cocked it, but before Kerry could shoot, the deputy pulled the trigger. The ten-gauge Greener roared and billowed smoke, and the load of double-aught shot hit Kerry in the chest, knocking him from his horse.

"Kerry!" the other cowboy shouted in alarm as he watched his friend go down.

Kerry lay motionless, his unfired pistol on the ground beside him.

"You son of a bitch! You killed Kerry!" the cowboy said. He started toward his own pistol.

"Don't do it, cowboy!" Hawke shouted, his own pistol now drawn.

"He killed my friend!" the cowboy replied. "He killed my friend in cold blood!"

"Your friend was given a choice," Hawke replied. "He could either follow the law or fight it. He made the wrong choice."

For a moment it looked as if the cowboy had a notion to draw his pistol, and his hand hovered in position.

"If you make one move toward that pistol, you will be dead," Hawke said menacingly.

The cowboy moved his hand away from his pistol, then pointed at Hawke, Deputy Foster, and Marshal Truelove.

"You'll be hearin' from us!" he said. "We ain't about to take this lyin' down!"

The cowboy turned then, and galloped out of town, leaving his friend lying in the road behind him. The dead cowboy's horse stayed behind, and Truelove walked over to look at the brand.

"Damn," he said. "There's going to be hell to pay now."

"Why?" Hawke asked.

"This isn't a Bar-J horse. That means we're going to have another outfit to deal with."

"What are we going to do with him?" Foster asked.

"He's not our problem now," Truelove said. "He's Robert Griffin's problem."

Kerry Parker, the young cowboy who was killed, rode for the Slash Diamond outfit. Tucker Evans owned the Slash Diamond, and neither he nor any of his men knew much about Kerry Parker, so there was no place to send his body. As a result, plans were made to bury him in the Braggadocio cemetery, and an invitation was sent out to all the cowboys in all the encampments around Braggadocio.

The invitation met with an overwhelming reception, and so many cowboys wanted to come that the owners had to select some to stay back and keep watch over the herds.

Almost fifty cowboys gathered on the road about one mile south of town.

"Where is the young man's body?" Jessup asked Tucker Evans.

"The undertaker said he would meet us with a wagon at the edge of town," Evans replied.

"A wagon? Not a hearse?"

"A wagon is what I wanted," Evans said.

Robert Griffin had brought the wagon to the edge of town, just as he promised. When he got it in position, he saw Marshal Truelove and Deputy Foster walking toward him. Both were carrying shotguns.

"Are you goin' out to meet them?" Truelove asked.

"No," Robert Griffin replied. "I told them I would meet them here. And I'm just as glad. I don't think I would care much about going out there all by myself. I feel a lot better waiting here with you and the deputy."

"Ha," Truelove said. "There's likely to be thirty or forty of them at least. Maybe more. If they wanted to start something, you don't really think Foster and I could prevent it, do you?"

"You mean you couldn't?"

Truelove shook his head.

"Then what are you doing out here with a shotgun?"

"It's my job," Truelove said.

"Marshal, here they come," Foster said.

"Yeah, I see 'em," Marshal Truelove said.

"Damn, how many did you say there would be?" Robert Griffin asked quietly.

"Thirty or forty," Truelove answered.

"There's a hell of a lot more than that. Looks like just about every cowboy in Nebraska is here."

When they reached the edge of town, Truelove stepped out into the street and held up his hand to stop them.

"You goin' to keep us from comin' into town, are you, Marshal?" Clint Jessup asked. "Are you sayin' we can't bury our dead?"

"You can come into town," Truelove said. "But I'm counting on you and the other owners to make sure none of your men are armed."

"We know the rules," Jessup replied. "None of us are carrying guns. We don't like it, but nobody is armed."

Truelove looked back along the road where the cowboys were riding two by two, almost as if in a cavalry formation. They returned his glance with stern gazes of their own.

"All right," Truelove said, stepping out of the way. "You can come in."

"You want me to lead the way in?" Robert Griffin asked.

"Yeah," Tucker Evans said. "But wait a minute."

Evans got down, then took something from the back of his horse. It was two signs, and he walked over to the wagon that was carrying Kerry Parker's coffin and attached a sign on each side.

"Now," Evans said as he remounted. "You lead the way in."

"Yes, sir," Robert Griffin replied, positioning the wagon at the head of the column.

With the wagon in the lead, the procession started into town. The sign on one side of the wagon read:

KERRY PARKER, KILLED WHILE DEFENDING HIS RIGHTS

On the other side of the wagon the sign read:

AN INNOCENT COWBOY MURDERED FOR NO REASON

As the wagon and large parade of cowboys passed down the street, the town stood still. The hoofbeats of the horses clopped loudly on the dirt street, echoing back from the false-fronted building that lined the way. Most of the citizens watched the procession from inside the homes and stores that lined the street, but several stood outside, watching silently.

The procession turned into the cemetery, then stopped beside a grave that had already been dug. Tucker Evans swung down from his horse and turned to face the assembled cowboys.

Gideon McCall had offered his services, but he was turned down by Tucker Evans, who told them that the cowboys would take care of their own.

Tucker Evans spoke over the cowboy's grave.

"Some of you fellas from the other outfits might have met Kerry Parker when you were in town together. Some of you might have even ridden with him at one time or another, because I know how you boys move from ranch to ranch.

"But for those of you who didn't know him, let me tell you what he was like. He would ride flank, or point, or drag, without complaint. He never crowded the chuck wagon, and you could roll him out of his blankets when he had nighthawk and you could count on him to do his job. He was a dependable worker and a good man, and he deserved a lot more than to be shot down in the street just for wanting to hang on to his own, private property.

"So now we're buryin' him here in the enemy's own backyard, so to speak. We're doin' that because nobody knows for sure where Kerry's folks are, or even if he has any folks. I guess that makes us his folks, so that bein' the case, I'm goin' to ask each of you now to sort of pray a silent prayer for our friend.

"Amen," he concluded.

A few of the riders tossed in their own amens.

After the burial, a sizable number of the cowboys stayed in town. They went first to the Nebraska House, where they occupied every table in the restaurant, intimidating the few diners who were already there and running them out.

After their meal, during which so many dishes were broken that it wound up costing the proprietor more money than he made from the meals he served, the cowboys went to Foley's. There, using an axe handle as a ball bat and empty beer mugs as a ball, they had a game of baseball. Foley watched in helpless despair as his glasses were broken and scattered all over the floor.

Their behavior was no more civilized at the Hog Lot, where they terrorized the girls by jerking down the top of their dresses and pulling up the hems of their skirts. When they finally rode out of town at around midnight, they announced their departure by loud whooping and yelling. Whooping and yelling was all they could do, because they had left their guns behind.

Chapter 13

"I'LL TELL YOU WHAT I THINK," JUBAL GOODPAS-
ture said to the group of community leaders who had been
called together. "I think we ought to form us a vigilante committee. 'Cause if we don't, things is goin' to get out of hand
just real quick around here."

"Jubal's right," Schermerhorn said. "A vigilante committee is just what we need."

"A vigilante committee?" Truelove said, and shook his
head. "No, sir. I've been around vigilante committees before. Once they get started, they can't be controlled."

"I didn't mean a vigilante committee exactly," Jubal said.
"I'm talking about something more like a posse. With you in
control, of course," he added. "You could deputize us."

Truelove shook his head. "No, you can put a mule in horse
harness, but it's still going to be a mule. Call it whatever you
want, but if you put a lot of armed men on the street and let

them think they have some sort of law enforcement power, you are just asking for trouble."

"Come on, Marshal, you aren't going to be able to handle all these men by yourself. They're coming into town now in groups of thirty to forty every time they come."

"But they are coming unarmed," Truelove said, holding up his finger. "Don't forget, when they come into town, they are not wearing their guns."

"The marshal is right," Gideon said. "The worst thing we could do now is put a lot of armed, untrained men in a position of authority over a bunch of prideful, young, and antagonistic cowboys. Let them come into town and make a little noise. If they aren't carrying guns, they can't really hurt anyone."

"Beggin' your pardon, Parson, but seein' as they ain't never come to your church, and seein' as how they ain't never goin' to, you don't have nothin' to worry about. But those of us who have businesses to contend with aren't all that happy to see 'em come into town and raise hell like they do."

"I agree with the preacher," John Harder said.

"You agree with him?" Jubal asked, surprised at Harder's position. "I woulda figured that you would agree with me. You've had more damage than just about anyone else in town, except maybe Foley."

"Yes, and so far it's just a few broken glasses," Harder said. "I can always get more glasses. What I don't want is to lose another girl the way I lost Cindy. And as long as the cowboys continue to come in without their guns, about the only thing we're going to have to worry about is a little noise here and there."

"I agree with John Harder," Foley said. "I'm doin' a good business with the cowboys right now, and as long as they don't shoot nobody, well, I can live with a few broken glasses."

"And a mirror and a window or two?" Jubal asked.

Foley nodded. "Yeah," he said. "Like I say. As long as there's no shooting."

"All right," Jubal finally agreed. "Matt, if you don't think you want a posse—"

"I don't want one," Truelove said.

"And if you other fellas are willing to put up with the noise and the fistfights and such, then who am I to say we must have a posse?"

"I think you are right to be concerned, though, Jubal," Marshal Truelove said. "These are violent men who are short-tempered and not very intelligent. While they are here, we'll have to do all within our power not to spook them."

"Sort of like walkin' around a herd of cattle when they're likely to stampede," Clemmons said. "Is that it?"

Jubal laughed. "I reckon that's about it," he said. "I don't think I could have said it any better myself."

"Of course you couldn't," Clemmons replied. "If you could have, I'd hire you as a reporter."

"The score is now three dead cowboys, all three shot by someone in town," Major Jessup said. "But the townspeople are armed and we aren't. Does that seem right to you?"

Jessup was talking to Evans and Townes, both of whom had ridden over to the Bar-J encampment in order to discuss the situation.

"It doesn't make that much difference whether it is right or wrong," Townes said. "The point is, it's the way things are, and we are just going to have to live with it."

"I don't agree," Jessup said. "People have never had to live with what's wrong. We fought the British to right what was wrong, and we fought the Yankees to right a wrong."

Townes and Evans both chuckled.

"Well now, Jessup, seein' as both Tucker 'n' me fought for the North, we might just have a different take on that war," Townes said.

"All right, but even the North fought to correct what they thought was wrong. My point is, we don't have to just sit out here and take it. We can make things right, even if we have to fight for it."

"Look, I don't know what started all this," Evans said. "But you and your outfit are the one who got here first. In fact, it was your men that got the town all riled up in the first place."

"Yeah," Townes agreed. "And now you're askin' us to join in a fight when we don't even know which side is right and which side is wrong."

"Let me remind you that Kerry Parker rode for the Slash Diamond," Jessup said. "And who was it that killed him? It wasn't the Bar-J. It was the people in town."

"I agree," Evans said. "But Jake was ridin' with Kerry when that happened, and even he says it was Kerry's fault, that instead of turning over his gun when he was told to, he tried to draw on the marshal."

"Why are you so all-fired worked up about it anyway?" Townes asked. "You have all your cows shipped out, you'll be pullin' out of here, leavin' us with the trouble you've started."

"You're right, we'll be pulling out of here tomorrow morning," Jessup said. "So it's not my men, or me, that I'm concerned about now. It's the right or wrong of the thing, and I just think that what the town is doing is wrong. What's right is right, and what's wrong is wrong."

Evans and Townes looked at each other for a long moment.

"Go ahead," Evans said.

"Go ahead what?" Jessup asked, confused by the way the two men were acting.

"This business about what's right is right and what's wrong is wrong," Townes said. "Do you really believe that?"

"Yes, of course I believe it," Jessup said.

"Uh-huh. Well, if you really believed that, you would have shared the trains."

"Share? What do you mean, share?"

"I mean, instead of you shipping three hundred cows each day, you would've shipped one hundred, the Slash Diamond would have shipped a hundred, and the Rocking T would have shipped a hundred. Instead, you kept the whole train for yourself."

"Will you two be sharing the trains?"

"We will."

"Well then, it's a moot point, isn't it? My cows are already shipped."

"Do you think that was right?"

"It's the way it has always been," Jessup said. "Whoever gets here first has first rights to the trains. I was here first."

"Normally, that wouldn't be a problem," Townes said. "But that was before you got the town stirred up so. They're actually talking about closing down the shipping pens. It would take us a month to six weeks to make other arrangements. Our cows would be so late that we would be at the tail end of the market, that is, if we made this season's market at all."

"Which means," Evans said, "that your cows, being the first ones there—and maybe the only ones there—will be getting top dollar."

"Gentlemen, if it is any consolation to you," Jessup said, "tonight is the last night my boys will be able to go to town. I plan to go to town with them to make certain that nobody gets into trouble."

"It's a little late for that, isn't it?" Evans asked.

"It's never too late for good manners," Jessup replied.

"Let's go, Charley," Evans said. "I wouldn't want us to overstay our welcome here. It wouldn't be . . ." He paused and looked pointedly at Jessup. ". . . good manners."

The two men started to leave, but Townes looked back. "Jessup, there may come a time when you need help from another rancher," he said. "If that time comes, don't be looking toward the Rocking T."

"Or the Slash Diamond," Townes added.

* * *

"This is the last night we'll be comin' into town," one of the Bar-J riders told Trudy. "Are you going to miss me?"

Smiling, Trudy put her hand on the cowboy's cheek and turned his face so she could look directly into it.

"I have no doubt but that I will cry for days," she answered.

"Ooowee, Abe, did you hear that?" Cracker asked. "She's goin' to cry for days. Why, I'll bet she'll be that upset that she won't have nothin' to do with any of the boys from the Rocking T or the Slash Diamond."

"Of course I won't," Trudy said. "I'm a Bar-J girl from start to finish."

Abe—the object of Trudy's professional attention—Tex, Brandt, Cracker, Carter, and Deekus, were all in the Hog Lot for their last Saturday night in town. The Hog Lot was filled, not only with Bar-J riders, but with cowboys from the other two cattle companies. It also had the regular compliment of locals.

"You know what I miss?" Cracker said. He looked toward the place where the piano had been, its spot along the back wall now replaced with a table. "I miss the piano playin'."

"I don't," Deekus said. "I hate that son of a bitch."

"Oh, I don't miss the piano player," Cracker said. "Just the piano playin'."

"Hello, boys," Jessup said, coming over to their table. "Are you having a good time?"

"Yes, sir," Abe said. "Major Jessup, I want you to meet my girlfriend, Trudy."

The others around the table laughed. "Your girlfriend?" Cracker said. "Why, hell, Abe, she's anybody's girlfriend that has the money. Ain't you, Trudy?"

Trudy leaned up against Abe, pushing her breasts into his face.

"That doesn't mean I can't have favorites," she said. "And Abe is my favorite."

"Honey, why don't you pick yourself a man?" Brandt asked. "Ol' Abe there is only seventeen years old."

"I like them young," Trudy said. "When they are young, they haven't picked up a lot of bad habits."

"What kind of bad habits?"

"For example, I don't like for anyone to grab one of my titties, unless I want him to grab it," Trudy said, and she put Abe's hand under the scoop of her dress so it was directly on the flesh of her breast. "Like this," she said.

The table broke into such loud and raucous laughter that everyone else in the saloon looked over to see what was happening.

"Well, you boys continue to behave yourself," Jessup said. "And, Trudy, you take especial good care of Abe. Oh," he pulled out some money and gave it to her, "and bring another round of drinks to the table."

"Thank you, Major Jessup!" Deekus said. The others around the table joined in the thanks.

Jessup walked away from the table, leaving the laughter behind him. He saw Hawke sitting alone at a table in the back of the room.

"May I buy you a drink, Mr. Hawke?" Jessup asked.

"If you want."

Jessup signaled one of the bar girls and held up two fingers. "Whiskey," he called.

The girl nodded and went to the place on the counter that was set aside just for them.

"Mr. Hawke," Jessup began. "I've come to apologize for the behavior of some of my men. I know you and I didn't get off on the right foot, but I was hoping we could part . . . well, if not friends, at least not as enemies."

"I have few friends, and fewer enemies," Hawke said.

Jessup chuckled. "Few enemies, huh? It's hard for me to believe that a man with your, let us say, volatile personality, doesn't make enemies."

"I didn't say I don't make enemies," Hawke said. "I said I have few enemies."

"Well, now, there is a conundrum for you," Jessup said. "You admit that you make enemies, but say that you have few. How can that be?"

"Because most of the time when I make enemies, I kill them," Hawke said calmly.

"Really?" Jessup said. "Well now, that is quite a philosophy."

"You are leaving tomorrow?"

"Yes. We got the last of our herd shipped out this morning. We'll pull out at first light tomorrow morning, provided everyone is sober enough to ride. I decided to let them come into town one last time, and I came in with them, just to keep them out of trouble."

"I'm sure Marshal Trueblood appreciates that," Hawke said.

One of the girls, Annie Mae, arrived with the two drinks. Jessup paid for them, including a generous tip.

"I never got to see you play the piano," Jessup said. "Of course, I'm not sure I would have fully appreciated it in here."

"Probably not," Hawke replied.

"Mr. Hawke, have you ever considered the unusual twists and turns a person's life makes? I mean, look at us. You, a classically trained pianist, reduced to playing a piano in a saloon—when the saloon even has a piano," he added.

"I, on the other hand, was sure that I would be a general by now. Maybe even President. After all, look at Grant. He went to West Point, I went to West Point. The difference is, I resigned my commission to fight for the South. A lost cause, and a lost career."

"You went to West Point?"

"Yes."

"You son of a bitch!" someone shouted, and Hawke and Jessup looked over to see a confrontation developing between one of the Bar-J riders and a cowboy from one of the other outfits. Hawke started to stand but Jessup held out his hand.

"One of them belongs to me," he said. "I'll take care of it. In fact, I think it's time I got everyone out of here. As I said, we'll be pulling out at sunrise."

Hawke watched as Jessup separated the two men, then gathered up all his riders. Within five minutes every Bar-J rider was gone.

"Good riddance," John Harder said.

Turning, Hawke saw that the saloon owner had come up to stand beside him.

"Are they like that every year?" Hawke asked.

Harder shook his head. "Not like this. They seemed especially wild this year. Like I said, good riddance."

Chapter 14

"DEEKUS," JESSUP SAID. "DEEKUS, WAKE UP."

It was still dark the next morning when Deekus opened his eyes to see Jessup standing over his bedroll.

"Something wrong, Major?"

"Get dressed," Jessup said. "Then step over behind the chuck wagon. We need to talk."

"All right, I'll be right there."

Jessup walked away then, disappearing in the predawn darkness as Deekus sat up on his blankets and pulled on his boots. A moment later Deekus left the other sleeping men and joined Jessup, who was leaning against the back of the chuck wagon.

"What's up?" Deekus asked.

"Sergeant, do you ever think back to the war?" Jessup asked.

Deekus, Poke, and Carter had all served with Jessup during the war, and sometimes Jessup used that military form of address to the man who had been his first sergeant.

"Yes, sir, lots of times," Deekus replied.

"Do you miss any of it?"

Deekus chuckled. "Well sir, I know it probably ain't right to miss somethin' like a war, but the truth is, I do miss it from time to time. We were one hell of a fightin' unit, I'll tell you that. Hell, if Lee had a whole army like the bunch you led, Major, the South would've won for sure."

"You remember what I told you when the war was over?"

"Yes, sir, I remember it well," Deekus said. "You told us that you was goin' to buy a ranch and that we'd all three have jobs as long as we wanted one. And that's exactly what you done."

"I said it, I meant it, and I haven't regretted it," Jessup said. "Of all the men I've got working for me now, you are the most dependable."

"Well, I appreciate you sayin' that, Major," Deekus said.

"That's why I'm going to ask you to do a job for me. That is, if you are willing to do it."

"Whatever you want, Major, I'll do it," Deekus said.

Jessup pointed in the direction of Braggadocio. "What do you think about that town?" he asked.

"Well, I don't rightly know what you mean."

"I mean the way they've treated us," Jessup explained. "They watered our drinks, they overcharged us for the goods that we buy, they turned their back on us in the street. And in your case they just stood by and watched that piano player humiliate you."

"He got the drop on me, Major," Deekus said. "I mean I wasn't expectin' him to pull a gun on me for no reason at all. If he hadn't had that gun, he would never have been able to do that."

"I'm sure he wouldn't have. But he isn't the only one to blame. In any decent town—any other town but Braggadocio—the sheriff or city marshal would not allow one of its citizens to use a gun for intimidation like that. And what angers me the most is that while they took away our guns, they let the only people who have actually used them keep them."

"Yeah, that don't seem right to me neither," Deekus said.

"You know, don't you, that they have threatened to close down the loading pens if there is any more trouble?"

"I hadn't heard that. But we're leavin' now, so there shouldn't be any trouble."

"I want there to be trouble."

Deekus regarded Jessup with a confused look on his face, and Jessup chuckled. "What?"

"Let me explain it to you, my friend," Jessup said. "I don't intend to let a bunch of ribbon clerks and shopkeepers get away with what they have done. I think it is time we taught them a lesson."

"But if they close the loading pens—" Deekus started.

"It will make no difference to us. We have already shipped our cattle," Jessup said.

"Yes sir, but—"

"Thank about this, Deekus. If neither the Slash Diamond nor the Rocking T is able to ship their cows, we will get a premium price for the cows we have shipped."

"How does that work?" Deekus asked.

"Don't worry about how it works. The only thing that concerns you is the five hundred dollars that's in it for you."

"Five hundred dollars for me?" Deekus asked. "What five hundred dollars?"

"If you can arrange for Braggadocio to close their loading pens before the other two cattle companies can ship their herds, I will give you five hundred dollars."

"Damn, that's a lot of money," Deekus said enthusiastically.

"We're going to pull out at daybreak. After the job is done, you can join up with us on the trail. I'll give you your five hundred dollars as soon as we get back to Cherry County."

"The only thing is, what should I do?" Deekus asked. "I mean, how am I going to get the town to close the loading pens?"

"You've raided towns before, haven't you, Sergeant?"

"Yes, sir, when we was at war I did."

"We *are* at war," Jessup replied. "It is the town people against the cattlemen."

"Yes, sir, now that you mention it, I guess we are in kind of a war at that."

"We aren't in kind of a war, we are *in* a war," Jessup corrected. "Now, Sergeant, if this was back during the war and I asked you to raid a town, what would be your plan?"

"Well, I guess I would gather up five or six good men, and then make a quick gallop through, shooting it up," Deekus said. He slapped his thigh and laughed out loud. "Damn if I ain't looking forward to this."

"I wish I were going with you," Jessup said. "But it wouldn't do for me to be seen. And, if possible, don't let anyone connect you to the Bar-J."

"Don't worry, Major, I'll take charge of things."

"I'm not at all worried, Sergeant. As I said, that's why I chose you," Jessup said.

Less than half an hour later Deekus and five other men were saddling their horses. When he saw Jessup watching them, he walked over to talk to him.

"Who do you have going with you?" Jessup asked.

"They're all good men, Major," Deekus said. "I have Carter, Tex, Cracker, Brandt, and Abe."

"Abe's a little young, isn't he?"

"Abe woke up while I was talking to Cracker and said he wanted to go. I figured it would be better to bring him along rather than leave him back to talk to the others."

"You did tell your men not to let anyone else know what is going on, didn't you?"

"Yes, sir. You said you didn't want to connect the Bar-J with this, so I figured the fewer that knew, the better off we would be."

"You figured correctly," Jessup said. "Very well, Sergeant,

I'm leaving this in your hands. Make it count. We won't have another chance."

Deekus smiled. "You don't worry none about that, Major. Mr. Townes and Mr. Evans might as well start movin' their cows to another place right now, 'cause after we get through with this little foray, they sure as hell ain't goin' to ship 'em out of Braggadocio."

"Deekus, you remember one of the tactics I used to drill into all of you during the war? What did I say was our best weapon?"

"Surprise," Deekus said.

"Surprise," Jessup said. "This is Sunday morning. The saloons are closed, and everyone thinks we are on our way back north. Whatever you do will meet with very little resistance. You will have your element of surprise."

"Yes, sir," Deekus said. "I was just thinkin' that same thing."

By the time Deekus returned to the remuda, all the others were mounted. Abe, who was holding the reins to Deekus's horse, handed them over to him.

"Is everyone ready?" Deekus asked.

"We're ready, Sergeant," Carter said.

"Sergeant?" Abe asked.

"We was in the war together," Carter said without any further explanation.

"Let's ride out of camp very quietly," Deekus said. "We don't want a bunch of curious people wakin' up to see what is goin' on."

Deekus led the small group until they were about half a mile out of town. There, he halted them and ordered them to dismount.

"We'll rest here for a while," Deekus said.

"Rest?" Abe said. "Why do we need to rest? I ain't tired. Let's do it."

"We'll do it when I say we'll do it," Deekus said.

"This don't make no sense," Abe said. "Why are we just waiting around?"

"Carter, you want to take care of your friend?" Deekus asked irritably.

"Abe, Sergeant Decker is in command."

Abe laughed. "Decker? Deekus's real name is Decker?"

"Do you know what it means when someone is in command?" Carter asked.

"It means he's in charge," Abe said.

"It means he is in charge, and everyone else shuts up and does what he is told. You're the one who wanted to come along, so shut up and do what you are told."

"All right, sure," Abe said. "I didn't mean nothin'."

The men lay in the shade of a thicket of trees for most of the morning. They heard the bells of the church calling the people to service. About an hour later they heard the bells dismissing the service. Not until then did Deekus get to his feet.

"All right, men, ever'body take a piss," Deekus said.

Abe laughed.

"What's so funny?" Carter asked.

"I figure he's in charge, but I didn't know that meant he could tell us when to piss."

"You ever been in battle, boy?" Carter asked as he began relieving himself.

"No."

"You don't ever want to go into battle without pissin' first. Otherwise, you'll wind up peein' in your pants ever' time."

"Oh," Abe said. Without further word he joined the others.

Before they mounted, Deekus ordered everyone to put on their dusters and tie kerchiefs around their faces.

"What's this for?" Brandt asked.

"It's so nobody will know who we are," Deekus said.

"You think they ain't goin' to know we're cowboys?" Brandt challenged.

"There's near a hundred cowboys camped around the town," Deekus explained. "They're goin' to know we're cowboys, they just ain't goin' to know which ones we are."

Chapter 15

THERE WERE MORE PEOPLE IN CHURCH SUNDAY morning than there had ever been at any time since Gideon McCall began his pastorate there. And as the parishioners filed out, nearly everyone commented on the music.

Lucy was sitting at the piano, while Gideon and Tamara were at the front door, saying good-bye to everyone. Lucy pushed a couple of the piano keys.

"C and A," Hawke said.

"What is C and A?"

"Those are the sounds you made," Hawke explained. He pointed to the keys on the piano, then to a piece of sheet music. "When you see this note on the paper, that means to play this note."

"But there are a lot of notes on the paper," Lucy said.

"And a lot on the piano. Look." Hawke pointed to a bar of music, then played the bar.

"Oh! What fun that must be!" Lucy said.

"It is fun."

"Would you teach me to play?"

Hawke hesitated for a moment. He had never taught anyone how to play the piano, but why not?

"All right," he said. "I'll teach you."

Lucy squealed with delight and ran back to the front of the church, just as Tamara and Gideon were coming back in.

"Oh, Mama, Mr. Hawke is going to teach me to play the piano!" Lucy said excitedly.

"Well, how wonderful that will be," Tamara replied with a broad smile.

Tamara and Lucy were wearing identical pink dresses, and Hawke commented on it.

"Tell me, Lucy, did you make those dresses for you and your mama?" he teased. "They're just alike."

Lucy laughed. "No, Mama made both dresses," she said. "I can't sew. I'm not old enough yet. But one day I will be old enough, won't I, Mama?"

"Oh yes, dear. Why, I'll bet you could make your own dress to wear when give your first piano recital."

"They were all talking about the music, Hawke," Gideon said. "Everyone who left the church talked about how good the music was. I don't know but what I'm a little jealous. I have been at this church for two years now, but my sermons—brilliant though they may be," he added with a self-deprecating chuckle, "have never drawn as many people as you have managed to draw with your music."

"I'm sure it is curiosity," Hawke said. "They have all come to see if I might suddenly start playing the 'Gandy Dancers' Ball' or something."

"Gideon," Tamara scolded. "Don't tease Mr. Hawke so. Whatever draws the people to church is fine. Now that they are here, it is up to you to keep them coming."

"Oh, thanks," Gideon said. "There's nothing like putting a little pressure on me, is there?"

"You'll do well, I'm sure you will," Tamara said. She

kissed her husband on the cheek. "Now, don't forget, Mrs. Rittenhouse has invited us down to her house for Sunday dinner. Lucy and I are going to walk there now to see if she needs anything."

"Sunday dinner with Mrs. Rittenhouse. How wonderful," Gideon groaned. "Shall I put on my hair shirt before I come down so that my penance is complete?"

"Oh, don't carry on so. I'm sure it will be a lovely dinner," Tamara said. She smiled at Hawke. "And, Mr. Hawke, I know that she would be very glad to set an extra place for you."

"Thank you, Mrs. McCall, but I believe I will pass on this one," he said. "I wouldn't want to put anyone out."

Gideon laughed out loud. "You don't want to put anyone out? You are a lucky man, Hawke. That dodge will work for you. I don't think it would work for me."

"Oh! You men are awful," Tamara said. "Gideon, darling, please don't be late. I can do my Christian duty and exchange pleasant conversation with Mrs. Rittenhouse only for so long. I will need you there to help."

"Ah-ha!" Gideon said, pointing at Tamara. "Admit it! It is as hard for you to be nice to that woman as it is for me."

"I just know that the Lord has put her here for a purpose," Tamara said.

"Oh, I don't doubt that. The Lord put her here to try my soul," Gideon said.

Clucking and nodding her head, Tamara called out for her daughter. "Lucy?"

"I'm out here, Mama," Lucy said, sticking her head in through the front door.

"Come, dear, we must go."

"You have a fine family, Gideon," Hawke said after Tamara and Lucy were gone.

"I am a very lucky man," Gideon said.

"Sometimes I . . ." Hawke started, but didn't finish the sentence.

"Sometimes you what?"

"I know that envy is wrong," Hawke said. "But I envy someone like you, someone who has a family, a purpose, and a steady life. Of course, the envy is tempered by the fact that I know it will never be like that for me . . . that it can't ever be."

"Because you are looking for your soul?"

"Something like that."

"Don't give up," Gideon said. "I was once where you are now."

"Really?"

"I told you that I wasn't born wearing a parson's cloth. I was in the war," Gideon said.

"I suspected as much. Your understanding of military tactics didn't seem to jibe with you being a preacher."

"And, like you, like many, I came away from the war scarred and dispirited. There were many trails to my future then, Hawke, and I could have taken any of them, including the outlaw trail. But I met Tamara, and my life changed."

"Tamara convinced you to become a preacher?"

"She convinced me to go back to the pulpit."

"Go back to the pulpit? You mean you were a preacher before the war?"

"Yes."

"From some of the things I've heard you say, you seem to have learned the art of war quite well, for a preacher."

"Before I was a preacher I was a regular army officer," Gideon said. "I graduated from West Point a few years before the war started."

"You were in West Point? Interesting. Last night Jessup told me he went to West Point. Did you know him?"

"In a manner of speaking."

"What do you mean, a manner of speaking?"

"His name wasn't Jessup then."

"Oh? What was it?"

Gideon shook his head. "If he thinks it is important to use a different name, I don't feel it is my place to interfere."

"I can understand that," Hawke said. "I've run across many who, for reasons of their own, have changed their name."

"I knew you would understand."

"How did you get into the ministry from the army?"

"I resigned my commission even before the war, and went to seminary to become a Roman Catholic priest. Then the war started and I left the priesthood to take up arms against the country I had once sworn an oath of loyalty to. I wore the gray." Gideon paused for a long moment before he continued. "I must tell you, Hawke, that violating that oath was one of the most difficult things I have ever done. My joining the Confederacy closed the doors on going back into the army, and I no longer felt as if I could perform the duties of a priest. I was a lost and wandering soul."

"But you are no longer lost and wandering."

"No, I'm not, thanks to Tamara," Gideon answered. "She convinced me to go back into the ministry. Obviously, since we were to be married, I could no longer be a Catholic priest. But that didn't mean I couldn't serve God."

Gideon took in the church with a wave of his hand. "So, here I am in a nondenominational church, serving the entire community."

"I'll give you this, Gideon. You have what writers would call a colorful background."

"Perhaps no more colorful than yours," Gideon said. "A classically trained pianist, a warrior, and now a traveling minstrel, playing saloon pianos for the unenlightened and unappreciative."

"From time to time I will encounter someone who has a genuine appreciation for music," Hawke said. "And those few bright, shining nuggets make it all worthwhile."

"I can understand that," Gideon said. "There are many who might not understand it, but believe me, I do."

"How many in town know your background?" Hawke asked.

"Tamara knows. So does Bob Gary. I haven't told anyone else."

"Yes, well, the sentiments in this town are definitely pro-Union. I can understand your hesitancy to let your congregation know that you fought for the South."

Gideon laughed. "The truth is, Hawke, in this heavily Protestant area, there are probably more who would be more put off by the fact that I was a Catholic priest than by the fact that I was a Confederate."

"So, Bob Gary was in the war with you?" Hawke asked.

"Yes, he was."

Hawke nodded. "That explains the odd friendship."

"Odd? How, odd?"

"Well, you have to admit that a friendship between a minister and a saloon bartender is rather unusual."

"Bob Gary saved my life, Hawke," Gideon said. "More than once. And if it ever came to a choice of giving up my ministry or turning my back on Bob Gary, I would give up my ministry."

"I don't think you will ever have to make such a choice," Hawke said. "But the fact that you would speaks more for your character than anything else I could imagine."

Gideon put his hand on Hawke's shoulder. "I knew you would understand that. You are a good man, Hawke. I pray that someday you will find the peace that you are looking for."

Tamara and Lucy McCall were walking from the church to the home of Evelyn Rittenhouse. It was at the south end of town, on the same route that had been used to bring the cattle in over the previous two weeks. Because of that, Tamara and Lucy had to walk carefully to avoid soiling their dresses.

"Mama," Lucy said as she lifted her skirt to step around one cow pod. "Why doesn't Daddy like Mrs. Rittenhouse?"

"Why, darling, what makes you think Daddy doesn't like her?"

"Because of the way he smiles—like this—whenever he

is talking about her." Lucy put on a strained smile to demonstrate.

Tamara laughed. "Is that how Daddy looks?"

"Yes ma'am, just like this," Lucy answered. She repeated the smile.

"Well, Mrs. Rittenhouse can be difficult at times, but Daddy likes her just fine. He likes all the members of our church."

"Oh, Mama, look at those men," Lucy said. "Why are they wearing slickers, it isn't raining?"

Tamara gazed in the direction her daughter pointed and saw half a dozen riders approaching town. "Those aren't slickers, dear, they are dusters."

Lucy laughed. "Look, they're wearing their kerchiefs tied across their faces too. Isn't that funny, Mama?"

Tamara felt a growing sense of unease at seeing six men coming toward them, wearing dusters and with their faces covered up.

"There's Marshal Truelove," Tamara said, with a sense of relief that he was on the job. "He'll find out what they are doing."

Truelove stepped out into the road with his hand raised, but before he could say a word, several shots rang out and Truelove went down. Immediately afterward, the riders broke into a gallop.

"Mama!" Lucy shouted. "They shot the marshal!"

"Quick, get behind me," Tamara said, but even as she tried to push Lucy behind her, she and her daughter went down under a fusillade of gunfire.

The riders galloped by them, the churning hooves kicking up dirt, mud, and manure that spattered their dresses.

Hawke had just left the church and was walking back to the saloon when he heard the shots. Reflexively, he reached for his pistol, but he wasn't wearing one. Then he remembered that he'd left it in his room, thinking it would not be proper to wear it to church. He watched as the duster-covered, masked riders galloped through the town, shooting indiscriminately.

"There's the piano player!" someone shouted.

"Shoot the son of a bitch!" another yelled.

At least three of the galloping cowboys began shooting at Hawke, and he could hear the bullets whizzing by him. With no way to return fire, the only option left for him was to flee.

Hawke ran toward the display window in the front of Robison's Hardware Store. He leaped into the window, covering his face with his arms as he crashed through the glass, then rolled across the shattered pieces of glass to get out of the way. Rising up to peer through the opening where the window had been, he saw two more citizens of the town go down under the hail of gunfire.

For a moment Hawke felt a sense of frustration over being unarmed, then he remembered that Robison's sold firearms. Running to the back of the store, he grabbed a rifle, dumped a box of shells on the counter and, grabbing a few, began loading.

"Let's go!" he heard a voice call from the street. "Let's get out of here!"

Hawke had managed to get only two shells loaded into the tube, but he jacked one of them into the chamber and ran back to the front window, getting there just as the riders turned and started galloping back to the other end of town. He fired, and saw one of the men slump forward in his saddle. The wounded rider reeled a bit but didn't fall from his horse.

Hawke jacked in a second shell and pulled the trigger, but this time the bullet misfired.

"Damnit!" he shouted in anger, and watched in frustrated rage as the riders got away.

Looking toward the south end of town, he saw two lumps of pink cloth lying in the street, and felt it in the pit of his stomach as he realized, instantly, what they represented.

"No!" he shouted in rage. "No!" He burst out of the store,

running toward Tamara and Lucy, and saw that Gideon was running toward them as well.

By the time Hawke reached them, Gideon was already there, on his knees, oblivious to the cow manure as he sobbed over the bodies of his wife and daughter.

"Deekus!" Tex called. "Deekus! Hold up!"

Deekus reined in his horse and the others stopped as well. One of the horses whickered, and all the horses were breathing hard.

"This ain't no time to stop," Deekus said. "What is it?"

"Abe's in pretty bad shape," Tex said. Abe was the only one who had been hit during their raid.

"How bad is it, Abe?" Deekus asked.

Abe's face was ashen and it was all he could do to remain upright in his saddle.

"I . . . I don't know," Abe said, his words labored.

"He needs a doctor," Tex said.

"A doctor?" Deekus said, scoffing. "So, what do you want to do, Tex? Do you want to just ride back into Braggadocio and tell the doc that Abe got shot while we was shootin' up the town?"

"I don't know," Tex said. "All I know is he needs a doctor."

"No doctor is going to look at one of us."

"Yeah, Deekus, what was that all about?" Brandt said. "I thought this was going to be like before, when you broke me 'n' Tex and Cracker out of jail. I thought we was just goin' to make a lot of noise. I didn't know we was goin' to actually shoot at people."

"You seen the marshal come out there, didn't you?" Deekus asked.

"Yes, but all he done was hold up his hand."

"So, was we supposed to stop?" Deekus asked.

"What do you mean?"

"Well, that would be a hell of a thing, wouldn't it, if we

had rode this far, then stopped just 'cause the marshal held up his hand?"

"Well, no, I wasn't plannin' on stoppin'," Brandt said.

"You thought we would do what? Just ride on through?"

"Yeah, somethin' like that."

"If we hadn't stopped, he would have shot us like he done that cowboy from the Slash Diamond. So, look at it like we just beat him to the draw."

"But what about them two women?" Cracker asked. "What did we shoot them for?"

"Yeah, and one of 'em wasn't even a woman. She was just a little girl," Tex said.

"Didn't nobody mean to kill them, ever'body was shootin' and they was just at the wrong place at the wrong time is all," Deekus said.

"We're goin' to have the whole town down on us," Cracker said.

"The whole town is already down on us," Deekus said. "The only thing is, they don't know who we are. Let's shuck out of these now," he added, taking off his duster. "No need in just callin' attention to ourselves."

"What about Abe?" Tex asked again.

"What about him?"

"If he don't get to a doctor soon, he's goin' to die."

"When he dies, throw him belly down across his horse," Deekus said calmly. "We don't want to leave him out here where folks can trace him to us."

"I ain't dead yet," Abe growled.

Chapter 16

〜〜

THE CITY COUNCIL, WHICH NORMALLY MET ONCE
a month, met for the second time in less than a week. The
subject of the meeting was the raid against the town the day
before.

"It was Jessup, I know it was," George Schermerhorn said
after the meeting got underway.

"I'm not so sure," Cornett said.

"Hell, Mayor, you know it was Jessup," Schermerhorn insisted. "He's the only one we've been having trouble with. I
mean, if you ask me, we should get a posse together and go
out there and clean out that nest of sidewinders."

"May I enumerate all the fallacies in that?" Webber asked.
The city attorney began counting off the points on his finger.
"Number one, the riders were wearing dusters and masks so
nobody was able to identify anyone. And number two, the
Bar-J outfit had already shipped all their cows and pulled out
yesterday morning. It hardly makes sense that they would do

something like this when they were on their way back to Cherry County."

"I agree with Webber," Cornett said. "There's no sense in going off half cocked."

"How many dead?" Jubal Goodpasture asked.

"Five," Cornett answered. "Including Marshal Trueblood, as well as Pastor McCall's wife and daughter."

"Damn," Cornett said, shaking his head. He sighed. "I'll tell you the truth, boys, this reminded me of some of the raids the Bushwhackers and Redlegs pulled during the war."

"That's why I think it was Jessup," George Schermerhorn said. "He was a Bushwhacker."

"What makes you say that?"

"Come on, James, I know you've heard the rumors. Everybody knows he is Jesse Cole."

"Like you said, George, they are rumors."

"He admits, himself, that he fought for the South."

"Lots of people fought for the South. That doesn't make them all Jesse Cole, or even Bushwhackers."

"Well, how about this? He paid cash for the Bar-J Ranch. Now, where do you think he got that kind of money if it wasn't something he stole during the war?"

"Hell, maybe his family had money. The fact that he paid cash for the ranch doesn't prove anything. Besides, first things first. We need to decide whether we are going to close the railhead to any future cattle shipment and disassemble the loading pens."

"If we're going to decide, we better decide it quick," Jubal said, looking out the window.

"Why?"

Jubal pointed. "Looks like the good folks of the town have already voted."

"Tear it down!" someone shouted. "Tear the son of a bitch down!"

With a roar in a hundred throats, the men and several boys

of the town began tearing down the loading pens. Axes, picks, and sledgehammers did their work until, within a few minutes, nothing was left of the pens but scattered pieces of broken wood.

"Here comes the train, boys!"

"Pile the wood on the track, stop the train!"

As the train approached, the engineer, seeing the commotion around the track, applied the brakes so he came to a halt a few feet short of the pile of wood. The engineer leaned out of the cab as several of the men approached.

"What is this?" he called down over the sound of percolating steam.

"Back up!" one of the townspeople shouted up to him. "We ain't loadin' no more cows in this town."

"I can't back up. The local will be coming along about an hour behind me."

"All right, then, go on ahead. The thing is, you can't stay here."

"I need to take on some water."

"Do it and be gone."

Half an hour later, as the train was pulling out of town, an armed posse of at least twenty men met the combined herds of the Slash Diamond and the Rocking T.

"What is this? What's going on?" Charley Townes asked.

"You can't bring your cows into town," now acting marshal Foster said. "The loading pens have been closed."

"They ain't just closed," one of the others in the posse said. "We've done tore them sons of bitches down."

The others in the posse laughed.

"I'll be damned," Townes said to Evans. "I don't know how the son of a bitch did it, but he did it. Jessup just doubled the price he'll be getting for his cows."

Back in town, Hawke was sitting at his table in the Hog Lot, staring morosely into his drink. John Harder, Mayor Cornett, and Millie were sitting at the same table.

"I'm with Schermerhorn," Harder said. "There's no doubt in my mind but that they were from the Bar-J. The only thing is, I can't prove it."

"I don't think anyone could prove it," Hawke said. "They were covered up pretty well with their dusters and kerchiefs. I saw them as well as anyone, and I couldn't identify a single one."

"Well, where else could they be from?" Harder asked.

"The cowboy that Deputy Foster killed was from the Slash Diamond," Cornett said. "It could've been a bunch of cowboys from that outfit, out to get revenge."

"You really think so?" Harder asked. "I mean, don't forget, the Slash Diamond and the Rocking T both tried to bring their cows to town today. It seemed pretty clear to me that they didn't know anything about what happened yesterday."

As they were talking, Robert Griffin came into the saloon. He stood just inside the door for a moment, as if letting his eyes adjust to the dim light. Then he went to the bar. Robert Griffin was a known teetotaler, so seeing him go to the bar got everyone's attention.

"Bob, can I talk to you for a moment?" Robert Griffin asked.

"Sure," Bob Gary said.

All conversation at Hawke's table stopped so they could hear what Robert Griffin had to say.

"You're a good friend of the parson, aren't you?"

"Yes."

"Maybe you can talk to him," Robert Griffin said.

"Talk to him about what?"

"He said he isn't going to preach any of the funerals, not for the marshal, not for Mr. Gates, or Mr. Lankford, not even for his own wife and daughter. In the meantime, I've got five decedents needing funerals."

"I'll see what I can do," Bob said. "Mr. Harder, is it all right with you if I step away from the bar for a while?"

"Sure, go ahead," Harder said. "I'll tend bar till you get back."

Bob took off his apron then looked over at Hawke. "Hawke, would you mind going with me?" he asked.

"No, I don't mind at all," Hawke answered. "If you think it will do any good."

"I know that Gideon sets a great store by you," Bob said. "I think it might help to have you come along."

As the two left, Harder got up from the table and walked behind the bar.

"Mr. Harder?" Robert Griffin said.

"Yes?"

"I'll have a drink, if you don't mind."

"Are you sure?"

"Yes, I'm sure."

Harder poured some whiskey into a glass and shoved it toward him.

"More, please," Robert Griffin said.

Harder poured a little more.

"More."

Harder filled the glass to the top. Robert Griffin paid for the drink, then turned it up and drank it all. Showing absolutely no effect from it, he slapped the glass back down on the bar.

"Thank you," he said.

Harder, Millie, and the others stared at him in silent surprise as he walked back out.

Hawke and Bob Gary found Gideon, not in the church, but in the parsonage. He was sitting in the parlor, the room darkened by the heavy shades drawn over the windows.

"That's far enough," Gideon said as Hawke and Bob approached him. Gideon was in a rocking chair with a shawl draped over his shoulders. His hair had not been combed, and he had a two-day growth of beard. His eyes were red-rimmed, his pupils dilated, his face drawn.

"Gideon, it's me," Bob said. "Hawke is with me."

"What do you want?" The words were cold and clipped.

"Well, nothing in particular. We were just checking on you," Bob answered. "We wanted to see how you are getting along."

Gideon didn't answer.

"Robert Griffin is getting worried. In fact, the whole town is getting a little concerned."

"Why?"

"Well, there are some funerals that need to be conducted. Matt Trueblood, Harlan Gates, Lymon Lankford." Bob paused for a moment. "And Tamara and Lucy."

"No," Gideon said. This time the word was strained and filled with pain. Gideon stared straight ahead as tears streamed down his face.

"Do the funerals, Gideon," Bob said. "They need them, the people of the town need them, and you need them."

"Why do I need them?"

"It will help God begin the healing process."

Gideon stared at Bob with a face twisted in anger and disgust.

"God?" he said. "Did you say it will help God begin the healing process?"

"Yes."

Gideon laughed, an evil, demonic laughter from hell.

"Why, you poor deluded son of a bitch," Gideon said. "Haven't you learned by now that there is no God?"

"Major—" Bob started, but Gideon held up his hand to stop him.

"Go away, Sergeant," he said. "Please, just go away."

There was no church service for any of the dead. Instead, they were buried in five adjacent graves in the cemetery, with James Cornett saying a few words.

After the abbreviated funeral, which Gideon McCall did not attend, Hawke returned to the Hog Lot. Technically, the Hog Lot was closed, a sign outside explaining the situation.

**THIS DRINKING ESTABLISHMENT WILL
BE CLOSED FOR THE REMAINDER OF THIS DAY
OUT OF RESPECT FOR VICTIMS OF THE
DASTARDLY RAID ON OUR TOWN**

There were some who were allowed in, but they hadn't come as customers. They came as John Harder's close friends. Mayor Cornett was there, and so was Deputy Foster, Jubal Goodpasture, Vernon Clemmons, and George Schermerhorn. They were sitting with Hawke, Harder, Bob Gary, Millie, and Trudy, two tables having been drawn together to accommodate them.

"You fired the preacher?" Millie asked, surprised by the announcement Jubal had just made.

"We didn't have any choice," Jubal explained. Jubal was a member of the church board. "We had to fire him. I mean, if you can't get a preacher to give you a decent, Christian burial, what's the purpose of having one in the first place?"

"Don't you think you could have given him a little more time?" Bob Gary asked. "After all, he just lost his wife and daughter. That's a hard blow for any man to take."

Jubal nodded in agreement. "It is at that," he said. "Bob, I know you 'n' the parson are close. And I'll tell you true, I was for givin' him a little more time. But the board voted five to one to fire him. The ladies don't have a real vote, but even they voted three to one to fire him."

"Let me guess," Hawke said. "The woman who voted to keep him was Mrs. Rittenhouse."

Jubal looked at Hawke in surprise. "You're right," he said. "How'd you guess that? She's been such a thorn in his side all this time, her votin' to keep him on surprised the hell out of me."

Hawke shook his head. "I'm not surprised," he said. "I'm not surprised at all. Evelyn Rittenhouse is a thorn in Gideon's side because she is serious about her religion.

That means she's also serious about such things as compassion."

"Yeah, well, you coulda knocked me over with a feather when she spoke out to keep him," Jubal said.

The bat-wing doors swung open then and a man stepped through, then stopped. He stood for a long moment just inside the saloon, making no advance toward the tables or the bar. His odd behavior caught the attention of those seated around the table.

"I'm sorry," Bob Gary called toward him. "But the saloon is closed."

"They did it," the man said.

"I beg your pardon?" Bob Gary asked.

"It was just like it was in the war. They did it. Only there ain't no war. I told the major it was wrong, but he told me it was none of my business. I was just to cook the grub and stay the hell out of it."

"Who are you?" Cornett asked. "What are you talking about?"

"My name is Westpheling, Stan Westpheling, but most folks just call me Poke. I cook for the Bar-J. That is, I did cook for the Bar-J. I just quit."

"Poke, come over here and have a seat," Harder invited. "Would you like a drink?"

"Do you have any coffee?"

"Coffee? Yes, I'm sure we do."

"I'll get it from the kitchen," Millie offered.

"And, ma'am, if you would," Poke said, "put a shot of whiskey in the coffee?"

Millie smiled. "I'll do it," she said.

"Now, what were you talking about?" Harder asked. "What do you mean they did it, and that it was just like the war?"

"You know them riders that come into town Sunday to shoot up the place? Well, they was all ridin' for the Bar-J."

"I thought the Bar-J had already left," Cornett said.

"Yes, sir, we had," Poke replied.

"So, what you are saying is, the entire Bar-J outfit turned around, came back, and shot up our town?" Harder asked.

Millie returned with the coffee then, and Poke reached for it before answering. He took a swallow, then nodded. "Thank you ma'am." Then he looked at Harder and answered his question.

"No, not the whole outfit," he said. "Truth is, most of 'em didn't know nothin' about it. The only reason I knew was 'cause I was up already and I seen 'em leave. Then, later, I seen 'em come back, only when they come back, young Abe had done got hisself kilt. He was belly down over his horse."

"But why?" Cornett asked. "Why would a bunch of riders come into a town on Sunday morning and kill five innocent people?"

"Did you close down the loading pens?"

"I beg your pardon?" Cornett asked.

"Did you close the loading pens?" Poke repeated.

"You damn right we did," Schermerhorn said emphatically. "That's why they did it."

"No, that can't be right," Jubal said. "We didn't close the pens until after the raid."

"You don't understand," Poke said. "Major Jessup didn't do it *because* you closed the pens, he did it to *make* you close the pens."

"Why the hell would he want to do that?" Cornett asked.

"I think I can answer that," Clemmons said. "With the pens closed, the other two cattle companies can't ship their cows. If they can't ship their cows, that makes the cows Jessup shipped more valuable."

Poke nodded. "The broker said if there was no more cows coming from here, he could get twice as much for Jessup's cows when he sold them."

"That sorry son of a bitch," Jubal said. "And we played right into his hands."

"The question now is, what do we do about it?" Schermerhorn asked.

"I know exactly what to do," Jubal said.

"Oh? What's that?" Cornett asked.

"I think we should form a vigilante committee and go after them."

"You sure are quick to want to form a vigilante committee," Cornett said. "You wanted to do that once before, remember? Matt Truelove and Pastor McCall talked you out of it."

"Yes, and where is Truelove now?" Jubal asked. He pointed in the direction of the cemetery. "I'll tell you where he is. He's lying down there under six feet of dirt, that's where he is. And so are McCall's wife and daughter. They'd all be alive today if you'd listened to me the first time I brought this up. I'm tellin' you right now, the only way to handle this is to overtake the Bar-J and kill ever' damn one of 'em."

"So, you think they wouldn't shoot back?" Cornett asked. "What about it, Poke, you know these boys. Will they shoot back?"

"They'll shoot back," Poke said. "And some innocent folks on both sides would be killed. I told you, most of 'em is good boys who don't even know what happened."

"I'll tell you now," Cornett said. "I'm not going to authorize any vigilantes from this town."

"What are you going to do about it, then?" Jubal asked. "Send Deputy Foster?"

"No!" Foster said, standing up so quickly that the chair he was sitting in turned over. He shook his head and stuck his hands out. "No, I—I ain't killin' no more. No more." He took his badge off and tossed it on the table. "You folks can just get someone else."

The others watched in surprise as Foster left the saloon, shaking his head. "No more," he was saying. "No more."

"What was all that about?" Jubal asked. "I never figured Foster to be a coward."

"I don't think it's so much that he's afraid for himself,"

Cornett said, "as it is he's afraid he'll have to kill again. Don't forget, he killed that cowboy from the Slash Diamond."

"Well," Jubal said, "if he felt like that, he shouldn't have taken the job in the first place."

"The mayor is right," Schermerhorn said. "Foster's not been the same since then. Trust me, he is not the person you want to send out for something like this."

"What about the county sheriff?" Jubal asked.

"Sheriff Sanders?" Clemmons said. "Ha, don't make me laugh. He's worthless as tits on a boar hog. The only reason he is sheriff is because he kissed more babies than Rufus Montgomery did."

"What about Montgomery? Maybe we could deputize him," Schermerhorn suggested.

"You want to go to California and find him?" Harder asked.

"He's gone to California?"

"He left last month," Harder said. "He dropped in for a good-bye drink before he left."

"Well, what are we going to do about it, Mayor?" Clemmons asked. "We can't just let Jessup get away with it."

"I'm a deputy," Hawke said quietly.

The others looked at him.

"What?" Cornett asked.

"I'm a deputy," Hawke repeated. "Truelove made me a deputy when I agreed to be a private guard for the Hog Lot. Remember?"

"Well, yes, but you aren't being paid to be a deputy," Cornett said.

"Maybe you could rectify that," Hawke suggested.

"What are you saying? Are you saying you want a job as deputy city marshal?"

Hawke shook his head. "No. As city marshal I wouldn't have any authority. But if the city wrote out warrants for Jessup and his men, I could serve those warrants as a private citizen."

"How could you do that?" Jubal asked.

"Bounty hunters do it all the time," Vernon Clemmons explained. "The only authority bounty hunters have is the authority of a citizen's arrest and the warrant declared when someone is put on a wanted list."

"Is that what you're saying, Mr. Hawke?" Cornett asked. "That you would be willing to go after these men as a bounty hunter?"

"Yes," Hawke said.

"Why would you do that?"

"Consider my situation, Mr. Mayor," Hawke replied. "There is no piano in here, and the preacher has just been fired, which means I have no piano to play in church either. It's time for me to move on, and a little traveling money would help make the move easier."

"I'd have to call a city council meeting," Cornett said.

"Why?" Clemmons asked.

"Well, to discuss this with them," Cornett replied.

"No need," Clemmons said. "For something like this, you could issue an executive order." Clemmons smiled. "Executive orders are one of the good things about being a mayor."

"How do I know Mr. Hawke can handle something like this? As far as I know, it might be like sending out Deputy Foster."

"Hawke can handle it," Harder said. "I've seen him in action."

"That may have been a fluke," Cornett insisted.

"It was no fluke," Clemmons said.

"How do you know?"

"I've researched Mr. Hawke here," Clemmons said. "Believe me, if he says he will take care of Jessup and the others . . ." Clemmons paused and looked directly at Hawke. ". . . he will take care of them."

"All right, so now it comes down to how much money do you want?"

"One thousand dollars should do it," Hawke replied.

"One thousand dollars for each man?" Cornett replied with a quick gasp.

"One thousand dollars total," Hawke said. "No matter how many are involved."

Cornett smiled broadly. "You've got a deal!" he said, extending his hand.

"In advance."

"In advance?"

"In advance."

"Well, if I give you the money in advance, how do I know you are going to bring them back?"

"I'm not going to bring them back," Hawke said simply.

"If you aren't going to bring them back, what are you going to do with . . . uh, I mean how can we be sure that—" Cornett stopped and stared at Hawke, whose expression had not changed.

"Oh," Cornett said, realizing what Hawke meant. "Oh," he repeated. He sighed. "All right. Come down to my office. I'll give you the money."

Chapter 17

WHEN HAWKE CAME DOWNSTAIRS FROM HIS room, he had his saddlebags draped across his shoulder, his bedroll tucked under his arm, and his rifle in his left hand.

"Aren't you going to have a good-bye drink with a friend?" Millie asked, meeting him at the foot of the stairs.

Hawke smiled at her. "I'd be happy to," he said. He looked around the empty saloon. "Is everyone gone?"

"Mr. Harder is back in his office. He told me to ask you to stick your head in to tell him good-bye. Bob is behind the bar, the others have gone."

When Hawke stepped back into Harder's office, the saloon owner looked up from his rolltop desk.

"You're leaving now?" Harder asked.

"Yes," Hawke answered. "They've already got a head start on me, I don't want to let them get too far ahead."

"Yeah, I don't blame you. Oh, by the way, you don't have to stop by the mayor's office," Harder said. "Here's the money."

Harder handed Hawke an envelope, and Hawke put it in one of his saddlebags.

"You aren't going to count it?"

"No need to."

"I truly enjoyed listening to you play the piano, especially those times in the middle of the night when you thought no one was around to hear. I don't mind telling you, Hawke, that I'm going to miss you," Harder said. "It's not every day someone meets a classically trained pianist. Especially someone like you."

"I've enjoyed working for you, John. You are fair to your employees and honest with your customers. This has been a good place to spend some time."

"But you don't want to settle here," Harder said. It was a statement, not a question.

"I don't think I'll be able to settle anywhere until the day I'm planted six feet under the ground. And Lord knows where that will be."

"Hawke, all I can say is, it must have been one hell of a war for you."

"It was no worse for me than it was for anyone else who was in it," Hawke said. "It's just that we all have our own way of dealing with it. And wandering around is my way."

Harder stood up and shook his hand. "If you ever come through Braggadocio again, you'll always have a job. Who knows, I may even have a new piano by then."

"I'll keep that in mind," Hawke said.

When he left Harder's office, he saw that Millie, Trudy, and the other two bar girls were standing by the bar, waiting for him. Hawke stepped up to the bar and set his load down beside him. "Mr. Gary, if you don't mind, I would like to buy a drink for all the ladies and me," he said, sliding a coin across the bar.

"No, sir," Bob said, pushing the coin back. "Your money is no good here. I'm buying the drinks."

"Well, thank you, Bob, I appreciate that," Hawke said as Bob began to pour.

"If you would, Sergeant, pour a drink for me as well," another voice said.

Turning toward the sound of the voice, Hawke saw Gideon McCall standing just inside the door. Hawk almost didn't recognize him. Gone was the black suit, ribbon tie, and wide-brim, low-crown hat. Instead he was wearing denim trousers tucked down into calf-high boots, a buckskin shirt, and a hat that was not unlike the hat Hawke was wearing. In addition, Gideon had one pistol in a holster and another stuck down in his belt. And he was carrying a Whitworth, hexagonal bore, .45 caliber sniper rifle, complete with scope.

"I'm going with you, Hawke," Gideon said.

It wasn't a request; it was a declaration of fact.

"Going where?" Hawke replied.

"After the people who murdered my wife and child," Gideon said. "I'm going with you."

"I don't think so," Hawke said.

"My drink?" Gideon said to Bob Gary.

Bob nodded, and poured a drink, then pushed it across the bar to Gideon. Gideon tossed it down.

"Maybe I had better explain something to you," Hawke said. "I have reason to believe that Clint Jessup is Jesse Cole."

"Is that a fact?" Gideon asked.

"Yes. And even though I know you were in the army during the war, I don't think you want to run up against a man like Jesse Cole."

"Jesse Cole is a tough bird, is he?" Gideon said.

"About as tough as they come," Hawke agreed. "Wait a minute. You knew that, didn't you? You said that you knew Jessup when he was at West Point, and you said that Jessup wasn't his real name. You knew who he was all along, didn't you?"

"Yes, I know who he is."

"I understand it all now," Hawke said.

"And what is it that you think you understand?" Gideon asked. He picked up the bottle and poured himself a second drink.

"I understand your feeling of guilt. You didn't tell anyone that he was Jesse Cole, so now you blame yourself for your wife and daughter's death, don't you?"

"You have it all worked out, do you?"

"I have to tell you, Gideon, getting killed is a poor way to assuage a guilty conscience."

"I'm going with you," Gideon said again.

Hawke shook his head. "No. I know how you feel, but I'm going to have a hard enough time looking out for myself. I don't want to play nursemaid to a preacher who thinks he can handle someone like Jesse Cole simply because he was in the war. This is an entirely different situation."

"Sergeant Kincaid," Gideon said in a commanding voice.

Bob Gary stood at attention. "Yes, sir?"

"Sergeant Kincaid?" Millie said as she and the other girls looked at Bob Gary, their faces mirroring their curiosity.

"Tell Mr. Hawke who I am."

"He is Gideon Mc—"

"Tell him who I am!" Gideon demanded in a loud and commanding voice.

"Major, are you sure you want me to do that? You've made a good life for yourself and—"

"Tell him, my friend," Gideon said, and this time his voice was quiet, gentle, and confident.

Bob Gary cleared his throat. "My name isn't really Bob Gary," he said. "My name is Glen Kincaid. I was first sergeant for the Third Missouri Brigade. The Third Missouri was also known as Cole's Raiders. This gentleman's name is not really Gideon McCall. His name is Jesse Cole."

"Oh my God!" Millie said, putting her hand to her mouth. "I was at Spring Hill. I was just a little girl then, but I remember it all."

Gideon looked at Millie, and there was genuine pain in his eyes.

"I'm sorry, miss," he said. "I'm truly sorry."

"You're sorry? That's all you can say, that you're sorry? My father and my brother were killed at Spring Hill. My mother died soon after. Do you have any idea how different my life may have been? You call yourself a preacher? I could be a wife and mother, living in my own house. Instead, I'm a whore, and it's all because of you."

Gideon looked as if he were going to answer her, to challenge her assertion or, perhaps, to accept the responsibility. Instead he merely nodded.

"I'm sorry," he said again.

It was obvious by the expression still on Hawke's face that he just now realized that Gideon was telling the truth.

"If you are Jesse Cole, who is Clint Jessup?" Hawke asked.

"You may have heard of him as Quint Wilson," Gideon said.

"Yes," Hawke said. "Yes, I've heard of Quint Wilson. Did you two ride together during the war?"

"From time to time," Gideon admitted. "I also rode with Quantrill and Anderson, as well as Sterling Price and Jeff Thompson."

"Why didn't you tell us who he was?" Hawke asked. "If the townspeople knew who he was, he might not have been able to get away with as much."

"I figured we had both started new lives for ourselves," Gideon said. "I thought Quint Wilson was dead, just as I thought Jesse Cole was dead. But I was wrong."

"Did you really attend a seminary? Were you a priest before the war, or is that just part of your cover story?"

"I was a priest."

"Gideon—"

"My name is Jesse."

"Jesse, I can understand how you must feel. But do you want to give up everything you've worked for now?"

"Everything I worked for is dead."

Hawke paused for a moment, then nodded. "All right," he said. "If you want to go with me, let's go."

The Bar-J had a two-day head start on them, and because the Bar-J wasn't pushing a herd, the cowboys were able to move fairly quickly. Hawke and Jesse rode hard through the first day, getting off and walking their horses frequently to spare them.

That night they had a supper of jerky and water.

"The piano at church," Hawke said. "How were you able to buy that?"

"I bought it the same way Quint Wilson bought the Bar-J," Jesse said. "I bought it with money I stole during the war."

"And you thought that buying a piano for a church would absolve you of all your sins?"

"What do you know about absolution?" Jesse asked.

"I know that I haven't found it yet," Hawke said. "And apparently, neither have you. All this talk of my soul still being intact and you finding peace with the Lord. What about that, Jesse? All lies?"

Jesse pinched the bridge of his nose. "I thought it was true," he said. "I really thought it was true. I thought God had made a covenant with me by giving me Tamara. But I know now that it was hollow, all hollow. You are right, Hawke. You were right all along. You and I, and everyone like us, have lost our souls."

"Come on," Hawke said, remounting. "If we are going to catch up with them, we're going to have to go all through the night."

If Hawke thought he would be able to cause Jesse to turn around because of hard trailing, he was mistaken. Jesse matched him step for step, and though it had been several years since the war, from his endurance and demeanor, Hawke could see why Jesse Cole became a name that was feared all through Missouri and Kansas.

Just before dawn Hawke caught a whiff of frying bacon and held up his hand.

"Yes, I smell it," Jesse said.

The two men dismounted, then tied off their horses and moved ahead silently until they came to a small hill. Getting down on their hands and knees, they crawled to the top, then looked over.

About one hundred yards ahead of them they saw ten men sitting around a campfire.

"Where are the others?" Jesse asked. "I know more than ten men ride for the Bar-J."

"They have no cattle to drive," Hawke said. "They probably split up. Or maybe these men aren't even from the Bar-J. Wait here, I'm going to go down and talk to them."

"What are you wasting time talking to them for?" Jesse asked.

"Just wait here," Hawke repeated.

Hawke went back to his horse, mounted, then began riding, slowly, toward the campfire. The cowboys saw him approaching and stood to face him as he rode into their camp.

"You're the piano player, aren't you?" one of them asked.

Normally, Hawke would correct people who called him that, assuring them that he was a pianist rather than a piano player. But this didn't seem to be the time or the place for that.

"Yes."

"I remember you," the speaker said.

"I remember you as well. But I never caught your name."

"The name's Clayton, not that it's any of your business."

"Are you all with the Bar-J?"

"What if we are? What's it to you? And what are you doing here?"

"Everyone has to be somewhere," Hawke replied. He nodded toward the fire. "The coffee sure smells good."

"Don't it?" Clayton answered. Neither he nor anyone else offered him a cup.

"I was wondering," Hawke said. "Did any of you happen to ride into town Sunday morning?"

"You people never give up, do you?" Clayton asked.

"What do you mean?"

"Did the town send you out here to roust us for that? I know you was a deputy or somethin' in addition to bein' a piano player. But I can't believe you come all the way out here after us, just because Deekus and some of the other fellas rode into town, as sort of a good-bye."

"A good-bye?"

"Yes, I know they horsed around a bit, shot off a few guns. But that was just to let you sons of bitches know that we didn't appreciate you trying to take them away from us."

"Is that what you call it?" Hawke asked. "Shooting off a few guns to say good-bye?"

"Yeah, that's what we call it. Only it turns out that your town don't take too kindly to us, because Abe Wallace got hisself kilt, just for havin' a little fun. Fact is, Abe ain't the only one got kilt. Shorty got kilt, and so did Frank Miller. Three men that come into town with us was killed, but you sons of bitches complain about us havin' guns."

"So Frank Miller was one of your riders," Hawke said.

"Yeah, he was one of us. What of it? I was one of the men who come into town that night. We didn't shoot nobody, we was just havin' a little fun. But Miller got killed. Now Abe got killed. What does it take to satisfy that town of yours anyway? You've kilt three of us, and we ain't done nothin' to any of you."

"Do you really not know?" Hawke asked.

"Do I really not know what?"

"The group of cowboys who rode into town on Sunday, just to tell us good-bye, killed Marshal Truelove, Mr. Gates, Mr. Lankford, the pastor's wife, and Lucy, the pastor's little girl."

Clayton looked surprised, and Hawke surmised immediately that the surprise was genuine.

One of the other cowboys shook his head. "You're a lyin' son of a bitch," he said. "Nothin' like that happened."

"I don't know, Billy," Clayton said. "If you think back on it, Deekus was—"

His words were cut short by a shot, and Hawke felt the concussion of a bullet passing within inches of his head, then saw a spray of blood and brain detritus spewing from the side of Clayton's head. That was followed by the sound of a rifle shot.

"What the hell?" Billy shouted in alarm. "Who's shooting us?"

While the cowboys stood around in shocked inaction, Hawke mounted his horse and galloped back to the hill. As Hawke rode away, bent low over the horse's neck and waiting for a bullet to tear into his back, he saw a flash of light and a puff of gun smoke coming from the hill in front of him. Twisting around in his saddle, he saw Billy go down. Not until then did the remaining cowboys react, not by returning fire, but by scattering for cover.

Hawke leaped off his horse just as Jesse was reloading the long rifle.

"Jesse, what are you doing?" he shouted in anger.

"Enough talk!" Jesse shouted back. "I'm going to send every one of those sorry sons of bitches to hell!" Jesse used his ramrod to tamp down the wad.

Hawke hit Jesse on the point of his chin, putting everything he had into the swing. Not expecting it, Jesse fell back with his arms flailing out to either side, his eyes rolling back in his head.

Chapter 18

WHEN JESSE CAME TO, HAWKE WAS SITTING QUI-
etly on a rock, staring at him. Jesse sat up and rubbed his
chin.

"What did you hit me with?" he asked. "A horseshoe?"

"What was that all about?" Hawke asked, pointing to the
rifle.

"I told you what it was about," Jesse answered. "They
killed Tamara and Lucy. I didn't ride all the way out here to
talk them to death."

"The men you killed had nothing to do with it," Hawke insisted. "The ones who came into town were Deekus and his
bunch."

"Emil Decker," Jesse said.

"What?"

"Deekus's real name is Emil Decker."

"You know Deekus?"

"Yes, I know him."

"I suppose you have ridden with him too," Hawke said.

"I have."

"I'll say this for you, Gideon—"

"Jesse."

"All right, Jesse. You are a man full of surprises. When you told me back at the Hog Lot that you were Jesse Cole, I wasn't sure I believed you. The preacher I knew didn't square with what happened at Spring Hill. But you made a believer out of me a few minutes ago when you shot down those two men."

"I'm not proud of what happened in Spring Hill," Jesse said.

"Were you in Lawrence, with Quantrill?"

"No."

"What about Sikeston? Were you in Sikeston?"

"No, Sikeston was all Quint Wilson. There is a big difference between Spring Hill and Sikeston."

"What was the difference?"

"At Sikeston, the killing was systematic and by design. Quint Wilson ordered the slaughter of every man and boy in the town, and Deekus took a particular delight in carrying it out.

"Spring Hill wasn't supposed to happen the way it did. We were just going to rob a bank then leave. But the whole town turned out against us, and we got into a full pitched battle. A lot of people wound up getting killed, but we had no choice."

"Tell that to Millie," Hawke said. "I think she would tell you that you are straining to draw a line between Spring Hill and Sikeston."

"As I said, I'm not proud of Spring Hill," Jesse said. "Anyway, why am I having to explain this to you? You were in the war, you know what it was like."

"I'm not sure that I do know what it was like," Hawke said. Standing then, he started toward his horse.

"Where are you going?"

"I'm going after Deekus."

"I'm coming with you."

Hawke paused for a moment, then turned and looked at Jesse Cole. "If you start shooting innocent men again, Cole, I'll kill you," he said calmly.

"You can't kill me, Hawke. I'm already dead," Jesse replied.

They had been on the trail for nearly six hours when the still of the afternoon was interrupted by several gunshots.

"Ambush!" Hawke shouted, but his warning was unnecessary. Jesse's training and experience, though long dormant, surfaced immediately, and he jerked his horse to the right of the trail, darting in behind a small grassy mound, even as bullets were clipping through the leaves of a low-lying sumac bush.

Hawke left the trail to the other side, finding cover behind a fallen tree.

"Hawke," Jesse called, loud enough for Hawke to hear but too quiet to be heard by whoever set up the ambush. "Are you hit?"

"No," Hawke replied. "How about you?"

"I'm not hit. Did you see where the shooting came from?"

"I saw a puff of smoke, but it was already drifting when I saw it. No telling where it came from."

"We need them to shoot again," Jesse said. "You keep a sharp look."

"All right."

Jesse put his hat on a stick and held it up, moving it back and forth, but there was no reaction.

Hawke chuckled. "I guess they've seen that trick before."

"I reckon so," Jesse said. "All right, I'm coming over to your side. You watch."

"Don't do it, Jesse, you'll be too exposed," Hawke said.

"You just keep an eye open," Jesse replied.

Hawke realized then that Jesse was going to do it no

matter what, so he kept his eyes peeled when the preacher stood up and darted across the trail.

At least three shots rang out, and Hawke saw all three muzzle flashes. The flashes were followed immediately by billowing puffs of smoke.

Jesse dived the last few feet and slid to a stop right beside Hawke.

"Please tell me I didn't do that for nothing," Jesse said as he sat up and began brushing rocks and dirt from his pants and shirt.

"I don't know how many are up there," Hawke said. "But I know where three of them are."

"Good. Point them out to me."

"You see the cottonwood there, just to the left of those two rocks?" Hawke said.

"I do."

"Follow the limb that comes straight out to the right, the one that runs almost parallel to the ground. Do you see it?"

"Yes."

"Now, when you get to the third branch that is pointing down, follow it down. You'll see that it is pointing directly at one of them."

"Glory be, you're right," Jesse said. "I can see him. Keep an eye on them, let me know if they move."

Jesse slipped down a little lower and, lying on his back, loaded his Whitworth. Then, with the load tamped down, he eased back up to the fallen tree limb and looked toward the rocks.

"Is he still there?"

"Yes."

"I don't see . . . wait, there he is," Jesse said. He lay the long rifle across the log, thumbed back the hammer, aimed, and pulled the trigger.

The rifle boomed and rocked back against Jesse's shoulder. When the smoke of the discharge rolled away, one of their adversaries was lying on his back, head pointed down on the small incline upon which the two large rocks were located. He had fallen forward, thus marking the location of the others.

"Holy shit! Where'd that come from?" one of the cowboys shouted, his words clearly audible across the distance.

"Let's get the hell out of here!" another said.

Moments later they heard the sound of retreating hoofbeats as the would-be assailants rode away.

Tex and Cracker rode hard to get away from the place where they had set up the ambush. Finally, when they were sure they weren't being followed, they slowed their horses to a trot, then to a walk.

"How many did Keefer say there was of them?" Tex asked.

"He said he thought there was only two of 'em," Cracker answered. "He said that while the piano player was talkin' to 'em, the other'n started shootin'."

"There must be at least three of them," Tex said.

"I only seen two," Cracker answered.

"That's all I seen too, but there must be another one."

"What makes you think that?"

"One of 'em was the piano player. Did you see who the other'n was?"

"Not so's I'd recognize him," Cracker replied.

"It was the preacher," Tex said.

"What was the preacher doing there?"

"You remember the woman and little girl we killed when we rode into town the other night?"

"Oh, no," Cracker said. "Not 'we' killed. I didn't have nothin' to do with that. I know damn well I didn't shoot no woman and little girl."

"Well, one of us did," Tex said. "So as far as anyone else is concerned, we're all guilty of that. Anyway, the woman was the preacher's wife, and the little girl was his daughter."

"So that's why he come along with the piano player," Cracker said.

"Yeah, but, like as not he's just along to see that things are made right. I can't see a preacher doing the actual shooting. Especially not as good a shot as this person is."

"Where's Brandt?" Jessup asked when Tex and Cracker returned.

"He's lyin' back there somewhere," Tex said.

"Dead?"

Tex nodded.

"They sent a posse after us, didn't they?" Jessup said. He shook his head. "I didn't think they'd do that without a marshal to lead them. How many were there?"

"I don't know," Tex said. "That's what Cracker and I were trying to figure out."

"Ten? Twenty men, maybe?" Jessup asked.

Tex shook his head. "We only saw two, but there might be one more."

Jessup looked up in surprise. "Two? You only saw two, and you ran?"

"After Brandt was killed, that left only two of us," Tex said. "And like I said, I'm pretty sure there was three of them."

"What makes you think that?"

"Well, one of 'em is the piano player," Tex said. "And like we said, Major, he isn't your ordinary piano player. But he wasn't the one who killed Brandt."

"Who was the other one? The deputy? Is he the one who killed Brandt?"

"I don't know," Tex said, "but I think there must be a third person, one that we didn't see, because the second man—the one that we did see—is the preacher. And it's not likely that the preacher did the killing."

"You don't think it was the preacher, huh?" Jessup asked.

"Hell no, I don't think it was the preacher," Tex replied. "I mean, can you see some preacher havin' the courage to pick up a gun and come lookin' for us?"

"You said Hawke is no run-of-the-mill piano player, didn't you?" Jessup asked.

"That's what I said, all right."

"Well, believe me, Gideon McCall is no run-of-the-mill preacher. Not by a long shot."

"What makes you say that? Do you know this preacher?"

"Oh, yes, I know him."

"You know the preacher?" Tex chuckled. "Why, Major, who would have ever figured you for a Bible-totin', gospel-singin' churchgoer? How long have you known him?"

"I've known him for a long time," Jessup answered. "Ever since we were plebes together at West Point."

"You mean this preacher went to West Point?"

"He did."

"I'll be damn. Who would've thought that? So, did you keep up with him durin' the war? Or did you fight on opposite sides?"

"No, we were on the same side. He fought for the South, just like I did. Actually, he made somewhat of a name for himself. In fact, I would be very surprised if you had not heard of him."

"His name is Gideon something, isn't it? Gideon McCarty, or McNeil, or something like that?" Tex shook his head. "No, I don't recollect the name."

"That's because Gideon McCall isn't his real name," Jessup said. "But if you heard him called by his real name, you'd recognize him."

"Well, if Gideon McCall isn't his real name, what is his real name?" Tex asked.

"He is Jesse Cole," Deekus said, coming up behind them then, and answering Tex's question before Jessup could respond.

"Damn! Jesse Cole? Are you sure?"

"I'm sure," Jessup said. "As I told you, I've known Jesse Cole for a very long time."

"Why didn't you say somethin'?" Tex asked.

"What would you have us say?"

"For one thing, you coulda told us who he is. If we had known who he was, maybe we would've been a little more careful," Tex said.

"Yeah, and if a frog had wings, he wouldn't bump his ass every time he jumps," Deekus said.

"You're the one that got us into this mess, Deekus," Tex said. "You're the one killed his wife and daughter."

Deekus chuckled. "It don't matter to Cole who it was that killed his wife and daughter, he's going to kill us all if he can."

"This ain't right," Tex said, pointing at Deekus. "You didn't say nothin' about anything like this."

"So, what do you want to do, Major?" Deekus asked Jessup, paying no attention to Tex's outburst.

"We don't have any choice," Jessup said. "We're going to have to kill them."

"That's what we've been trying to do, isn't it?" Tex asked.

"Yes," Jessup agreed. "But now we'll try a little harder."

"Have you got any ideas, Major?" Deekus asked.

"Maybe," Jessup replied. "Cracker, look over there in my saddlebag and bring me that map, will you?"

"All right," Cracker agreed.

"Deekus, how many men do we have with us right now?" Jessup asked.

"Well, let's see. Some of the men have gone on ahead, some quit soon as they were paid out, and a couple have gone off to visit family. I reckon we've got around twenty or so who are still with us."

"Here's your map, Major," Cracker said, returning with the document.

Jessup opened the map and looked at it for a moment, then put his finger down on a point. "Right here," he said, "right here where Eureka Creek comes off Snake River. This is where we will bait our trap."

"Bait our trap?" Tex asked.

"Yes, bait," Jessup answered. "You do know what it means to bait a trap, don't you?"

"Well, yeah, I know what it means to bait a trap."

"Say, you wanted to catch a rat. What would you put in the trap?"

"Cheese?"

"Very good," Jessup said. "And if you wanted to catch a rabbit?"

"I don't know, maybe a carrot."

"Right again. The point is, if you want to catch something, the best bait is normally food. Now Hawke and Cole have been coming after us at a pretty good clip for two or three days now. And unless I miss my guess, they've been eating nothing but jerky."

Jessup put his finger on the map again. "There is a line shack right here that's in pretty good shape. And it's near fresh water. They are bound to stop and take a look around when they get there. What do you think they would do if they found some flour, a side of cured bacon, a few potatoes, and some salt and pepper there?"

"Ha!" Tex said. "I see what you mean! It would be just like baitin' a trap for a possum."

"While they're in there, feeding, we'll be outside, closing the trap."

"Yeah!" Tex said. "Damn, that's a good idea!"

"Deekus, get ten good men."

"Just ten? I tell you what, Major, if it was up to me, I'd get every rider we've got. I mean, why take chances with these guys? We've already seen what they can do."

"Have you ever heard of Euripides?" Jessup asked.

"You rip a what?"

"Euripides," Jessup repeated. "He was a Greek philosopher

and military strategist. He is also the author of one of the most important maxims we learn at West Point. According to Euripides, ten men wisely led are worth a hundred without a head."

"Ten men wisely led are worth a hundred without a head," Deekus repeated, letting the words jell in his mind. After a moment of concentration, he smiled broadly. "Hey, that's a good one," he said.

"Do you see any sign of life?" Hawke asked. He was referring to a ripsawed and weathered structure that sat on the bank of the creek, just before the creek joined the river.

"There's no one there that I can see," Jesse answered.

They didn't have a pair of field glasses, but Jesse did have the scope on his rifle, and he was using it as a spyglass. "I would say that the shack is empty."

"Then what do you say we ride down there and check it out?" Hawke suggested. "If they came through here, we might get a lead on how far ahead they are."

The two men rode across a small opening until they reached the line shack, approaching it not from the front, or even from a windowed wall, but from the blind side. And there, on the blind side of the shack, they dismounted and ground-tethered their horses.

Hawke pulled his pistol and noticed that Jesse had done the same thing. How vastly different this efficient warrior was from the mild-mannered, almost meek preacher he had met several weeks ago.

They moved quietly along the wall until they reached the corner. Then, stepping around the corner, they approached the window. Hawke looked inside.

"Anything?" Jesse whispered.

"I don't see anything."

The two men moved to the door. Hawke pushed it open hard, then stepped back out of the door opening.

There was no reaction.

Cautiously, the two men entered, looked around, and then, satisfied that it was empty, put their guns away.

There was a woodstove in the center of the single room, and Hawke went over to smell it. "It's been used in the last few days," he said.

"By the people we're after?"

Hawke shook his head. "I don't think so. Look around. The dishes are washed, the floor is clean. Nobody who is on the run would leave it like this."

Jesse began looking through the cabinets. Seeing a sack, he opened it, then sniffed its contents and smiled broadly. "Hey, Hawke, there are some coffee beans here. How'd you like a cup of coffee?"

Cracker couldn't believe his luck. Jessup had sent him back to see if he could spot the two men following them, and he saw their horses tied to the front of the old line shack Jessup had chosen as a trap but that they hadn't gotten to yet. A wisp of smoke was curling up from the chimney. Hurrying back to report what he had found, he overtook Jessup and the others about a mile up the trail.

"Did you see them?" Jessup asked when Cracker rode up to make his report.

"Yes, sir, I seen 'em," he said, and smiled broadly. "They are at the shack."

"Damn," Jessup said. "I thought we had more of a lead on them. We'd better get there before they leave."

"Major, you don't understand," Cracker said. "Looks like they just got to the shack. And they got 'em a fire goin', which means they're goin' to stay for a while."

Jessup nodded. "All right," he said. "That's good. Let's go. This is where it ends, once and for all."

"I'm going to like this," Deekus said. "I'm going to like this a lot."

* * *

Hawke had just started to take a swallow of his coffee when a fusillade of shots rang out. They crashed through the two windows and the door.

"Get down!" he yelled, though his warning wasn't necessary as Jesse was already on the floor, gun in hand, crawling toward one of the windows.

Hawke crawled to the other and the two men began returning fire.

For the next several minutes there was a ferocious exchange of gunfire, and Hawke had the satisfaction of seeing at least three of his targets go down. Jesse was as accurate, as Hawke saw more than one of his targets fall.

"Hawke, how many bullets do you have left?"

"I just reloaded and I have about four more," Hawke replied. "How about you?"

"I'm out, but I have some more in my saddlebag. I'm going to get them."

"No!" Hawke said. "You'll never make it!"

"We'll both be out in another minute, then all they'll have to do is come in here and shoot us like rats in a trap."

"Jesse, no, don't try it," Hawke said, but even as he was calling out his warning, Jesse dashed toward the front door.

He didn't make it. Hawke saw a mist of blood fly up from his chest as he was hit. Jesse fell back inside, and Hawke, crawling, went over to him, pulled him out of the doorway and away from the line of fire.

"You were right. I should have listened to you," Jesse said.

"How badly are you hit?" Hawke asked.

"I'm dying, Hawke," Jesse replied in a strained voice.

"Maybe it's not as bad as you think," Hawke said.

"You and I have both been around a lot of dying men," Jesse said. "I always wondered how they knew. Now I know. I'm dying."

More bullets slammed against the outside wall and crashed through the window.

"I wonder if God will accept a prayer of contrition from me?" Jesse asked, exerting himself to talk.

"Who is the prayer of contrition for, if not for people like us?" Hawke said. "You start it, I will say it with you."

"I'm going to say it in Latin."

"Deus meus, ex toto corde," Hawke started.

"You know Latin?" Jesse smiled, then picked it up as they continued to pray together.

"Paenitet me omnium meorum peccatorum, eaque detestor, quia peccando, non solum poenas a Te iust statutes promeritus sum, sed praesertim quia offendi Te, summum bonum, ac dignum qui super omnia diligaris. Ideo firmiter propono, adiuvante gratia Tua, de cetero me non peccaturum peccandique occasiones prosimas fugiturum. Amen."

"Thank you, Hawke," Jesse said. Then he gasped for breath a couple of times and quit breathing.

"Are you both dead in there? Or are you just out of ammunition?" a voice called from outside.

Staying low, Hawke crawled back over to the window and looked outside. He saw someone rise up to get a look, and Hawke fired, but missed.

His shot had the effect of bringing on another fusillade.

Hawke rose up and fired three more times, mostly to let them know there was still someone left and that he still had ammo.

He opened the cylinder and punched out the three empty cartridges, then replaced them. Now his pistol was fully loaded, but he had no bullets beyond that.

"Son of a bitch, they still have some fight left," Jessup said.

"Yeah, but it don't seem like there's as much shootin' as there was," Deekus said.

"All right, Tex, now is the time to light the fire," Jessup ordered.

Tex nodded, then started out, running behind the ridgeline so as not to be seen from the shack. He spotted stacks of dry weeds, sticks, and wood at the corner of the house. Someone could approach here without being seen, and a fire could be started that would involve the entire house within moments.

Tex lit the fire, then ran back around the ridgeline to rejoin Jessup, Deekus, and Cracker. There were only four left of the ten who had come to spring the trap.

By the time Tex got back, the little line shack was burning fiercely.

"Seen anybody come out yet?" Tex asked.

"No, but they'll be coming out soon," Jessup said. "So be ready for them."

Hawke was trapped. He couldn't go out the front door or one of the front windows without being shot. And he couldn't stay in the house.

The smoke was getting unbearable, and he had to get down on his stomach and keep his nose to the floor in order to breathe. He moved to the back corner of the house, though he knew there was no place he could actually go.

Then, as he lay there, he felt a breath of fresh air coming in through the cracks of the floor planking. As he examined it, he saw that it was more than cracks, that there was a trapdoor in the floor. When he opened it, he saw water. The house had been built over a small tributary and this was the water supply!

"Yes!" he said happily. He crawled back to Jesse's body, grabbed him by the foot, pulled him to the hole, then dropped him through. Hawke went down after him, falling into the water below.

The water was nearly waist deep, and he followed it to the edge of the house, then ducked down and swam underwater until he cleared the edge. Coming up on the other side, he waded down to the junction of the tributary and the creek, then crawled up the bank and sat there a moment while catching his breath.

From where he sat, he had an excellent view of the shack,

which was now nearly totally consumed by the fire. He also saw Jessup, Deekus, Tex, and Cracker standing about fifty yards away, watching it burn. All four were holding pistols in their hands, waiting for someone to try and escape.

Hawke dropped back down behind the bank and went downstream several yards, then crawled up the bank again for another view. This time he was behind Jessup and his men. He climbed over the bank and began walking toward them, as casually as if he were strolling down main street.

"I hope they ain't dead yet," he heard Deekus say. "I want 'em to burn."

"Yeah, like they're in hell," Tex added.

"Funny you should mention hell, since that's where I'm about to send you," Hawke said.

Startled, the four men turned around. Then, seeing that Hawke's gun was still in his holster, they smiled.

"Well now, would you like to tell me how you are going to do that, with your gun in your holster?" Jessup asked.

"I think I'd rather show you," Hawke replied.

Before the last word was out of Hawke's mouth, the gun was in his hand. Not one of the four had even raised their pistols yet, thinking they had the advantage.

"What the hell?" Jessup shouted, bringing his pistol up too late. He was the first to die, and Deekus was second. Neither one of them managed to get off a shot.

Tex and Cracker both got off shots, but both missed.

Hawke didn't.

Hawke waited until the fire had burned down and the timbers cooled enough for him to go back. He found Jesse's body underneath, preserved by the water.

He buried Jesse at the point where the creek and the river joined. Making a cross from two timbers that had not been completely consumed by the fire, he erected it over Jesse's grave. Then he used a piece of charcoal to write on the cross, choosing the words of the Good Thief.

LORD, REMEMBER ME WHEN THOU COMEST INTO THY KINGDOM

Leaving the others unburied, Hawke mounted his horse and rode away knowing that somewhere, on the other side of the next range of hills, just over the horizon, there would be another town, another saloon, another piano.

A chill wind blew down from the north. There would be snow in the higher elevations soon.

Maybe he would go south.